Past Imperfect

Past Imperfect

Kathleen Hills

Poisoned Pen Press

Copyright © 2002 by Kathleen Hills.

First Edition 2002

10 9 8 7 6 5 4 3 2 1

Library of Congress Catalog Card Number: 2001098489

ISBN: 1-59058-007-9   Hardcover
ISBN: 1-59058-022-2   Trade Paperback

Poisoned Pen Press
6962 E. First Ave. Ste 103
Scottsdale, AZ 85251
www.poisonedpenpress.com
sales@poisonedpenpress.com

Printed in the United States of America

To Richard

Acknowledgments

Much appreciation to those who so generously gave of their time and expertise in answering my questions: Michigan historian Jim Dompier, Lake Superior fishermen Walt Sve and the late George Falk, attorney Shelly Marquardt, and retired police officer Jerry Larson. A special thanks to my friends and colleagues at Lake Superior Writers for their patient support and suggestions, and to the ladies and gentleman of The Butler Did It book club for their inspiration and insight into all things mysterious. Lastly, I thank the geography of the Upper Peninsula of Michigan and the people of its past, and I beg the indulgence of the people of its present.

I

Constable John McIntire leaned into the rail on the *Frelser's* forward deck, closed his eyes, and let the sharp morning air ease into his lungs. A brief and violent spasm engulfed his body. The barely perceptible rolling of the boat did nothing to ease the more pronounced waves in his stomach, and he breathed a prayer of thanks that the call had at least come before breakfast. Eight months into his career as keeper of the peace in St. Adele township, and already this was the second death to require his sanction. He didn't feel himself in danger of getting blasé about such missions, but right now he wasn't sure which caused his greater anguish, the lifeless body in the cabin below or its unfortunate location on a boat. *Any* boat.

Anchored in the wide mouth of Huron Bay, nose to the open lake, the *Frelser* faced a boundless expanse of mirror-smooth water. Phantoms of mist waltzed over its unruffled surface, filtering the rays of newly risen sun and wrapping the scene in a soft luminescence. It was a setting to inspire poets and painters, mysterious, serene, and, as far as McIntire was concerned, purgatory on earth. Ten more minutes on this tub and he'd be as prostrate as the man he'd come to see.

He thought of the day, now literally a lifetime ago, when he first met Nels Bertelsen. *Met* was not exactly the right word; the boy had come to ask for water and had spoken only to McIntire's mother. It was Nels' hair, milk-white and almost to his shoulders, that had so fascinated the six year old Johnny McIntire as he watched from his observation point on the woodpile, waiting while his mother split the kindling that he would carry to the kitchen woodbox. McIntire could see him still, trotting into the yard on an enormous black workhorse, his bare feet dangling, and those gossamer locks flying out behind, like the fairies in his Granny Kate's nightmare-inducing tales.

This stranger had answered Sophie McIntire's questions solemnly, in accents not unlike her own. His family had just come today. Yes, it was they who had bought the Association farmland. He had a sister who was twelve. Her name was Julie. No, his father wouldn't be looking for work in either the lumber camps or the mines—they were going to plant apple trees.

McIntire smiled to himself as he remembered his mother's reaction when she realized that the newcomers intended not only to *plant* apple trees—everybody did that—but to make their living at it. As she put it to her husband, "Those simpletons will starve to death long before they even get a sniff of their first apple."

Ole Bertelsen hadn't quite realized his dream of becoming Michigan's most prosperous fruit producer, but he didn't starve either. If in some winters the family had little more than potatoes and the occasional piece of deer meat on its table, they were not that much different from most of their neighbors. And Nels, at least, had survived and gone on to oversee the orchard operation himself before abandoning it to take up his father's original occupation, fishing.

McIntire hadn't been around to witness Bertelsen's transformation from fruit grower to fisherman, but had not been surprised when he heard of it. Like the rest of the Bertelsens, the young Nels had been a slave to the family business. But regardless of the hours he put in pruning, planting, and picking, it was never too late, too dark, or too cold to squeeze in some time on the lake. His allergy may have been the goad that pushed him from the fields to the water, but McIntire couldn't imagine that he had needed a very forceful push.

From the first day of the spring fishing season, Bertelsen had been persistent in inviting McIntire to spend a day on the *Frelser*. McIntire was equally emphatic in declining. The last boat trip he and Nels had taken together was the one that carried them across the Atlantic in the fall of 1917 aboard one of the world's largest luxury liners, unhappily pressed into service as a U.S. Army troop ship. Memories of that passage had kept McIntire out of anything bigger than a rowboat since. The mere sight of a whitecapped wave was sufficient to send him plummeting back through time to those interminable nights spent curled in a cramped bunk in the belly of the *Leviathan* as she plunged in darkness through cold black seas. He was only half joking when he said it was that hellish experience that had kept him from returning to the United States until air travel became a reasonable option. He'd found that air sickness was also no picnic, but flying cut the trip and the view was almost worth the loss of a little gastric lining.

Nels, McIntire recalled, had suffered no such agonies during that long ago voyage. On the few occasions that McIntire had left his evil smelling cot to stagger to an open deck— and hastily to a railing—Nels had been there ahead of him, ruddy face to the wind and an expression that clearly showed he'd fallen in love. "Someday," he'd informed McIntire, "we'll be taking a ride on *my* boat." The inward smile came again, a rueful one. Since his return McIntire had discovered that it was a rare event in St. Adele to hear the name Nels Bertelsen uttered without the added designation, "that bullheaded Norwegian," and Nels had stayed true to his reputation to the end. He'd gotten his damn boat and had lured McIntire on board it at last, even if he had to die to do it.

A half dozen gulls wheeled and careened past his ears, engaged in a fray over some distasteful looking flotsam a few yards off the bow. Their shrieks were countered by a chest-wrenching cough, reminding McIntire that he was not alone on the tiny deck. He wiped his sleeve across his mouth, pushed his glasses farther up on his nose, and turned to Simon Lindstrom, an elderly man of dwarfish proportions and gnome-like features, features rosy and unlined, belying a lifetime spent on the water.

Lindstrom sat hunched on the rail, resplendent in yellow waterproof overalls and a red wool shirt. He nodded to McIntire and emitted another stream of raucous coughing, rocking on his perch and crowing like a brilliantly hued rooster. McIntire swallowed bile and the urge to leap forward and yank the old man down to a more stable position. "Thank you for waiting, Mr. Lindstrom," he said. "Was it you that found him?"

Lindstrom struck his chest with his fist, cleared his throat, and leaned at a perilous angle to spit over his shoulder. His response, when it finally came, was in a creative merging of languages that took McIntire several seconds to unravel as, "Oh no, not me. It was Jonas there." He waved the stem of his pipe in the general direction of two skiffs snugged up like nurslings to the *Frelser's* side. In the stern of the nearest, an anemic-appearing youngster huddled in his Mackinaw, picking at a frayed spot on the knee of his dungarees. "My son Benjamin's boy. He's work with Nels two year now." Lindstrom added this last with eyes cast down, the better, McIntire supposed, to negate any unbecoming note of grandfatherly pride.

"You mean Jonas was here on the boat with Nels when he died?" No wonder the kid looked so peaked.

Lindstrom shook his head. "Nah, we just come out. I come in the skiff here, to pick my bait nets, and I take the boy along to Nels. Then he don't need no ride to Nels' place, you know. I go home to bait-on for Ben and me, but with this big fancy boat Jonas just sit by the stove and cut bait while Nels take her to the banks."

But Simon had not gone home, and it was tragically evident that Nels Bertelsen hadn't taken anything much of anywhere on this morning. McIntire braced himself against the rail and pressed on. "Let me be sure I've got this straight. Nels was waiting for Jonas and netting bait fish here in the bay before going out to the fishing banks. You intended to drop Jonas off at his boat when you came to pull in your own bait nets?"

"Ya," Lindstrom's head bobbed emphatically, "that is what I just tell you. We pull up to the *Frelser* here, but damn if we see Nels nowhere. His nets is just hangin' out the hatch, and still the fish is in, and nobody is pulling. We yell out, and Nels, he don't say nothing. So the boy, he climb in the hatch too, and was right back out, quick as a wink. 'Nels is just sittin' with his pants down,' he says, 'and he ain't breathin' *ay*tall.' So I get on board and by golly there sits Nels, dead as the doornail. I tell Jonas he better hop back in that skiff and high-tail it home lickety-split. 'Call the constabulary,' I tell him, 'Talk fast and talk Swede!'"

The boy had indeed talked "Swede" when he made that crack-of-dawn call. It was a common ploy when ringing the constable on his six-party line with information the caller hoped to keep confidential. It seldom kept anything really interesting out of the public domain for long, but might have worked in this case. Jonas's Swedish had been considerably less comprehensible than his grandfather's English.

"Go ahead and talk Swede too, if you like," McIntire suggested, and began to do so himself. "What time was it when you found Nels?"

Lindstrom nodded and replied in the vaguely Gallic tones of his native Varmland. "It was getting pretty light already, after four, maybe almost four-thirty. I don't wear a watch on the lake—might lose it, you know. Jonas was out of here like a shot. I suppose it took him about twenty minutes to get home and call you."

"So Jonas went for help immediately after you found the...after you found him?"

"Well, yes, he did. What do you think, we stopped for coffee? Maybe read the paper?"

"I mean," McIntire explained, "did you try to revive him or anything?"

Lindstrom dismissed the question with gutteral "ech" and a flip of his chin. "There was no chance of that. I could see right away that he was dead. If I hadn't been sure of it, I'd have told Jonas to get the *doctor*. But I see you brought him along anyway." He paused briefly, as if to underscore the folly of summoning a doctor to minister to a dead man, before going on. "What did he say happened? Was it a heart attack? Nels was still young. But he was a great one for letting himself get all worked up over things. That's not good for the old pump, they say."

Dabbling at four o'clock every morning in the liquid ice that was Lake Superior water couldn't be too beneficial to that "pump" either. "I don't think he's done with his examination yet," McIntire told him. "To tell the truth, it was Dr. Guibard brought me out. I don't have a boat." McIntire's confession of boatlessness brought a droop to Lindstrom's mouth, an expression of profound pity mirroring McIntire's feelings toward those who *were* compelled to travel on water.

One of Lindstrom's remarks still mystified him. When he'd first boarded the *Frelser* and entered the dark cabin below, he'd tripped over a wooden box—a box that was stacked to the rim with the posterior halves of small herring, each wearing a large hook where, in the natural order of things, its head would be. It accounted for the seagulls' breakfast, but didn't quite fit with Jonas Lindstrom's aborted plan to "sit by the stove and cut bait." Not that it really mattered, but if McIntire was going to be here he might as well make some pretense of filling his office.

"I understood you to say," he said, "that Nels and Jonas caught their bait here in the bay, and Jonas baited the hooks while they were on the way to their fishing grounds. But there's a box of baited hooks down there. Does that mean that Nels was waiting longer than usual for Jonas? Did he have time to string up those herring himself before he died?"

"Oh, no. Like I said, Nels only got his nets half pulled in. But he made a good catch, and he sure won't be needing any bait today, so I kept myself busy while I was waiting for you to get here. And I can save my nets for tomorrow." Lindstrom pushed himself off the rail, landing with a thump and setting in motion a shudder that ran along the deck and rippled upward through McIntire's stomach to his throat. While the fisherman's complexion might have escaped the ravages of icy wind and water, his joints obviously hadn't. McIntire could almost hear the grating as Lindstrom painfully shifted from roosting position to standing. He then settled the suspenders of his overalls more securely on his shoulders and rapped the bowl of his pipe on the rail, sending a smoldering black lump hissing into the water. A sharp-eyed gull swooped in and downed the tasty morsel in a gulp. Lindstrom stuffed the pipe into his pocket and rubbed his hands briskly together. They were as gnarled as cedar roots with knuckles the size and color of ripe plums.

"I have to be going now," he announced. "I fish with Ben, you know. He'll think it's me that's had the heart attack if I don't get back soon. We should have been on our way an hour ago." He called down to his grandson, "Jonas, get your ass in gear! Bring that skiff up now. Then I think you take the *Frelser* on."

So, if McIntire had deciphered this correctly, he wasn't expected to pilot the big boat back into town himself. It was the best news he had gotten so far that day, but it was adding to his growing suspicion that Lindstrom's reasoning was as convoluted as his speech. "Mr. Lindstrom," he asked, "if your grandson can handle this boat, why didn't he just head back into St. Adele when you first found Nels? Why make two trips?"

And why drag me all the way out here to risk losing half my guts in the lake? he might have added, had he been a less charitable man.

"Well, hell, I think I can't let Jonas do that all by hisself. And Nels, he ain't in no shape to have the whole town come trooping in to have a look." Lindstrom's overlarge boots made a hollow sound as he crossed the deck, then turned once more to McIntire. "Nels Bertelsen was ornery as they come, but... well, you know, he didn't hafta hire just a dumb kid like Jonas."

With that, he disappeared into the vessel's pilot house. Seconds later, he emerged through the hatch in the side of the hull and dropped with a grunt into the skiff. Jonas scrambled in through the opening and heaved the bait box out to his grandfather, who settled it lovingly against his knees. The outboard roared, the little boat gave a leap, and Simon Lindstrom sped off toward the brightening shoreline.

II

McIntire took one last lungful of air and himself reentered the cabin.

It was as if a bag had been pulled over his head. The *Frelser's* interior was a murky cavern choked with odors of coal smoke, motor oil, and fish, overlaid with the acrid smell of human excrement. McIntire felt his gullet threaten to erupt and edged nearer to the open hatch. The space would not accommodate his entire height, and he stood with knees slightly bent and his head and shoulders painfully cocked to one side as he regarded Dr. Mark Guibard, semi-retired physician and Flambeau county coroner.

The doctor had apparently completed his examination and had assumed a similarly contorted position, not from any lack of headroom, but the better to sight along the deck and under the pot-bellied heater in the attitude of one who had dropped a dime and wasn't sure where it had rolled to.

Behind him, in a weak pool of electric light, Nels Bertelsen sat on the damp deck boards with his back against the door of an unpainted pine cabinet, and his feet, in heavy rubber boots, extended before him. His wool shirt lay discarded at his side, and his waterproof overalls and woolen longjohns were pushed down to bunch around his knees, exposing a torso that glowed stark blue-white, ironically reminiscent of the fish he had come seeking. The pallor of this ample mid-section gave way abruptly to a deep purplish-brown on his throat and forearms. The contrast was even more pronounced between his weathered face and the fringe of white hair that straggled, scarecrow style, from under the tattered gray stocking cap. His eyes, staring out through the hatch, were the hazy blue of a winter sky. Fully clothed, Bertelsen's stockiness, ruddy cheeks, and snowy hair had always given him something of a clown-like appearance. This morning the watery light revealed chest and shoulders wrapped with muscles like steel bands—a body that radiated vigorous masculinity. McIntire could scarcely comprehend that there was no life in it.

The doctor turned back to Bertelsen and tugged at the overalls to cover the soiled underclothing. He picked up the hypodermic syringe that rested against the lifeless fingers, and stood erect, his feet wide apart on the wet deck boards. At the sight of the constable, he boomed, "Christ Almighty, if you weren't more or less standing up, I'd think I had two corpses on my hands! I'd sure as hell hate to see what you'd look like if we were actually out in the lake—in a moving boat—with maybe a wave or two thrown in."

McIntire put a hand against the boards of the hull to steady himself. "I'd hate to be feeling what I'd feel like if we were really out in the lake, and I'd appreciate it if you'd avoid making references to undulating water."

The doctor chuckled at McIntire's discomfort, his verbiage, or both. He could afford to laugh, McIntire thought. For all that Guibard had spent a lifetime dealing with death, disease, and traumatic injury, it seemed that such human misfortunes could never touch him personally. He had the body and constitution of a man half his age. And the vanity. Even this morning he was pressed and polished and brushed to perfection, and exuded a cloying aura of Old Spice and Wildroot Cream Oil. McIntire would have paid money to see how he had managed to effect such sartorial splendor between the time his call had roused the doctor from his bed and the fifteen minutes later that he had come charging over the water to snatch McIntire off the end of Bertelsen's dock.

"Don't worry," Guibard advised, with a hint of a smile still lurking in his eyes, "I know it's hell, but in all my years of practice, I've never seen anybody die of *mal de mer.*" He dropped the syringe into his bag. "I have come across quite a few who would have liked to, though." His expression became marginally more sympathetic. "But take a few deep breaths and try to pull yourself together. We're going to have to lay him out straight before too much rigor sets in. And the term 'dead weight' is an apt one—he'll be heavy and every bit as uncooperative as he was in life. You think we should get...?" He nodded toward the thin back of Jonas Lindstrom, just visible through the opening to the pilot house.

McIntire considered, and shook his head.

A deck a few feet wide ran around the perimeter of the boat's interior. Straight down the center was an area open to the bowels of the vessel, revealing the engine, some components of the steering mechanism and, McIntire supposed, a place for holding fish. The boards on which Bertelsen sat were water-soaked and slimy with the residue of Simon Lindstrom's "baiting-on."

"Let's get him over to a dry spot." McIntire stepped over a pile of soggy netting and grasped the slick, rubber-clad legs, leaving the exposed flesh of the shoulders to the other man. Together, accompanied by panting and grunts, they maneuvered the body along the deck and around the still hot potbellied stove to place it in front of a closed hatch opposite the one where Nels had been retrieving his catch. As the doctor eased his burden gently to the deck, McIntire retrieved the fisherman's crumpled shirt and slid it under his head.

Guibard extracted a gleaming white handkerchief from his coat pocket and pressed it daintily to his brow. "I'll zip back into town and call for the ambulance. I'd as soon get well back into the bay before the wind starts to kick up. Simon tells me Jonas drives this beast all the time, so he should be able to get you back okay. But take your time, eh? Once I get in, it'll be at least another half an hour before the ambulance can make it out from Chandler. We don't want to be hanging around the dock attracting a crowd any longer than necessary." He made a circuit of the deck, frowning slightly as he surveyed the surroundings a final time, peering down into the greasy mechanical innards. He turned back to McIntire with abrupt severity. "Oh, and be sure you leave everything the way you find it here. Don't take anything off the boat." Before McIntire could respond he added in a milder tone, "If Nels had life insurance there might be questions."

McIntire nodded. Curses! The looting and pillaging would have to wait for another day. He pulled the string that switched off the single naked bulb, plunging the cabin into twilight. They didn't need a dead battery. "Will you be doing an autopsy? Hold an inquest or anything?"

"What for? There's no doubt about what killed him. I'll give him another once-over when I get in some better light, see if I can find the stinger. But bees don't always leave their stinger behind." The doctor looked down upon the inert body. "He spent the last ten years of his life scared shitless of this happening. Took every reasonable precaution and a hell of a lot of unreasonable ones, and for what? Made life miserable, looking over his shoulder every minute, and in the end one of the little buggers nailed him anyway. We might have been able to desensitize him, but he went into conniptions every time I brought the subject up. Wouldn't have anything to do with it. Damn fool."

"What about the antidote or whatever you call it? Didn't he give himself the shot?"

"Epinephrine—adrenaline. He must have gotten some of it in anyway. There's a mark on his leg from the injection. But there are no guarantees." He pulled the bib of the dead man's waterproofs up a little higher over the pale abdomen.

"Not a very dignified way to die, eh? I told him to put the shot in his thigh. I wanted him to get it into a good-sized hunk of flesh. If he'd tried to jab himself in the shoulder and tensed up, he'd have snapped that needle like a toothpick. His muscles were like concrete."

McIntire swallowed. "How long would you say…?" He let the question trail off.

Guibard shrugged. "Oh, I'd figure he's been dead between an hour and an hour and a half—not more than that for sure. It couldn't have happened very long before he was found. He'd already started to pull in the nets when he died, and he wouldn't have got out here much ahead of the Lindstroms."

It didn't take a coroner to figure that out. "I meant to ask," McIntire said, "how long did it take for him to die? *How*, exactly, did he die?"

Guibard rubbed his palms with his handkerchief and gazed out over the water. McIntire followed his line of sight. The sun had burned away the last of the vapor. Superior stretched away to merge imperceptibly with the horizon, interrupted only by the distant Huron Islands, the interplay of light and shadow on their steep cliffs creating misty castles suspended in air, unreal as a desert mirage. A light breeze was now teasing the lake with sporadic gusts, sending intermittent streams of ripples skipping across its surface.

The doctor cleared his throat and touched the handkerchief to his lips before he spoke. "Anaphylaxis is a complicated reaction, but basically it boils down to one thing, the tissues swell and cut off the airway and the victim chokes to death. I can't say he never knew what hit him, but he wouldn't have suffered long. If the epinephrine had no effect at all he would have passed out within fifteen minutes or so and probably not lived long after that."

Fifteen minutes? The way Nels had been sitting it didn't look like he'd lasted much more than fifteen seconds. "But why wouldn't the epinephrine have an effect? Why didn't it work?"

"How the hell would I know? I'm a doctor, not a magician!" Guibard balled the handkerchief and stuffed it into his pants pocket. "Maybe the sting went straight into a vein or artery. Maybe he didn't get the shot in soon enough. Maybe some of it ended up on the floor. The shot didn't help much. If it had, he'd have had time to get his pants on and start to head back in. At least he'd have still been alive when Jonas showed up."

"Are you sure he wasn't?" McIntire asked. "He might have only been unconscious. Maybe if they'd put *him* in that motorboat and gone in 'lickety-split' you could have saved him."

The doctor picked up his bag. "It's possible, but not very likely. It looks like he lost consciousness within minutes. The syringe was lying like he'd just dropped it. Simon was sure he was dead. He did what he thought was best. That's all you can ask."

"It sounded a bit to me like old Simon did what he thought would be the least time consuming. Did you notice that he even went so far as to help himself to Nels' hooks and bait? Sat right next to him and chopped the heads off those fish, couldn't even be bothered to cover the poor man, just let him lay there half naked in his own…"

"*Shit,* John. You can say it. You're not in some duchess' drawing room now." Guibard looked at McIntire with an air of astonishment mingled with that same patronizing sympathy he had shown at his sea-sickness. "And, Jeez, come down to earth. The Lindstroms weren't headed out to make a few casts and have a goddamn picnic lunch. This time of year they're working eighteen hours a day, seven days a week, just to stay alive. The time Simon spent hanging around here means it'll be midnight before he gets to bed tonight, and he'll be up again at three o'clock tomorrow morning."

The wiry coroner climbed up into the pilot house, lowered himself with enviable agility out the narrow door into his bobbing motorboat and departed, leaving a somewhat chagrined McIntire alone with a fourteen-year-old boy and the body of his childhood friend.

McIntire slid the door of the hatch into place and called up to Jonas that they could go. Without a word, the young man cranked up the anchor and started the engine. They moved off at an agonizingly slow crawl. Guibard need have no worries about their having a long wait for the ambulance.

With the hatch closed, the mélange of odors combined with the monotonous grumble of the engine to make the space even more claustrophobic. The only light entered through the narrow doorway to the pilot house and four tiny portholes, two near the bow, two in the stern. McIntire bent his head under the low ceiling and shuffled unsteadily toward the rear, where an arrangement of cupboards covered by a wide shelf for a countertop made a rudimentary kitchen. The "galley," he reminded himself, and wondered why ordinary things always seemed to have out-of-the-ordinary names when they happened to be found on a boat: the galley, the cabin, the head. Sailors were, by and large, a pretentious bunch.

The boat gave a sudden lurch, and McIntire lunged for a small hinged box that came skipping across the counter toward him. Its interior was cushioned and contained a long strip of soft rubber, a small bottle with a handwritten label—"isopropyl alcohol"—a wad of absorbent cotton, and a hypodermic syringe with a piece of adhesive tape wrapped around the barrel about a third of the way up. These were accompanied by a folded paper which proved to be a type-written list of instructions. Bertelsen was to have used a tourniquet between the site of the sting and his heart, if pos-sible. He was to fill the syringe to the level of the bottom of the tape, and, after swabbing off the spot with alcohol—a step Nels had apparently chosen to omit, the cotton was dry—inject the entire contents into the thigh area. He should then briskly rub the area around the site of the injection to improve absorption, and immediately seek medical attention. McIntire held the syringe up to the beam of light coming through the porthole. It was empty and appeared to be dry, not the one Bertelsen had used that morning. A spare maybe? The instructions didn't say anything about a second injection, just admonished Nels to SEEK IMMEDIATE MEDICAL ATTENTION. There was no sign of a bottle or other container that might have held the epinephrine. Maybe Guibard had taken that, too. He returned the syringe to its case and snapped it shut.

The only other objects in evidence were a barn-shaped black metal lunch pail and a red thermos, held in place by a sort of wooden box affair nailed to the counter. A folded copy of *Grit*, dated February 7, was wedged between them. He stuck the bee sting kit in next to the thermos, and, grasping the edge of the counter to steady himself, opened the cupboard doors one by one until he located a slightly musty blanket woven with a flamboyant Indian-inspired design.

As he started to turn away, he became aware of a barely audible but persistent buzzing noise, higher pitched and independent of the steady rumble of the engine. It was only inches from his ear, and seemed to come from the clothing that hung on the wall, a yellow slicker, a couple of shirts, and the top half of a set of wool underwear. He listened for a moment, then reached over and shook out the tucked-up sleeve of a heavy plaid shirt. A bee emerged at the wrist and began a laborious climb toward the shoulder. Its fat body was banded with yellowish brown stripes. It was an unremarkable insect, hardly McIntire's idea of an instrument of death.

McIntire contemplated its sluggish movements. Did bees really die after they sting someone? He picked up the flimsy tabloid and rolled it into a tube. "Well, here's one that will," he murmured. A swat sent the insect spiraling to the counter where it continued its angry buzzing, twirling helplessly on its back. He gave another whack, somewhat harder than necessary, and tucked the paper, with the squashed bee fused to page one, back into its spot. Then he clutched the blanket to his chest and teetered back to where the fallen fisherman lay.

Kneeling beside the body, he unfolded the blanket over it. When he reached the smooth, hairless chest he stopped. A narrow bluish scar snaked from the dead man's collar bone across his shoulder, a relic of another battle perhaps, one that had a happier outcome. McIntire placed the palm of his hand on one of the sun-browned cheeks. There was unexpected warmth in the skin and he recoiled as if burned. He sat back on his heels and contemplated the features: the network of tiny broken veins, the stubble of beard, the deeply carved lines around the slack mouth. There was nothing left of the intensity, the determination—admittedly the obstinacy—that had been written on that face in life. It was the face of a tired and defenseless old man—the old man that Nels Bertelsen would never be.

"Well Nels, you stubborn son-of-a-gun, if you're listening, I'm here on board the *Frelser*. You got your way, as usual." His words were swallowed up by the grumble of the engine. "But I really think you've gone to extremes this time."

The *Frelser*, savior, liberator. An ignominious death was surely not what Bertelsen had anticipated when he shucked off the burdens of his father's farm and took to the open waters.

McIntire reflected with regret on the limited acquaintance he had had with the adult Nels Bertelsen. That wood sprite on the fiery stallion was more real to him than the body lying here with the warmth of life ebbing away. "*Farvel, gamle venn, og takk for alt.*" Thanks for all, old friend. He smoothed back the hair and pulled the blanket up over it.

III

McIntire decided to take a short detour on his way to take the news of her bereavement to Lucille Delaney, Nels Bertelsen's…Nels Bertelsen's what? She was popularly referred to as his "mail order bride." This was a misnomer on at least one count; while Lucy had shared Bertelsen's home for quite a few years, she had not become his wife. On the other hand, the romance may well have been conducted with the aid of the U.S. Mails. Bertelsen had not been known to travel far abroad—at least not since his soldiering days—and Lucy was definitely not a locally grown product. Her background was shrouded in secrecy, although universal speculation held that she was Southern.

McIntire considered himself a compassionate and tactful person, but he had little faith in his ability to console a grieving widow, legitimate or not, and no desire to be closeted alone with Lucy Delaney under the best of circumstances. It wouldn't hurt to have a woman along, someone to provide comfort and sympathy. His own wife would be that perfect someone, but Leonie preferred to live by what she called the "continental clock." The time it would require to render her upright and functional before ten in the morning was time that probably shouldn't be spared right now. He turned off the aptly named Orchard Road, which would have taken him from Bertelsen's dock straight to his home, and traveled a half mile or so down the township's main thoroughfare, the Swale Road. With any luck he might recruit the notoriously early rising Mia Thorsen.

McIntire asked himself, as he had many times before without receiving a satisfactory answer, what demon could possibly have been in possession of his faculties when he agreed to this constable business. He had been astonished when the contingent of neighbors descended on him the previous autumn to request that he complete the tenure of the venerable George Armstrong "Walleye" Wall, who had suffered a fatal heart attack when attempting to hoist up a large hog for butchering.

They were most persuasive in their arguments. As a "military man," and the flesh and blood of Colin McIntire, he was the perfect choice for the job. The constable, they emphasized, wasn't reviled the way, say, a game warden was. And after all, how hard could it be? Track down a stray cow now and then, break up the occasional beer party at the gravel pit. Anything really serious was a job for the county sheriff. Old Walleye had handled it okay, and he was past eighty when that sow had taken her revenge. Besides, only a few months were left in his uncompleted term.

There were also added benefits: a telephone at township expense, the opportunity to keep up on the latest news of the neighborhood, and a little extra cash from the odd fine. They graciously avoided mentioning that, unlike most of the able-bodied men thereabouts, John McIntire appeared to have plenty of time on his hands.

Admittedly, McIntire was not only surprised, but more than just a little flattered, although not particularly encouraged by the implied comparison to his late father. Most of all he welcomed the opportunity to become an active member of the community. So after demurring only as strenuously as courtesy demanded, he had allowed himself to be persuaded. "Allowed himself"? Hell, he had pounced on it like a cat on spilled milk.

The job had kept him busier than he had anticipated and was far more burdensome than the pittance in compensation reflected. He had not endeared himself to the town's adolescents, but once their fall party season had drawn to a close and the countryside became buried under several feet of snow, he expected things to settle down. He had neglected to consider the resourcefulness of the Upper Peninsula folk. Hardly a day—and, more to the point, a night—went by that he wasn't dragged away from the warmth of his home to investigate some nefarious goings-on or settle some petty squabble, invariably finding, upon reaching the scene of the alleged crime, that the issue had resolved itself. The frequent summonses came to a suspicious halt following the December town board meeting, where he had presented a meticulous report of each incident, along with a detailed record of the expenses he had incurred. Not a single further call had come until that night in mid-February when things did indeed turn serious. A local farmer was bludgeoned to death with a manure shovel, without a doubt a job for the county sheriff, if there had happened to be one handy. On this particular evening, Sheriff Koski and his deputies were up to their armpits in snow some thirty miles away. By the time they reached St. Adele around noon the next day, McIntire had, through some fortunate alignment of the stars, apprehended the criminal who had obligingly confessed.

Shortly after this event, when the constable's term was drawing to a close, the McIntires embarked upon an extended sojourn in warmer climes, giving St. Adele's criminal element free rein. After a month spent visiting McIntire's mother in Florida and driving leisurely through a southern spring of soft warm nights and hills ablaze with mountain laurel, they had returned to find Northern Michigan still held in winter's implacable embrace, and John McIntire elected to a full term as constable on a near unanimous write-in vote.

It was barely possible that this vote of confidence was the result of his rapid resolution of the homicide, but McIntire couldn't help but feel that he somehow had been the victim of a well organized version of "put one over on the new guy"— a sort of civic snipe-hunt. Well, at least the blackfly hatch had been a bit early this year, nipping the spring gravel pit parties in the bud.

He left his car at the end of the Thorsens' rutted driveway and walked up to the house.

He had driven past many times since his return, but, for one reason or another, had not actually visited. And his passings-by hadn't given him a clear view of the structure, shielded as it was by a grove of spruce. Now he stopped in the shelter of those trees and gazed with interest upon the familiar slate-gray asphalt siding and solid brick chimneys of the house in which he'd spent the first six years of his life.

It was within those walls that, from the time he first realized that *minulla an jano* would get a dipperful of water from Mama Saarinen as quickly as *jag ar torstig* did from his own mother, he began the love affair with languages that had become such a dominant force in his life. It was also here that he'd formed that other bond that had played its own part in shaping his destiny…he pushed the thought aside.

Except for the screening in of one of the two wide porches, the home looked much as it had in his boyhood.

The sound of a light but steady hammering intruded on his thoughts and reminded him of the reason he had come. The tapping emanated from a building added since his youth, a low-roofed structure of unpainted concrete block, sunk deep in the shadows of spruce and giant hemlock. Even on this bright June morning a faint glimmer of electric light showed through the open doorway. This must be the new workshop, which Mia insisted upon referring to as her "studio."

His approach took him past a garden in which the first shoots of green beans and sweet corn were emerging optimistically from the earth, but appeared to be condemned from the start by an already flourishing crop of pigweed and quack grass. He reflected that if Mia Thorsen's garden was any indication of her nurturing skills, her childless state might not be a complete tragedy. He had some fleeting second thoughts about the wisdom of asking her to minister to Lucy.

Four or five geese lounged near the pumphouse that stood at the end of the garden, taking advantage of a brief period of sunlight reflecting off the white walls. It was clear that the fowl frequented this path, too. McIntire grimaced and stepped carefully as he crossed to the studio and stood in the doorway. He searched the gloomy space for the source of the light. It proved to be a single lamp at the end of a long arm, aimed at a littered work bench where the angular figure of Mia Thorsen was bent over a piece of wood, hammer and chisel in hand. As a child, McIntire had once heard his father voice the baffling opinion that young Mia Vogel looked "like she'd been conceived through a sheet." In the dusky workshop, with the meager lamplight imparting a frosty translucence to her silver-gray hair and fair skin, her aspect was even more wraithlike than usual. He held his breath until the delicate tapping sounds ceased, and Mia straightened up. "Come on in, John, you're blocking the light."

"What light?" McIntire questioned. "It's darker than the inside of a cow in here, as Ma used to say. It beats me how you keep from chopping your fingers off."

Mia bent to blow the piece she was carving free of shavings, and squinted critically at her work. "This is a clock case for *Madame* Sylvia Hollander. What Madame wants Madame gets, and she wants it to look 'just like Eban did it himself.' If I want to carve like Papa did, I have to see like Papa did. He used kerosene lamps, and his eyesight was almost as bad as yours. But he was sure a heck of a lot more observant." She dropped the tools onto the bench and held up her hands, which were curiously out of keeping with her overall appearance of fragility. They were square, blunt-nailed, and strong, and bore the healed scars of a score or more minor mishaps and at least one major calamity: they comprised nine and a half fingers.

She waggled the stub of her left forefinger. "This is what happens when people sneak up on me."

She switched off the light. "But come on out, I was about to take a break anyway. How're things going with you?"

"Maybe you should get a watchdog, if you don't want unexpected visitors," McIntire stalled. For reasons he wasn't telling himself, he shrank from bringing up the purpose of his visit.

"That's what the geese are supposed to be for."

McIntire looked at the droppings that littered the path and the grass of the yard. "I would imagine they do keep the Fuller Brush Man on his toes," he observed.

"Worthless critters. Arnie Johnson swore to me that they would sound the alarm the minute anybody set foot in the yard, *and* they'd keep the weeds out of my garden, too. 'You'll never pull another dandelion,' he said." At McIntire's inadvertent glance in the direction of the garden, she smiled. "And you can see, he was right about that."

She removed her canvas apron and began vigorously shaking out the collection of sawdust and shavings, but McIntire's expression must have been easy to read; looking directly at him for the first time, she froze in mid-shake.

"I take it this isn't a social call," she said. "Don't tell me Nick's run afoul of the law again. What's he done this time—dumped the Sears catalogs in the lake?"

Her tone remained light, but her grasp on the apron had accelerated to a deathgrip.

McIntire hastened to reassure her, "So far as I'm aware, your husband hasn't been treating either Sears-Roebuck or the mighty Gitche-Gumme with anything other than the respect they deserve."

Mia looked at him through narrowed eyes before she tossed the apron in the general direction of a peg inside the door, shrugged when it landed on the concrete floor, and brushed off the sleeves of her flannel shirt. She wore baggy twill work pants that obviously belonged to her husband, barely reaching mid-calf, but bunched up where they were belted around her narrow waist. McIntire had never gotten quite used to seeing grown women wearing trousers, and he stared in fascination as he followed her to the porch.

"He did have his so-called barber shop quartet practice last night," she was saying. "There's no telling what those yahoos will get up to when they get turned loose together. I thought when Wylie joined them he'd kind of keep the lid on things, but he's turned into a regular Good Time Charlie himself. They're worse than a bunch of high schoolers, and they must have made quite a night of it last night. This morning Nick could hardly keep awake long enough to make it out the door. Well, he always says he can drive that route with his eyes closed—and no doubt he has, many times. I thought I noticed a new dent or two in the car, too, but it's kind of hard to say."

When McIntire was seated on one of the worn wicker chairs with Mia regarding him expectantly across a scarred metal table, he hesitated once more. In his anxiety over the necessity of informing Lucy about Bertelsen, he hadn't considered what Mia's reaction might be. She, too, had known Nels since they were children. They had lived practically within shouting distance of each other for over forty years. She might have much stronger feelings about the tragedy than Lucy herself, who, after all, was a relative newcomer, practically a stranger by comparison. For that matter, McIntire himself was a stranger in many ways. He felt the familiar pang of envy that always struck when he was reminded that St. Adele and its inhabitants had not been sealed in a time capsule on the day he boarded that ship in

Hoboken. They had inconsiderately lived on for thirty years without McIntire's participation, or even observation, except through his mother's letters. The sadness that he felt at Bertelsen's passing was for a young man who had been dead and gone for three decades. Mia had just lost someone who had been a consistent presence over the entire course of her lifetime, a circumstance McIntire could not even imagine.

"How much longer are you going to keep me hanging?" she finally asked. "Let's have it."

Undiluted terror, transient but unmistakable, leapt into Mia's eyes when she heard that Nels Bertelsen was dead, but her only response was a stiff, "How?" The news that he had died from a bee sting brought an incredulous look. Silence then descended, a silence that McIntire attempted to fill by relating the story of the morning's events in scrupulous detail. When he finished up by lamely informing her that Nels seemed to have netted quite a few herring that morning, she remained unmoving, her water-blue eyes fixed on his, frowning slightly while she slowly wound her single long braid around the fingers of her right hand in the old familiar gesture McIntire remembered from high school. She could appear to be concentrating furiously, but whether she was comprehending, or even listening, was impossible to tell. He wondered if this compulsion might be the reason she continued to wear her hair in that juvenile style, defying the dictates of fashion and, in his admittedly non-authoritative opinion, good taste.

When she spoke, her voice sounded tired and distant. "I just didn't think it would happen so soon."

"You were expecting this?"

"No, no." She waved her free hand impatiently. "I mean *us*, people our age. We just buried Nick's mother last fall. She was the last of our parents. It would have been nice to have a little breather before our own generation started dropping off."

"Nels didn't exactly die of old age, Mia. It could have happened any time. When you think about it, it's probably surprising that it didn't happen sooner."

Mia stared in the direction of two towering white pines that stood at the edge of the yard and twisted the braid more tightly. "I realize that, and I know that none of us is going to live forever. But if anybody could, I'd have put my money on Nels Bertelsen. He was just too ornery to die. I know he was allergic to bees. Cripes, he was so blasted picky about staying away from them that he could drive you nuts. Well," she admitted, "he did get really sick from bee stings once. He hit a nest of yellow jackets with a mower, and was stung about a dozen times. He was in a coma for a couple days."

"A dozen stings? From yellow jackets? Hornets?" Yet he'd survived.

Mia nodded. "How many stings did he get this time?"

"Only one, so far as I know," McIntire told her, "and that was from an ordinary bee." And minutes later he was dead. An allergic reaction would get worse with each exposure, but this was still remarkable. "When he was stung by the yellow jackets, how long did it take before he lost consciousness?"

"Why? What difference does it make?" Her fingers froze on the braid and the fogginess passed from her eyes.

"No difference, really." McIntire searched for an answer. "I was just hoping that Nels didn't suffer too much."

"Oh. I don't know how long he was conscious. He was alone. He managed to stay upright long enough to drive into Karvonens' store and get help. It was after that happened that he decided to lease the orchards to Wylie and take up fishing. I always thought it was just a convenient excuse to quit farming. I couldn't see that it would keep him away from bees anyway. Papa used to use dead fish to trap wasps."

She turned to McIntire almost accusingly. "Who would have thought just one bee sting could actually *kill* him? How much poison can there be in one of those dinky little things, anyway?" She gave up persecuting the braid and leaned back in her chair with a sigh. "It seems so unfair. Anybody with the guts to survive being young should be guaranteed the right to grow old." She gave him a limp smile. "How's Lucy taking it?"

McIntire was relieved to change the subject to more practical matters.

Once they were in the car, Mia's remoteness returned. She sat stiffly at his side, her hands gripping the edge of the seat as if she expected the modest Studebaker to suddenly rocket off over the treetops.

"Lucy might have already heard, you know," she finally said. "She takes that hike into town every morning to pick up her mail, and once the ambulance showed up the news would be out."

"I hadn't thought of that." McIntire slowed down and swerved to avoid a snowshoe hare that bounded erratically ahead of the car before it disappeared into the bushes at the roadside. "Maybe we won't need to be the ones to tell her after all."

She turned to him in amazement. "Are you actually saying that you prefer that Lucy hears about this through gossip, or maybe sees them packing the body into the ambulance?" She shook her head. "What is it about Lucille Delaney that seems to strike fear into the hearts of even the bravest men?"

"Besides the fact that she's a witch, you mean?"

Mia's whoop of laughter momentarily dissolved the years and transported McIntire back to earlier spring mornings when this road was only a wagon track winding between stump-strewn fields and their travels down it together had been on foot.

"I've heard plenty of Lucy stories," Mia said, "but witch-craft is news to me. Well, you're a man of the world. I guess you would know."

McIntire assumed his most superior tone. "Are you actually so gullible that you think it was mere coincidence that Elsie Karvonen slipped and broke her ankle at her own birthday party, to which, incidentally, Lucy had not been invited? And what about the time that Otto Wilke put his car in the ditch right after he passed Lucy on the road without offering her a ride? 'If you treat people badly, bad things happen to you,' that's what Lucy told Leonie. Naturally she denied wishing Elsie and Otto any bad luck, she said that's just the way things work out. 'As ye sow, so shall ye reap.' Of course Lucy didn't use those exact words. I don't suppose witches go around quoting from the Bible."

"Kind of makes you wonder," Mia remarked, "what poor old Nels did to get that bee sicced on him."

"What could possibly be worse than providing bed and board to a witch?"

Mia's laughter this time was cut short. "Lord, will you just listen to us? No wonder people used to find us so aggravating. Nels probably isn't even cold yet and already we're making jokes about it."

They traveled the rest of the way in silence.

Until this morning, McIntire had not really thought about just how much Nels' allergic condition might have affected his daily life, but now he saw the Bertelsen home from a new perspective. The house was set back from the road, a narrow, tidy building covered with the ubiquitous asphalt "brick siding." No trees shaded its green-shingled roof; no shrubs or flowering plants obscured its stone foundation. The closely-trimmed lawn that spread out around it was interrupted only by a border of evenly spaced spruce stumps along the north side. Several outbuildings occupied the clearing: a garage which dwarfed the residence, a diminutive white painted structure that McIntire remembered as the "summer kitchen," and the long, low greenhouse and with its attached fruit-packing shed. This cluster of buildings, along with various implements of modern husbandry, of which McIntire was able to identify *tractor* and *wagon*, was enclosed by a low white board fence.

On the other side of the fence, contrasting exuberantly with the bleak homestead, lay the orchards. Hundreds of trees were now in full bloom. Billowing clouds of pink and white sprawled over the hillside and out of sight. The air was filled with their perfume and with the twittering of cedar waxwings as they fluttered from tree to tree in an avian feeding frenzy. A half dozen ewes, looking diminished and vulnerable as a consequence of being freshly denuded of their winter wool, lay under one of the nearer trees, placidly chewing, while their lambs formed a line to take turns trotting up the slanted bed of a two-wheeled cart to leap with abandon off the higher end.

Into this scene of bucolic tranquility suddenly strode Lucy Delaney. Her squat body advanced down the slope with a wobbling gait which, combined with the red and blue stripes of her skirt, gave the effect of a child's top teetering in its rotation just before it comes to a complete stop. Her hair, black and wiry, flared out above her ears like the cap of a mushroom. Sagging beige-colored stockings covered her legs, and on her feet were sturdy men's boots.

"Mine eyes have seen the glory!" McIntire said under his breath. "She looks like a stump all got up for the Fourth of July."

"Careful!" Mia warned. "You don't want to spend the rest of your life squatting on a lily pad munching flies."

If Lucy felt any surprise at seeing her two visitors, she gave no indication of it, but greeted them heartily, ushered them with dispatch into her kitchen and strapped on a yellow-flowered apron. She had gotten down the cookie jar and filled the coffee pot with water before McIntire was able to break into her stream of pleasantries. On hearing his news, she stood staring from his face to Mia's for a full minute before she seemed to crumple like the stuffing was being sucked out of her robust body. She dropped into the nearest chair, put her face in her apron, and commenced sobbing, her body shaking with violent spasms.

Mia took over the brewing of the coffee and, after giving Lucy's shoulder an awkward pat, McIntire moved to the window. The lambs had given up their attempts at flying and were expending no less energy in nudging their mothers to their feet to provide a mid-morning meal. As he stood watching, a sudden breeze stirred the trees, creating a shower of petals that swirled like mammoth snowflakes to the ground.

When the sobs had subsided to an occasional hiccup, McIntire turned back to Lucy. Her broad face with its florid complexion was little altered by the extended bout of tears, but her usually strident voice had fallen to barely more than a croak.

"He was always so careful, especially when the trees are blooming. He never went anywhere without his medicine. Why didn't it work? Why were there bees on the boat, anyway?" She looked up at McIntire. "What can I do now? Will I have to find somewhere else to live?"

McIntire had no answer for any of this, and after his feeble attempts at consolation were waved away by Mia, he left the two women and went home to write out a report for the town board.

IV

When McIntire arrived for the funeral the church was already overflowing. A steamy heat rose from the jammed-in bodies, filling the space with a claustrophobic incense, a palpable offering of the community on behalf of its fallen brother. Leonie had spent the morning putting together the week's edition of what she bravely called her newspaper, and had agreed to meet him here. He searched the crowd for her best navy blue hat, praying that she, too, had been late and was seated near the back. Such unworthy supplications were not likely to be acknowledged; he ultimately spotted her waving genteelly to him from the third row. He squeezed in beside her and winced as the St. Adele Zion Lutheran Church choir raised its collective voice in *Children of the Heavenly Father*. It was a sound calculated to speed anyone a wee bit faster on the road to eternity, McIntire reflected.

He used the advantage of his height to quickly and unobtrusively survey the crowd. Although he presumed that most of the mourners were local residents, there was an astonishing number he knew only by sight and some he did not recognize at all, such as the elderly couple seated next to Lucy Delaney in the front pew. As far as he knew, Nels Bertelsen had no living family. Maybe these were friends or relatives of Lucy's. He craned his neck to get a better look, thinking to glean some clue to her arcane background. His optimism was short-lived; Leonie, following his gaze, murmured that the pair were a Mr. and Mrs. Paulson.

"So how do they fit in?" McIntire bent low and whispered back.

"Mr. Paulson was Captain Paulson in the Great War. He was Mr. Bertelsen's commanding officer, and he was the one that saw to it that Mr. Bertelsen was decorated, that he was awarded the Distinguished Service Cross."

Neither Paulson's hearing nor his appreciation of an attractive woman seemed to have dimmed much with the passage of time. At the mention of his name he turned and, upon spying Leonie, grinned widely, exposing a substantial set of sulphur-hued dentures. Leonie smiled in return and waggled her fingers.

"I interviewed the captain this morning," she said. "I'm including the complete story in the obituary."

That could make for interesting reading. Nels himself had been reticent when it came to discussing the incident, and the details were not universally known.

"So what is the whole story?" he asked.

"Well," Leonie whispered, "in a battle near Teirny-Sorny in September of 1918, Nels made no less than eight trips through open country under heavy fire to carry messages between the front lines and his battalion headquarters. He was decorated for his courage, sense of duty, and coolness under fire."

"And there he lies in a box, brought down by a bee."

He hadn't spoke as quietly as he'd intended. An assortment of heads swivelled in his direction, including, at the far end of the pew, that of a shrunken, silver-haired woman.

Even after all the time that had passed, McIntire recognized her immediately. Laurie Post, St. Adele's pre-Lucy scarlet woman. It was difficult to imagine that this wisp of a human being, her body straight-backed but diminished to the size of a child, had ever provoked in her neighbors the kind of animosity that McIntire knew she'd endured. Laurie had radiated strength and vitality when she first entered the community—and the Bertelsen home—all those years ago, as a private duty nurse come to care for Nels' ailing mother, Christina.

Mrs. Bertelsen had eventually succumbed to her illness and Mr. Bertelsen, apparently, to the charms of Laurie herself. She had stayed on for some twenty years, seemingly impervious to the comments of some of her less broad-minded neighbors. Sophie McIntire, in her lengthy letters to her son, had described the cruelties Laurie tolerated without complaint, and how, at the death of the senior Bertelsen, she had fed the mourners, given the house a thorough cleaning, packed the single bag she had brought with her two decades earlier, and left. Now an old woman, she sat with her hands resting in her lap, her fixed look never shifting to left or right, bloody, but unbowed.

Living without benefit of clergy must run in the family, but looking at the heaving of Lucy's black-cloaked shoulders as she snuffled into her handkerchief, McIntire couldn't help thinking that the father had made a better job of it. He chuckled softly to himself and received Leonie's elbow ever so slightly in his ribs.

As the service drew to a close and the pall bearers approached the flag draped casket, McIntire was once again reminded of his status as an outsider.

"Who are they?" Leonie asked.

"Who?"

"The casket bearers. What are their names?"

McIntire was forced to admit that of the six men who were honored by being selected to escort Bertelsen on his final earthly journey, McIntire could name only four. The three generations of Lindstroms were there, hair slicked back and faces flushed above starched white collars, flanked by two others whom McIntire couldn't remember having seen before.

The sixth he had grown up with, Wylie Petworth, the neighbor who had taken over the management of the apple business from Nels. Wylie's empty left sleeve testified that Nels' courage under fire—literally—hadn't begun with World War I. A blaze started by an exploding kerosene heater had long ago cost Wylie his arm, but, thanks to quick action by Nels Bertelsen, not his life.

Today Wylie's black double-breasted suit camouflaged the underdeveloped shoulder and minimized his usual slightly off-balance appearance. He grasped the folded American flag and ceremoniously presented it to Lucy.

Pastor Ahlgren spoke the final goodbye in the language of Bertelsen's fathers, "*vi lyser fred over ditt minne,* Nels Bertelsen," and the casket was moved out of the church to the waiting hearse.

McIntire extended his arm to Leonie and joined the sluggish procession toward the open doors. He heard a muffled "Good afternoon," and looked down to see what appeared to be an oversized tuft of cotton bobbing around the vicinity of his left elbow. It was the snowy locks of Laurie Post.

"So Johnny's come marching home, at last. You were just a squirt when you left, but I'd have recognized you anywhere. I don't suppose you know who I am?"

McIntire assured her that he did, indeed, remember her, and proceeded to introduce his wife. "Miss Post took care of Nels after he lost both his sister and his mother," he explained to Leonie. "Nels was almost a grown man by then, but he'd have been helpless without her."

Laurie smiled and patted his arm. "Thank you for saying so, John. Not everyone felt that way."

"You were always my favorite adult," he added, "because up until today, you were the only one that *didn't* call me Johnny."

Laurie tittered politely, and after extracting a promise that McIntire give her regards to his mother and come to visit her at her house in Painesdale so that she might hear all about his life in Europe, she made a swift dash for the side exit.

Small groups were clustered in the back of the church and on the steps and grass outside, having the customary discussions concerning transportation to the cemetery and back to the town hall for the luncheon. As the McIntires were carried by the tide out onto the lawn, they were approached by Dr. Guibard, natty in kid gloves and bow tie, his generously oiled hair gleaming in the sunlight. He greeted them cordially, holding Leonie's hand and remarking on the beauty of her English complexion.

"Lovely day for a funeral," he went on, "as long as it's not our own, eh? Ah, before you know it I won't have any patients left. Then I suppose it'll be time for me to shuffle off, too. By the way, John, I found your culprit. Too bad he's already dead—you could give him the chair. Left his stinger right in the poor man's armpit." He produced a small match box from his pocket and extended it to McIntire with a flourish. "Just for old times sake."

McIntire opened the box to disclose a bedraggled looking bee resting on a bed of gauze. He smiled at the doctor. "I'm afraid I already performed this particular execution, Mark. How'd you end up with it?"

"It was in Nels' shirt. The one you so thoughtfully put under his head. Not that it made any difference to him. He must have left the shirt on the boat or in the fishhouse, and the bee got into it. I suppose it was in the shirt when he put it on. What are the odds of that?" He shook his head.

McIntire experienced a moment of confusion. If this bee was entangled in the shirt under Nels' head, then it was not the same one he had discovered trapped in the clothing that hung on the wall. He settled his glasses higher up on his nose and inspected the insect more closely. It was a honey bee, about half the size of the one that he had slain, but so like it in appearance that it might have been its baby sister—and probably was.

"What are the odds of two of them finding their way into Nels' clothing without a little help?" he responded. "And coincidentally, just at the time his adrenaline decides not to work? Doctor," he said, lowering his voice, "you just might want to catch that hearse!"

V

As it turned out, McIntire's dramatics were ignored and the burial went ahead as planned. According to the doctor, no useful information was likely to be obtained from Nels' embalmed body, at least not enough to make it worthwhile to send the entire town into an uproar on the basis of some "half-assed" suspicions.

Despite Leonie's vehement protestations, McIntire skipped the trip to the cemetery and, leaving her in the company of the only too willing Guibard, drove to the center of Bertelsen's fishing operations.

Nels had been gone only three days, but the aura of desertion was complete. The net drying racks sat empty on the sand like the beached bones of some gargantuan fish. The windows of the fish house stared out over the sun-dappled water with a doleful air. The *Frelser* was tied, bow and stern, to the stone dock. In the shadow of her barn-red hull was a small motor boat. An even smaller skiff lay bottom side up on the shore.

McIntire found the doors to the fishing boat securely latched but not locked. He boarded with some trepidation, treading softly as if the vessel could sense an alien footstep on its deck. It didn't help. With every step the dried planks let out a complaining creak that reverberated through the dusky space.

At first glance, the interior looked to be as he had last seen it, but now felt bleak and lifeless as a tomb. Maybe it should have been one. They could have given Nels a Viking burial—placed his body in the boat, floated it out into the lake, and sent him to greet his ancestors on wings of fire—except that the *Frelser* probably wasn't yet paid for.

He turned on the light. The thermos and newspaper were wedged into their spots. The rubber slicker had fallen from its hook and lay in a heap against the wall. The bee that he had so summarily dispatched was still stuck fast to the paper, providing emphatic punctuation to the report of a two-headed calf born somewhere in West Virginia. He held the paper up to the light, and saw what he should have recognized right away, what he might have recalled from his translating of that scintillating Finnish work, *Beekeeping for the Backyard Gardener*, had his brain been operating at full capacity. This bee was a drone. He used his pocket knife to scrape free the mangled carcass and placed it in the matchbox next to its partner in crime.

The lunch pail was still in place and judging by its weight and its aroma, had not been emptied of its contents. However, one of Nels' colleagues must have come on board to take care of such housekeeping duties as he deemed vital. The bait nets had been dried and heaped into a wooden box, and the gas tank had been brought inside from its customary place on the open deck. The bee sting kit, with its syringe and tourniquet, was gone.

The shirt in which the falsely accused had been lurking still hung on the wall. He lifted the fabric to his face and inhaled deeply. It smelled only slightly fishy. Were bees attracted to the smell of fish? As Mia had mentioned, wasps or hornets might be, which did raise the question of why Nels had supposedly turned to fishing to escape them, but surely honeybees had no interest in dead fish. As he let the shirt drop back against the wall, he realized that it was no longer hanging directly over the counter as it had been when he swatted the bee off its sleeve. He couldn't be positive, but he'd have bet that the sweater and long underwear that he'd noticed on his first visit had also been moved. Picking up each of them in turn, he pulled the sleeves inside out and gave a vigorous shake—nothing. How could bees have gotten into the boat anyway? He tugged on the string that switched off the light. No telltale glimmer showed up a gap around a hatch or porthole. If Nels had indeed kept things closed up—and given his reputation for vigilance in such matters, it certainly seemed that he would have—it was unlikely that any insects had found their way in on their own. Had Nels been wearing the shirt harboring the bee that killed him when he boarded the *Frelser*? A six-legged critter crawling up your arm is hard to ignore. He hadn't been wearing an undershirt. If he'd put that shirt on at home, he'd have felt the bee long before he got out on the lake. And it probably would have stung him sooner. Guibard thought he must have put the shirt on *after* he was on the boat. So what had he been wearing when he left home? McIntire turned the light back on and began opening the cupboards. He found tea bags, a few cans of soup, a jar of coffee, a blanket similar to the one that had become Nels' shroud, and, stuffed into a lower cabinet, a pair of faded corduroy trousers and still another wool shirt.

He left the boat and walked the length of the dock. Except for the lazy droning of flies around the fish house door, only the soft lapping of water and the occasional creak of rope against wood intruded on the stillness. Even the lone herring gull was silent as it regarded him from its perch on a weathered post. He strolled back toward the twin buildings, the fish house and the ice house, both painted the same barn red with white trim as the *Frelser*.

The fish house was built with half of its length resting on land and its front extended over the water on pilings. A walkway attached at a right angle to the dock ran the full width of the small structure's front wall. Even standing outside, there was no ignoring the redolence resulting from a decade of cleaning fish. McIntire thumped the screen, turning a curtain of flies into a cloud, and opened the door the minimum necessary to squeeze through. Inside the closed building, the temperature had risen to tropical proportions, and the stench was overpowering. A quick look around showed an interior of bare wood, tables built along three sides, buckets, knives, stacks of wooden boxes, nets on the walls, an oil can on a windowsill, a metal toolbox and a gasoline can, kerosene lanterns suspended from a wire strung along the ceiling. A large sprayer for insecticide sat prominently on a shelf near the door. Heavily stained canvas coveralls hung on a hook nearby. A few flies crawled on the work surfaces. Probably those that McIntire himself had let in. Nothing seemed out of place here—not that he would be likely to know if anything *was* out of place. He lunged for the door and oxygen.

The ice house was set some distance back from the water, a windowless building constructed of square-hewn logs. McIntire didn't open the heavy door, but stood contemplating its solid facade as he fingered the matchbox in his pocket. Everything here was just so...ordinary. Could this sun-drenched setting really have been the scene of a monstrous crime? Was it conceivable that someone had stolen onto Nels' boat and planted bees in his clothing? It was almost too bizarre to comprehend. Still what other explanation was there? *Two* bees, and the way that sleeve had been so oddly folded back on itself in a manner that kept the one he'd swatted imprisoned. That should have struck him as peculiar right away. Being a drone, it shouldn't have been out wandering around in any event. And the clothing had been moved since Nels' death, he was sure of it. Someone had preceded him in his search of the *Frelser*. Someone looking to get rid of superfluous bees?

But who could have done such a thing, and why? Was it an ill-fated practical joke or some kind of ingenious murder plot? And the most baffling question: If Nels had injected the adrenaline, why had he dropped dead as the proverbial stone? Why had he died so *quickly*? McIntire didn't remember seeing a bottle that might have contained the antidote itself, only the syringe, which the doctor took away.

The sound of steady traffic moving on the nearby gravel road signified that Nels Bertelsen's remains had been duly committed to the earth, and McIntire left the tranquility of the lake for the St. Adele town hall.

He found Leonie waiting solicitously upon Lucy and the ancient Paulsons. He asked her to save a chair for him and excused himself for a surreptitious consultation with Mark Guibard over the necessity of examining the residue left in the syringe and the locating of any remaining antidote. Guibard took his elbow and led him into a corner near the stage. Before speaking he pulled back the dusty curtain for a quick glance behind.

"John, I would never have figured you for somebody to go off half-cocked like this. Nels died from anaphylactic shock, pure and simple. The world is full of bees. He couldn't have avoided them forever."

"When was the last time you had a bee in your shirt?" McIntire asked.

"I haven't taken up with a batty woman that makes me change my clothes outdoors."

So Lucy was the reason that the cabin of the *Frelser* resembled a backwoodsman's haberdashery. Guibard might have a point, although considering the heady floral bouquet in which the doctor kept himself steeped, McIntire couldn't imagine why he wasn't overrun with nectar-sucking pests. "Well," he persevered, "it can't hurt to take a good look at whatever might be left in that syringe and the bottle of medication. Can you do it yourself, or would it have to be analyzed in a lab somewhere?"

The doctor sighed. "The epinephrine was in a small vial. I never found it. Maybe it ended up in the lake. I gave the kit to Lucy along with Nels' other effects, his wallet and his watch. Maybe we can come up with some plausible excuse to get it back." Before McIntire could open his mouth to offer a suggestion as to what that excuse might be, he added, "*But not today.* This is neither the time nor the place, John."

McIntire muttered something reassuring and entered the line snaking through the buffet, marveling at Guibard's knack for reducing him to the level of chastened schoolboy. What did the doctor think he was planning to do? Slam Lucy up against the wall and frisk her? He piled a plate with a hefty scoop of each of the assembled dishes and went to rejoin his wife. Here the discussion in progress—calculated, he supposed, to take Lucy's mind off her grief—centered on the sumptuousness of the repast.

"This chicken is delicious," Leonie was saying. "Did you bring it, Inge?"

Inge Lindstrom blushed and cast her eyes to her plate. "Ya," she said, "but it was last year's bird. I thought it might have got a little bit dry."

McIntire swallowed. "You know," he ventured, "I have heard that a hypodermic syringe can be useful for basting poultry." His contribution was greeted with a gasp from Mrs. Paulson, a delicate cough from Guibard, and look of pure horror from Leonie. But Lucy's head shot up. "You don't say? How would a body go about doing that?"

McIntire ignored Leonie's heel on his instep. "Well, you fill it up with…," with what? "With melted butter and a little lemon juice and,"—he mimicked a thumb on a plunger—"just squirt it right in."

Lucy slapped four fingers to her chubby cheek. "Well, who'd a thought it? And I just pitched Nels' needle and stuff in the trash. If that ain't the berries!"

"You could get it back out."

"Too late. It's already been carted off to the dump." She turned to Guibard. "Maybe you could get me another one?"

The doctor's fork clanked against the enameled plate as he stabbed a pickle. He smiled graciously. "Certainly."

"And perhaps one for my husband?" Leonie purred. "He seems to have talents of which I never dreamed."

Leonie's pleasure with her husband did not increase when he rose and, parting reluctantly with his uneaten lunch, made straight for the township dump. There he spent the remainder of the day sifting through the latest additions with no success.

The sun was low in the west when McIntire returned home carrying a perfectly serviceable colander and a green glass vase, which had only the smallest of chips, as peace offerings.

He must have presented a pathetic sight, shivering on the front porch in his underwear—his gray pinstriped suit being best left in the open air for the time being. Leonie's good will grudgingly returned.

"Are you sure you want to do that?" she asked through the screen door. "Wasn't it the habit of changing his clothes in odd places that brought Mr. Bertelsen to his doom?"

Before entering McIntire paused to give a gentle prod with his bare toe to the bristly black heap that occupied the single remaining spot of late afternoon sun. A tiny portion of the mass lifted and thumped the floor three times. Satisfied that Kelpie, the spaniel he had acquired from his mother along with her house, was still breathing, if not, strictly speaking, living, he opened the door. "I daresay," he responded philosophically, "that more than one man has come to grief by disrobing in the wrong spot."

"Not likely," she observed, "when they smell the way you do!" She hustled him off to shower while she hummed along with Hank Williams and reheated pot luck leftovers until the various tuna hot dishes were indistinguishable from those that had hamburger as the featured ingredient.

Between bites McIntire agonized over how he was going to convince a skeptical county sheriff that, although it was remotely possible that one bee had gotten past Nels' line of defense, two of them, and one a drone, was too much of a coincidence.

"And for that matter," he said, waving his fork at Leonie, "why didn't that medicine work? Guibard says it should have saved his life, but that even if it didn't, it probably would have kept him alive for a short while, at least long enough for him to start up the engine and head for home. The last time he got stung it was by hornets—quite a few of them—and he was able to drive himself into St. Adele for help. But from the sting of a single honey bee he dies within minutes! Very few minutes. The syringe was right by his hand like he had just dropped it."

"Maybe he didn't get it all injected. Maybe he was so nervous he spilled some of it."

"I couldn't find the medicine bottle, but they usually have a rubber cork." McIntire smoothed back an errant strand of wet hair. "You just stick the needle through it, so it can't spill. He had a mark on his thigh where he gave himself the shot. I suppose he could have ended up squirting some of it out before he got the needle in. It was wet all around so there was no way to tell. But it just doesn't seem right, Leonie. He shouldn't have died so fast. Guibard hasn't really said so, but he agreed we should try to get the syringe and vial of antidote back. I'm pretty sure he thinks there's something fishy about this, too."

The feeble pun was unintended. Leonie rolled her eyes. "Well," she responded, "he didn't seem to think there was anything peculiar before he packed Mr. Bertelsen off to the undertaker."

"That can't be helped now." He dug his spoon into a dish of Jello containing some unidentifiable shreds of what he hoped were either fruit or vegetable, but looked disturbingly like shredded wheat. "Maybe Guibard could have been a bit more thorough, but it seemed perfectly simple. He knew that Nels was violently allergic to bees, and he knew that he was stung by a bee. He found the stinger *and* the bee itself. *Ergo*, the bee sting killed him."

Leonie removed his empty plate and sat down. "The doctor also knew that Nels' life depended on the medication that *he* provided to him. Nels gave himself the medication. Nels is dead. *Ergo*, maybe something was queer about the medicine…or maybe it was just too much for him. Epinephrine is strong stuff. If Mr. Bertelsen had a heart condition or something, maybe it could have been the medication that killed him."

The Jello laden spoon stopped in mid-air as her implication dawned on him. "And the good doctor wanted to cover it up? Leonie, your cynicism never ceases to amaze me!"

"*My* cynicism? I'm only suggesting that an elderly doctor might feel a bit of guilt at the death of a long-time patient. That's a far cry from what you're hinting at! But whether it was the bee sting or its cure that caused his death is sort of beside the point. It was still a honey bee in his shirt 'what done it.'" She picked up the teakettle and headed for the sink. "John." She turned to face him. "You don't honestly think someone deliberately set out to kill Nels Bertelsen?"

"I don't quite know what to think," he replied. "This isn't something I want to have to think about at all, and I sure as hell don't want to get people all stirred up over what could very well be nothing. But first thing tomorrow I'm going to pay a visit to Lucy."

"I think that's a good idea," Leonie told him. "I don't recall that you stopped long enough to tender your condolences at the funeral today."

VI

McIntire found Lucy splitting firewood for the winter that would come all too soon. He stood well back and watched in awe while she braced a chunk of maple with her booted toe, swung the ax high, and brought it down with a crack. She tossed the two pieces haphazardly onto a stack before squaring her shoulders and turning a bulldog countenance to him. Once McIntire made it clear that he hadn't come with an eviction notice, she exhibited no qualms about dropping her ax and her truculent aspect and inviting him into her kitchen to discuss Nels Bertelsen's last days on earth. She bustled about, placed two cups of coffee and a plate of funeral brownies on the oilcloth covered table, and began responding blithely to his questions without seeming to wonder in the least at his reasons for asking them.

"He gen'rally got up about three-thirty when he was going way out on the lake. He always ate breakfast at home first, even though it was the middle of the night. He had to get out to his bait nets by daylight—around four or four-thirty."

"Did he leave at his regular time on Friday?" The doctor had speculated that Nels died shortly before the Lindstroms found him because he figured that Nels and Simon would have come to pick their bait nets at about the same time, and Nels had already started to haul his nets in when he died. Of course, they only had Simon's word for that. They also only had Simon's word for it that Nels was dead when they found him.

"Well, I'd guess that he did," Lucy replied. "Leastwise there weren't no reason why he wouldn't of, that I know. But I didn't hear him leave, so I can't say for certain what time it was. He was always careful not to make a lot of racket when he left. We had separate rooms, you know." She spoke these last words with such an intimate air that McIntire felt a transitory twinge of guilt before he continued his prying.

"It must have been annoying for such a fastidious house-keeper as you obviously are to have someone coming home everyday smelling like fish." McIntire bestowed what he hoped was an admiring smile upon his hostess and helped himself to a brownie.

"Oh gracious sakes, no." Lucy fairly bounced with enthu-siasm. "Nels was always such a darlin' about that. He changed clothes on the boat, or sometimes out in the summer kitchen, and no matter how tuckered-out he was, he always washed up before he came into the house." Her lips trembled a little, and she paused to dab at her eyes with the corner of her apron. "If he hadn't been so thoughtful, he'd probably be alive today. I can't, for the life of me, figure out why a honey bee would of got on the boat, and it was actually *in* his shirt, the doctor says."

"Maybe the bee got in when it was hanging on the clothes line." McIntire had just thought of it.

"That does happen now and again, bugs and spiders and such on the clothes, but I always turn everything six-ways-to-Sunday, and shake it out good."

"Could Nels have taken the shirt off the line himself?"

Lucy's jaw dropped. "Nels never took in the washing," she said.

McIntire had to admit that the image of the stolid fisher-man retrieving laundry did defy credibility. "You say sometimes he left his clothes in the summer kitchen. Could the shirt with the bee in it have come from there?" Maybe Nels had taken the shirt with him but had not changed until he was on board.

Lucy looked even more astounded at this suggestion. "Believe-you-me, Nels made sure that there was no way a bee was about to get into any building on this place! He's always been careful, but after last fall…October, I guess it was, he found a nest of hornets in the biffy." Her lips began to quiver once more, but this time McIntire saw no hint of tears in her eyes. "It was in the hole. Only thing we could figure is that it was up under the roof and fell in. Nels heard the buzzing before he sat down, or he might have gotten quite a surprise." She gave in to a bout of hearty laughter, in which McIntire joined her.

"Well, Wylie sprayed them, but after that Nels really went all out. He tarred up cracks that a chigger couldn't squeeze through, and put hooks or locks on both sides of every door, so nobody could leave them open accidentally. The springs on the screen doors are strung so tight I'd be whacked in the rear ten times a day if I didn't step lively!"

McIntire could well believe that it would take some fancy footwork to keep that ample caboose ahead of a slamming door.

"You cannot imagine," Lucy went on, "just how aggravating it is to have to unlock a door every time you want to go in or out, and lock it again after you go through. I must admit I didn't always do it when Nels wasn't around. But," her fist thumped the table, "I did *not* let any bees in that summer kitchen!"

"No, I'm sure you didn't," McIntire agreed hastily. "Do you lock the doors to the house when you're not at home?"

"Nels started insisting on doing that this spring, too. We never did before. Course we used to have a watchdog. Hit by a car."

"What about the *Frelser*, did Nels keep her locked up?"

"I reckon so," Lucy answered, "but I've never once set foot on that boat, so I can't say for sure. Nels was always after me to take a little spin, but I just couldn't bring myself to do it. I swear, I get the heebie-jeebies just looking at the waves on that lake."

McIntire decided that witch or no, Lucy was not without her good points.

"So you don't hail from the seacoast, I take it?" It was worth a try.

For a split second Lucy froze like a doe caught in the headlights. Then she smiled and lowered her eyelids demurely. "No," she replied. "My man always said I came straight from heaven."

McIntire knew when he was beaten. Lucy's roots would remain solidly underground for the time being.

"You and your—you and Nels were both early risers, weren't you? I don't imagine you see many other people out and about when you go to town in the morning."

"Oh, you'd be surprised, not everybody can afford to lay in bed half the morning like you retired folks."

"Who? Who gets the jump on me?" McIntire assumed an air of indignance, an expression that came readily, although his pique stemmed less from unwarranted assumptions concerning his sleeping habits than from the reference to his unemployed state.

Lucy sipped her coffee and gazed at the ceiling. "Well, the mailman. I see him lots of times at the railroad crossing. Course he's headed for the post office, same as me, and you'd think he'd offer me a ride, wouldn't you? He never does, no matter what the weather. I could be toes-up in the ditch freezing to death, and he'd drive right on by with his nose in the air. How does he keep that job anyway? I don't think he cares whose box he puts that mail in as long as his bag is empty at the end of the day. Maybe he is a little off in the upper story, but that's no excuse for treating your neighbors poorly." She leaned forward and lowered her voice, her black eyes locked on McIntire's. "I'm not one to gossip myself, but I've heard from those that do that he's a mite free with the ladies, too…well, people like that always get what they have coming to them sooner or later. Bad manners bring bad luck, I always say."

McIntire resisted the urge to cross himself and to inquire if Nels had done anything to upset Lucy before he died. "So who else do you see out early…like Friday morning for instance?" He groaned inwardly at the blatancy of the question, but Lucy's wariness had melted away.

"Friday, the day my dear man died, you mean? Let's see… David Slocum was out in the orchards when I left. He's been doing some work for Wylie. Nels and Wylie had a real set-to about that, let me tell you. Nels didn't want the kid on the place, said he was lazy and no-good, and after that business with the Culver girl…they had to send her away, you know."

McIntire remembered that Earl and Sandra Culver's oldest daughter had gone off to care for a motherless family in Chandler while she finished her schooling. If he had thought about it at all he would have supposed the reason for the move to be economic. "Oh, my no," Lucy informed him. "They sent her there to keep her away from David. It happened after the dance last fall—the Hunters' Dance, you know."

Ah, yes, the Hunters' Dance, the biggest event on the St. Adele social calendar, bar none. Pinning on his badge and leaning against the wall watching those Hunters dancing had been McIntire's first official duty after taking his oath of office. Now that he thought of it, the necessity of having a body with a badge leaning against the wall during the soirée may well have been behind the townspeople's haste in finding a replacement for old Walleye. Other than confiscating a case of cheap beer from the trunk of the Wilke boy's car, McIntire didn't remember confronting any problems involving youngsters. Most of the kids were too busy trying to ensure that their parents embarrassed them as little as possible to stir up any trouble of their own.

"They left the dance together," Lucy was saying, "David and the Culver girl *and*"—she gave a satisfied "tsk" before delivering the climax to her tale—"didn't get back until eleven o'clock Sunday morning!" She sighed and dropped her hands in her lap, for a moment seemingly overwhelmed by the enormity of it all. "Anyway, when David started working around here this spring, Nels got all wound into a tizzy over it, but Wylie said the orchards were his business now and Nels didn't have a blessed thing to say about it. Then he brought in sheep to keep the grass down, and Nels really raised Cain about that. He hated sheep, always getting out and trampling through the garden. I sometimes think Wylie just did it to show him who was boss. He seemed to sort of enjoy getting Nels riled."

As McIntire recalled, getting Nels riled was not exactly something that took a hell of a lot of effort. He steered the conversation back to the hired hand. "Did David always turn up so early? From what I've heard he's not known for being the industrious sort."

"Well, I'd have to say I haven't noticed him here before ten o'clock or so very often, now and again maybe. But it's a big orchard, I might not always see him." She picked up a brownie and shoved the plate toward her guest. "I think Nels was wrong about David. Wylie says he's a good worker, and he's always been a perfect little gentleman to me. He was considerable help cleaning things up to get ready for the funeral." She chewed and swallowed. "He's quiet as a mouse though. It's like pulling teeth to get a word out of him, but such a nice looking young man, just as cute as a bug's ear. It's a shame he can't seem to make anything of himself."

Lucy had more anecdotes concerning encounters with various neighbors, leaving home early or coming in late, but, though fascinating, all had happened at least two weeks prior to Nels' death. McIntire decided to branch out into another subject.

"As I recollect from the good old days, Nels wasn't always the easiest person in the world to get along with. Some might think you must be a saint to have put up with him."

"Well," Lucy admitted humbly, "he could get a mite cantankerous at times, but, like I say, I had my own room. I'd just go in and shut the door and let him rant 'til he got it out of his system."

"Did Nels have disagreements with anybody else before he died—outside of Wylie and David?"

Lucy let out a snort. "Let's see…there was the butcher, the baker, the candlestick maker…Tom, Dick, and Harry… the doctor, the lawyer, the Indian chief. No, I reckon that ain't quite right, he got along okay with Warner Godwin—and Charlie Wall, too—but he *had* been a little miffed at the doctor."

"Miffed at Guibard? Why?"

"Oh, he had some cockamamie notion about grinding up dead bees and feeding them to Nels. Said it would cure his allergy. Nels said he never did trust the guy, and now he was beginning to sound like a witch doctor. He was going to start getting his medicine from the druggist instead of directly from the doctor."

"Did he do that?"

"No, he still had the stuff Guibard gave him last winter. Anyway, Nels was a sweet man, rest his soul, but he did like to complain. He was always in a snit over something. It would be easier to count up the folks Nels *wasn't* on the outs with. He probably griped to the undertaker about the way his suit was pressed. But I think most people did the same as me, ignored it. Everybody was used to the way he was. There was a big crowd for his funeral."

After a final half-cup of coffee, McIntire bid Lucy good-day and left, taking a short stroll past the summer kitchen, which was not now, and probably never had been, a kitchen.

Christina Bertelsen had kept a stove here for boiling down maple sap in the spring, and she would likely have done her laundry in it during the few warm weeks of the year. Now it contained a staggering assortment of garden tools and shelves packed with bottles and cans, most bearing a skull and crossbones on the label. If Lucy had wanted to rid herself of her paramour, she wouldn't have had to bother with bees.

The building did indeed appear to be impervious to any type of vermin.

VII

McIntire returned home to find his wife up and bright-eyed, sipping tea in her lace-collared housecoat. She foiled his attempts to join her by reminding him that there was someone else to whom he had not "tendered his condolences," the only other person who had been really close to Nels—Wylie Petworth.

"He kept asking for you at the funeral, and you hardly spoke to him when he did catch up with you. I know he thought you were avoiding him."

"Well, maybe I was," McIntire admitted. "I just didn't know what to say to him. He and Nels have been close friends for a long time."

"Closer than Nels and Lucy? You didn't seem too tongue tied around her. 'Needles and stuff!' I came close to having a heart attack myself!"

"I wouldn't dare speculate on whom Nels felt a closer relationship with. The choice between Lucy Delaney and Wylie seems pretty cut and dried to me." Leonie's eyes crinkled over her teacup, and he went on. "I know it's no excuse, I just have a hard time facing a sorrowful Wylie Petworth."

McIntire could count on the fingers of one hand the times he'd seen Wylie unhappy or angry, but every one of those times was indelibly etched into his brain. Since they were babies together, the sight of Wylie in a negative mood had filled him with a kind of foreboding. He tried to explain. "If Wylie's not smiling, things aren't quite right with the world. It's like that opera, you know, the one with the clown."

"I don't quite see Wylie Petworth as a clown."

"Maybe not, but he was always the cheerful one. Compared to Mia he was a regular Emmet Kelly, even through all his misfortunes."

"Losing his arm?"

"It started long before that, about the time the Association broke up."

McIntire was only six years old when the dissolution of the Gitchi-Gumme Association occurred. He had no knowledge of the events leading up to it, but its aftermath would be with him forever: the confusion and sadness of separation, and the bewilderment when Ragna Petworth chose to leave, not with her husband and son, but in the company of one of the group's unmarried men, a laconic soul known to the children only as "Uncle Joe."

A wan and silent Roger Petworth had moved with Wylie into the home of his aged parents. His wife was heard from only once again, when she came forward to claim her share of the proceeds from the sale of the Association's holdings. The following winter Roger Petworth died when his gun apparently accidentally discharged while he was hunting rabbits. To make the tragedy complete, the coming of spring brought with it the dismal discovery of the bodies of Ragna and her lover, spewed forth from the waters of Lake Superior, lashed tightly together, each with a single gunshot wound to the head.

After hearing the story, Leonie regarded him with sadness, almost as if it had been he that had suffered those adversities. Then she patted his hand and spoke with her customary briskness. "All the more reason he could use a friend now."

McIntire sighed and raised her fingers to his lips.

Minutes later he was traveling between fields where the rows of Petworth's Small Fruits and Vegetables stretched lush, green and arrow-straight.

Wylie's forebears had not been farmers. His great-grand-father, St. Adele's founder, was a seafaring Scandinavian first attracted to the region by its fishing and sheltered harbor. He later attempted to exploit the area's slate deposits, an enterprise that soon foundered, but one that provided him with a Welsh son-in-law. When the slate business fell victim to the financial panic of 1873, that son-in-law, Llewellyn Petworth, left the community to turn his attention to other minerals. After a lifetime spent mining iron and copper, he'd retired here, a retirement that was cut short by the necessity of raising his newly orphaned grandson.

McIntire felt a twinge of sadness as he turned into the drive—for the little boy who had gamely persisted in the face of calamity, and for the unfortunate transformation that his eventual success had wrought upon this small portion of the earth.

After the turn of the century, the Petworth land had been one of the few wooded tracts left in a countryside as stripped and burned out as a war zone. But now, while forest was steadily reclaiming most of St. Adele's fields, the patch of ancient timber that had escaped the first round of the log-ging onslaught had vanished, replaced with raspberries and potatoes. Only the few acres surrounding the old homestead were virtually unchanged. McIntire looked with envy at the house, solid as the day Grandpa Petworth had constructed it of massive logs and native stone, using the mast of his father-in-law's schooner as a ridge pole. To its rear, spreading oaks, a rarity in the Upper Peninsula, still shaded open grassy spaces, and the creek still gurgled over rocks on its way to the pond that was just visible through a drape of willows.

Together with Wylie and Mia, the young Johnny McIntire had spent long hours in this child's paradise, playing cowboys and Indians, catching minnows in the creek, and vainly endeavoring to construct rafts that would actually float in the pond—rafts, he recalled, to escape the vile pirate "Gutter," whose inspiration reposed just on the other side of a rusty iron fence in the form of the earthly remains of Captain Guttorm Gulsvagen, the earliest resident of what had become the St. Adele cemetery. In life, Gulsvagen must have been that great-grandfather who had first put down European roots here, but to the three adventurers, he was the personification of evil—the all purpose villain, a ready adversary for every game. They never tired of creating new tales of Gutter's sinister exploits, but they carefully avoided straying too near his grave after dark.

Odd, how it seemed that it was always summer then, especially considering that the reality was so much the reverse. Maybe those long frozen months only served to make the temperate days more memorable, but when McIntire let his mind wander back to his boyhood, as he did with increasing frequency, he remembered days filled with warm sun and blue water, and mellow starry nights chasing fireflies and executing hair's breadth escapes from old Gutter Gulsvagen.

He found Wylie seated at the table in his small, rigidly neat kitchen. He looked up unsurprised when McIntire walked in without knocking.

"Mornin' Mac. I'm afraid you didn't catch me in the best of spirits." He ran his right hand down the front of his shirt and up over his hair. "I just can't get used to it. The whole business hardly seemed real, right up until the time we put him in the ground. It only really hit me last night that he's not coming back." He stood up for a moment, then sank heavily back into his chair. "I have to get these books in order—maybe somebody else will be taking over the orchard—but I haven't had the heart to even open them."

Wylie did indeed have the appearance of one without a functioning heart. He looked worse alive, McIntire thought, than Nels had dead. Seemingly not one drop of blood had found its way to Wylie's face. Its only color came from the gray semi-circular smudges under his eyes. His usually chiseled features sagged like putty left in the sun. The thick waves of his russet hair and the back of his rumpled white shirt were damp with sweat.

McIntire yanked open the curtains on the two windows. The high-beamed room was flooded with light, causing Wylie to recoil and revealing three identical stacks of leather-bound ledgers on the table alongside an open bottle of Seagrams. McIntire helped himself to a mug from the cupboard and filled it with coffee. He took a couple of quick swallows of the viciously black brew before he sat down opposite Wylie.

"It's been quite a shock for everybody," he started awkwardly. "Of course, I know you and Nels were especially close," he added. He didn't want to appear unsympathetic.

"Closer than most brothers." Wylie lumbered to his feet, dumped the coffee from his own cup down the drain, thoroughly rinsed both cup and sink, and placed the cup on the counter to refill it. He added a splash of the whiskey and extended the bottle to McIntire. "Facemaker?"

McIntire shook his head. "I remember," he said, "how you two were always together when we were in high school. You deserted Mia and me for Nels. We were in awe of the way you stood up to him. He had quite a temper in those days, as I recall."

"Oh hell, that never changed." Wylie took a swallow of coffee and another swipe at his hair. "As a matter of fact, he flew off the handle the last time I saw him alive."

"About the Slocum kid, you mean? Lucy told me Nels didn't like him working on his place."

"Actually it was about the sheep. Nels couldn't stand sheep, raised billy hell about those few scraggly ewes. He was a real horse's ass about David, though. Didn't want *him* anywhere on the place either—always harping that he was a lazy bum and accused him of being a thief."

"A thief?" Lucy hadn't said anything about that. "Nels didn't report it to me. What did he steal?"

"Not a gol-damned thing that I know of. He thought David had gone into his house or left some building open, something like that. Nels was always bellyaching about something or other, and I didn't pay a hell of a lot of attention. It's not like he had anything a kid would want bad enough to steal it. Davy has his faults, but he seems trustworthy enough to me and works to beat the band as long as I make damn sure he knows what I want him to do. Nels just didn't care much for him."

"Is that why David went to work at the crack of dawn? To avoid Nels?"

A look of mild confusion brought a faint spark of life to Wylie's face. "I don't know what time he went to work. I just gave him a job to do and paid him when it was finished. Most of the time I didn't even see him. But he'd hardly need to plan his work schedule to stay shy of Nels. Nels was usually out on the water by four or five in the morning and generally didn't get home until after dark. Anyway, this is the first time I heard anybody accuse Davy of being an early riser."

"Lucy says she saw him already hard at work when she left for town the morning Nels died."

Wylie smiled slightly for the first time. "Oh well, you know Lucy—sees sprites and fairies too, I don't doubt. She's even more of a dingbat than most of her gender. Will she be leaving now, do you know?"

"She's just staying put for the time being, afraid that every knock on the door is going to be the evil sheriff come to throw her out in the street. Do you know if Nels left a will?"

"I would imagine he must have. He wasn't the type to leave things to chance, and he was most assuredly aware of his own mortality. Ever since that first really bad bee sting reaction he was terrified he was gonna keel over any minute....I kind of wish now I'd been a little more sympathetic, but it seemed almost funny to see that tough old buzzard scared like that...anyhow, will or no will, once the dust settles there might not be much of anything left for Miss Lucy. He mortgaged himself to the gills to buy that boat."

"He must have wanted to get out of bee territory pretty bad, to risk all that," McIntire observed. "In the end, how much good did it do him?"

"Well, he wanted to fish, that's for sure."

"What kind of bees did he have in the hives in his orchards?"

Wylie's eyes widened. "Kind?"

"What breed, I guess I mean."

"Just regular Italian honey bees, same as everybody else around here. Is that what stung him?"

"It looks like it. For what it's worth, he died quickly. It doesn't appear that he suffered for very long."

Wylie grunted and pulled one of the stacks of ledgers towards him, an action McIntire took as his signal to go. Before he left he toasted and buttered two slices of bread, placed them in front of Wylie and watched while he ate. Some color seemed to be coming back into the haggard face.

VIII

McIntire decided to stop at home for a bite before seeking out David Slocum. Aside from a few glimpses of denim-covered backsides rapidly disappearing into the brush, his working knowledge of adolescent boys was derived mainly from old Andy Hardy movies and a few contacts with some excessively polite, stiff-backed sons of Leonie's friends. Somehow he felt that David would not fit either of those molds.

There was also the problem of coming up with a plausible reason for asking the kid any questions at all. Clearly, any interview with the young man needed some mental preparation, preparation that could best be accomplished over something more substantial than a brownie.

His apprehensions were wasted. Upon entering the kitchen, McIntire found a message in Leonie's exuberant handwriting informing him that Dorothy Slocum had rung. Her son "Davy" had not returned home for the past two nights, and she was beginning to get worried. As McIntire digested this information along with a baloney sandwich, the crunch of tires sounded on the gravel driveway. He walked outside to see Mark Guibard's Plymouth coupe jolt to a halt in the yard.

The doctor opened the door and swung his legs out but did not rise to his feet, leaving McIntire to scrunch down against the side of the car in an awkward attempt to get on a conversational level with him. A tackle box and assorted fishing rods lay on the tiny back seat.

"John," Guibard began without preliminaries and without lifting his gaze from his shoes, "I just remembered something that maybe you should know. Nels lost one of his bee sting kits a few months ago. It was back in February or March, so it wasn't like he had to be overly worried about being stung, but he was concerned—to put it mildly—said he thought somebody had taken it. I figured he'd just misplaced it, or maybe Lucy moved it when she was on one of those cleaning sprees women seem to be so fond of, but looking back on it…he guarded that stuff with his life, and Lucy wouldn't have dared mess with it. Although, who knows? If she had accidentally thrown it out she might not have had the guts to tell him. He insisted that I get him a new kit right away. I told him that it might be just as well to wait until spring so it'd be fresh when he might need it, but he'd have none of that."

"*Could* the epinephrine he used have been too old to work?" McIntire asked.

"No. If it had been I'd have given him a new supply." The gruff response squelched any further questions, and McIntire straightened and stepped away from the car. Guibard removed his glasses, breathed on the lenses, wiped them methodically with his handkerchief, and held them up to the light at arm's length. Apparently satisfied, he donned them again, looked directly at McIntire for the first time, and continued in a more normal tone. "Anyway, I figured I'd better let you know that he lost his adrenaline last winter. It might not mean a thing, John, but on the other hand it could mean plenty."

"Mean what? You think someone could have filched Nels' medication hoping he'd be without it if he was stung? But that would never have worked. Nels always seems to have made damn sure he had it. If he missed it even in dead of winter, there wouldn't be much chance of anybody putting something like that over on him."

"What I mean, Sherlock, is that someone could have taken the kit, replaced the epinephrine with plain water, or maybe even something more lethal, and later switched it with his new one."

McIntire thumped the heel of his hand against his forehead. "Were they exactly alike? They weren't dated or anything?"

"The date was on the case, but not on the vial itself. He wouldn't have noticed the switch."

McIntire remembered Leonie's suggestion of the previous evening, that maybe it was the epinephrine that had killed Bertelsen. "Had Nels had occasion to use the antidote before? I mean, has it *ever* worked?"

"He'd never injected himself before, no. He only had that one life threatening reaction, and then he wasn't treated until he got to the hospital. It's not like bees go around hunting for people to sting just for the hell of it. I can't remember the last time I was stung by a bee."

The doctor seemed to be changing his tune a bit. At Bertelsen's funeral he had put forth the argument that the world was "full of bees" and the fatal sting was bound to have happened sooner or later.

McIntire lounged against the car again. "If Nels had some other medical problem," he ventured, "say, a heart condition for instance, could the adrenaline itself have killed him?"

"There was nothing wrong with Nels' heart." The doctor turned back into the car. McIntire jerked out of the way of the slamming door. Guibard reached for the starter, then abandoned it and sank back into the seat. "Maybe I *have* bungled this, John," he said through the open window. "Could be I'm just getting too old. But in forty years of practice I've never had anyone try to do away with one of my patients." He gave a short grunt. "That I know of anyway. Maybe I've just had the wool pulled over my eyes and they've been bumping each other off right and left."

"If somebody wanted to kill Nels Bertelsen, you couldn't have done anything to stop them." McIntire straightened up and peered at Guibard down the length of his nose. "On the other hand, who would have had more opportunity than yourself, prescriber of powerful brews *and* medical examiner? The perfect crime!"

"What? Knock off my bread and butter? I have few enough patients left as it is…and no more Bertelsens." He spoke as if that realization had just come to him. "And every last one taken on my watch."

"So who else could have been on watch? That's what happens when you're the only doctor around."

Guibard looked at McIntire for a long minute. Then he started the engine and grasped the gear shift. "I suppose you're right. If this was murder—and I'm not saying I think it was, not by a damn sight—if it was, I probably couldn't have prevented it, but if I'd been more suspicious I might have at least been able to show that it *was* murder. The way things stand now, I doubt that we'll ever know for sure."

"Unless," McIntire said, "it was 'something more lethal' in that syringe. I sure wish we could get our hands on that bottle of adrenaline. Or maybe the body could be exhumed?"

"We'd need some kind of real evidence, before we could take a step like that."

The doctor made motions to put the car into gear, but McIntire stopped him with a hand on his arm. "What about the second syringe? The one in the box didn't look like it had been used. Does that mean that Nels should have given himself a second dose?"

"I gave him two syringes, just in case he broke the needle on the first try. Well, frankly, I did tell him that if he seemed to be getting worse instead of better after fifteen or twenty minutes, and he couldn't get medical help, he could try another shot. There was enough epinephrine in the vial for at least two doses. But he didn't do it. There was only the mark of one injection on his leg."

"So he died quickly then?"

"Very quickly."

With that, the doctor threw the little car into reverse, spun it around, and took off at a reckless speed in the direction of the bay.

McIntire returned to the house and, with slightly shaking hands, put through a call to Sheriff Pete Koski in Chandler. The phone was answered in the high-pitched voice of deputy Cecil Newman. The surname was singularly appropriate. Cecil was a recent addition to the sheriff's department, and, from McIntire's point of view, to the family of man. Newman informed him that the sheriff had been called out but should be back around two o'clock. "Would you like me to track him down, or," he offered eagerly, "maybe I can help?"

McIntire declined both offers and said he'd come in himself later. In the meantime, he turned his attention to Dorothy Slocum and the absent David.

The Slocums lived several miles northeast of town in a white frame house badly in need of paint. For starters, it was situated at the end of a long drive that, as a result of its position at the foot of a half-mile of downhill, was alternately choked with snow or awash in a sea of mud, depending on the season. McIntire shifted into first gear and charged through the remaining vestiges of the spring runoff. On the left side of the driveway was an obviously well-tended vegetable garden. On the right, a tangle of lilac, plum, and unpruned apple trees, despite their neglect, bloomed in feral splendor.

Clifford Slocum had been a year or two behind McIntire in school. He had gained a certain amount of fame when he attempted to put into practice a pet theory of Arnie Johnson's: If you get a newborn calf and go out and pick it up every day, you'll be able to lift it even when it's a full grown animal. The experiment continued for several months until the husky young man finally gave it up, admitting that he "just couldn't get a decent grip on the bastard."

Cliff had been dead for seven or eight years now, killed when a tree he was cutting fought back. He left his widow with three children, David being the youngest. The two older were married and on their own now—a girl lived in Milwaukee and the other son was a barber in Chandler.

As he brought the car to a stop, Dorothy Slocum stepped out of her front door, ordered the two mongrel dogs to "lay down," and stood waiting for him on the sagging porch.

McIntire had a photo-like recollection of Dorothy in a long-ago performance at the St. Adele Township School's annual talent show. She had worn shiny black shoes and a white dress with a huge bow, and had sung something about going to the fair. She must have been about five years old, and now, in her faded dress and ruffled apron, her moonlike face surrounded by sausages of tight brown curls, she looked so much the same that it was eerie.

She said a brief hello and led McIntire directly into her living room without the customary offer of coffee. From the radio in the corner came the static-ridden announcement that Helen Trent was just "setting out to prove what so many women long to prove in their own lives—that romance can live on at thirty-five, and even beyond!" McIntire smiled to himself as Dorothy turned the volume down just a notch. Miss Trent could get a few pointers from Leonie.

Dorothy seated herself daintily on the edge of the balding plush davenport. McIntire chose a spot on its companion overstuffed chair and soon discovered that his hostess' tenuous parking job was probably not occasioned by either nerves or formality. His bottom contacted the seat and continued firmly in the grip of gravity until he found himself several inches off the floor regarding Dorothy between his knees. Mustering what little professional dignity he could, while wondering if removing his glasses would reduce his resemblance to a praying mantis, he asked her to tell him what had happened.

David had gone off to work Sunday morning, she told him, and she hadn't seen hide nor hair of him since. "I didn't think nothing of it when he didn't come home Sunday night. He's stayed out all night plenty of times before. But he didn't show up last night neither." She looked apologetic. "I'm probably just putting you through a lot of trouble for nothing."

"Did he take anything with him?" McIntire asked. "Pack a bag or anything?"

Dorothy shrugged. "Most everything he's got is in his car anyway. He keeps a little money in a drawer, and that's gone, but that don't really mean anything. He would of taken it if he was planning on going out on Sunday night."

"Does David have his own car?"

"Cliff bought it the year before he died. I suppose I could of sold it, but I thought I might learn how to drive it myself. Then Al, that's my older son, taught Davy—just on these country roads, he wasn't old enough to get a license then. Al thought one of us should drive, in case of an emergency, you know. It's been handy, having Davy able to take me in to town when I need to go."

"Have you called any of his friends, people he might have been with?"

Dorothy twisted the wedding band, which she wore on her right hand. A dark red line was visible where it cut into her plump flesh. "I don't have a telephone. I called your house from the Lindstroms'. To tell the truth," she went on, not looking up, "I'm not really sure who my son's friends are. They never come here to the house. I don't seem to know a thing about Davy no more. Maybe I never did. He was always different from the other two even when he was a baby. He didn't seem to care much about anything...except his dad. He took it real hard when Cliff died." She wiped her hands on her apron. "He was there when it happened, you know."

"No," McIntire said. "I didn't know."

A fleeting smile crossed Dorothy's face. "Davy was crazy about his father, followed him everywhere from the time he learned to walk. He should of been in school that day, but Cliff took him along to the woods for a special treat. It was Davy's birthday, you see. He was nine years old. After it happened—after the tree fell on Cliff—Davy hitched the horse to it and pulled it off. Cliff still didn't get up, and Davy wouldn't leave him. Of course we didn't look for them until suppertime. It was almost ten before they got found. Davy could of froze to death himself. The doctor said it wouldn't of done any good if Davy *had* gone for help. He said that the tree fell across Cliff's chest, and he was probably already dead by the time Davy got it off, but who knows?" She shrugged again.

"Anyway, after that there ain't nobody been able to tell Davy what to do, 'specially me. He wouldn't go to school unless he was dragged there. We gave up on it when he was fourteen. Sometimes he don't even come out of his room for days at a time. This job with Wylie is the first time he's stuck with anything for more than a couple weeks. That's why I can't believe he'd just take off. And Wylie still owes him money. If he planned on leaving, I think he would of waited until he got paid."

"What time of the morning did David usually go to work at the orchards?"

"Different times," Dorothy answered. "He didn't exactly keep regular hours. That was okay with Wylie, long as he did the work. When he was up and ready to go, he'd go. He didn't leave until about nine-thirty on Sunday. Usually he waited until he was sure he wouldn't run into Nels." She looked up. "No chance of that on Sunday, though…well, at least Nels didn't leave any children."

McIntire wondered if any blood was getting to his legs at all. When he tried to rise would he find himself sprawled at

Dorothy's feet? He asked, "Had your son quarreled with Nels, then?"

"I wouldn't say quarreled. Well, you know how Nels was. A couple months ago he accused Davy of going into his house when he wasn't there, and leaving the doors open on his garden shed or something. Davy said that Nels just started yelling at him and that he wasn't making any sense. But he told Davy that he'd better not catch him near his house again, and that everybody in town was going to hear that he was a thief. Course he said it like 'teef.' That made Davy laugh."

"What did Nels say was stolen?"

"That's just it, he didn't say. At least if he did, Davy didn't tell me, but he still swore up and down that Davy had broke in." She lifted eyes of a pleading basset hound to McIntire's face. "Davy wouldn't of done that. He may have his faults, but he's a good boy. He wouldn't steal." She sighed. "I don't think he would steal."

"Did your son have trouble with Nels, or anybody else, more recently? Did anything happen to upset him in the past few days?"

"Not so far as I know," Dorothy replied. "But he probably wouldn't of told me....No, I think things were fine. He seemed like his normal self—maybe even happier. He was excited on Sunday morning because Wylie was going to let him take his big Buick into Chandler to pick up that old couple from the train, you know, Nels' old army buddy. He kept after me to be sure to remind him when it was time to go."

So David had gone into Chandler that day, and Chandler was where the girl who'd been "sent away" from him now lived.

McIntire took a deep breath and let it out slowly before asking, "What about the Culver girl, might he have told her where he was going?"

A flash of anger appeared in Dorothy's eyes. "People around here always have to have something to talk about! If anything happened between Dave and Cindy Culver why put all the blame on him? I mean, if that's the kind of girl Cindy is you can't blame a young man for…" She slumped back to sink into her own seat. "I don't know if he went to see Cindy. I didn't want to call with Inge Lindstrom listening, along with everybody else on her line! Like I said, people around here talk too much anyway."

"I'll check on it," McIntire assured her, "and I'll let the sheriff know to keep a lookout for his car. Maybe you could describe it for me. Do you know the license number?"

Dorothy twisted the ring again. "The sheriff knows Davy's car."

McIntire gripped the arms of the chair and flung himself to his feet. "Before I go, maybe I could have a look around his room?"

Dorothy led him to the stairwell and left him to go up alone.

David's was one of two upstairs rooms that opened off either side of a short hallway. It was lit by a bare light bulb at the end of a cord which was draped, with a possible attempt at whimsy, over an over-sized ornate frame containing within its borders the motto, *The Lord is My Light*, written in elaborate white and gold lettering on a green background liberally ornamented with lilies. Furnishings consisted only of a small chest of drawers with white circles embellishing its rippled oak veneer surface and a bed, three quarter size with head and footboards of iron scrollwork. The brown lacquer of the headboard was missing from a number of dime-sized areas, the result, undoubtedly, of chewing gum being placed there and later removed, either for the sake of hygiene or for further chewing pleasure.

A threadbare quilt made of irregularly shaped scraps of fabric covered the bed, which was strategically placed near that feature that would give the room the status of being the most desirable in the house: the opening in the floor fitted with an iron grate, which was situated directly over the wood-burning heater in the living room below. As McIntire remembered from his own youth, such a floor register not only provided some measure of warmth on freezing nights, but afforded excellent year-round possibilities for keeping up on the late-night conversations of one's elders.

A radio sat on the floor at the side of the bed. Its aerial ascended the wall and dangled over rods holding the yellowed lace panels that dressed three tall windows. McIntire looked out over the unkempt orchard and beyond to the road where it wound up the hill. A spume of dust appeared over the rise, followed shortly by a battered Dodge meandering languidly from one side of the road to the other like an immense black beetle in no particular hurry to accomplish much beyond admiring the wild flowers that grew in the ditches—Nick Thorsen on his daily rounds.

The large windows did not help to dispel the aura of chill that permeated the room even at midday. Except for the radio, it was bare of personal possessions. Odd, considering Dorothy's report that her son spent a great deal of time here. The large drawers of the chest held little more than a moth-eaten sweater and some dingy long johns. In the smaller top drawer was a heavy leather belt, the length of which indicated that it had probably belonged to the robust Cliff Slocum. A cigar box lay under it, empty but for a rusty skeleton key. The only other article in the chest was a small carved wooden boat, painted with red and white enamel.

McIntire turned to the closet and was surprised to find it locked. It opened readily with the skeleton key to reveal a few articles of winter clothing on hooks, rubber buckle overshoes, and a couple of pairs of worn out oxfords. A narrow shelf above the hooks yielded only a heavy layer of dust and the desiccated bodies of some unfortunate insects. McIntire methodically inverted each shoe with a vigorous shake and peered beneath each grime-encrusted insole. He then turned his attention to exploring the pockets of the shirts and jackets. He repressed a whoop when, secreted in the lining of a green plaid Mackinaw—very large, probably also Cliff's—he found a bundle of letters.

The envelopes were addressed in small, square printing and included the name and return address of David Slocum's older brother. In part this proved to be a ruse. Closer inspection revealed that, while two of the letters had come from Al Slocum, half a dozen others were signed "Cindy." The postmark showed that the most recent had been mailed about six weeks earlier.

McIntire sat down on the bed and hastily scanned all six. Far from being tortured messages of thwarted love, they were simple friendly letters, describing the advantages of the "city," and informing David that he really should get out of "that one-horse town" and go where life had more to offer.

Nonetheless, following a hasty examination of conscience, McIntire pocketed the letters before relocking the closet door. After taking one last look around the room—nothing under the bed save a once-white metal chamber pot and dust bunnies of dimensions that would have sent Leonie back to London if she'd had to swim for it—he removed the toy boat from its hiding place and positioned it in the center of the chest. Then he left, closing the door behind him.

IX

Mia Thorsen pulled off her coverall apron, hung it on the wall, and pushed open the studio door. Although the calendar said that summer was at last upon them, the nights were cool, and the rays of the sun did not penetrate the studio's concrete walls. A fire was necessary to take off the early chill, but as the day wore on the shop became uncomfortably warm, and every inch of her felt coated with sawdust. She lifted her hair to let the breeze fan some of the dampness from her neck and drank in several deep breaths. Then she slid a rock against the door to brace it open and, after placing a discarded window screen across the lower half of the opening to keep out the marauding geese, passed under the shadow of the evergreens into the welcoming light of the open yard.

She had been working since Nick left at six o'clock, and it was now past eleven. Her hunger pangs were becoming increasingly insistent, but still she shrank from going into the house and facing the inevitable rumpled bed, dirty dishes, and unironed laundry. Cool mornings notwithstanding, Nature seemed to be making amends for a spring that had been late and wet even by Upper Peninsula standards. For the past few days the weather had been as close to perfect as could ever be expected in this part of the world. Even Nick, after weeks of cursing muddy roads, snowplow-destroyed mailboxes, and the incessant peeping of the season's orders of day-old chicks, had little to protest except the sun in his eyes. He'd left the snow shovel, rubber boots, and the wool cap with earflaps in the front porch. And he had replaced the thermos of blackberry brandy under the front seat of his car with one of dandelion wine, irrefutable evidence that summer was indeed on its way.

Mia reveled in being out of doors without the bothersome preparations and encumbrances that were necessary for just stepping off the front porch during eight months of the year. She brushed a wisp of hair from her eyes and told herself that life was short and the Benign Season a whole lot shorter. Following that rationale, she entered the kitchen and put together a lunch of a sandwich, an apple, and a copy of *Tales of the South Pacific*. She then went back outside, closing the door on the clutter of living.

She dragged the old wooden lawn chair from the gloom of the pines into the sun, careful to face it away from the errant vegetable garden. Leaning back gingerly to avoid splinters, she unbuttoned her shirt, took a bite of the home-made bread and peanut butter, and brushed the small shower of crumbs off her chest. She had sliced the crust from each end of the loaf of bread to make her sandwich, a slovenly practice which was always accompanied by a mental apology to her long-dead mother, but one that she had never been able to resist, especially when peanut butter was involved.

Peanut butter, John McIntire had told her, was one of the main things he had missed about home. During all those years in England, he said—a country where the most creative aspect of cooking is lighting the fire, where on Monday morning they make enough toast to last all week—the food he really craved was not fried lake trout, his mother's pot roast, or blueberry pie. It was peanut butter. A fact especially amazing when you consider the gritty stuff that passed for peanut butter in those pre-Peter Pan days.

Mia smiled to herself when she thought about John McIntire and admitted grudgingly that she was, after all, glad that he had been resurrected. And glad that there was so little awkwardness between them considering his long absence… and considering what they had formerly been to each other.

When he returned to St. Adele with his new wife, Mia had at first put off the welcoming visit—put it off so long, in fact, that the situation was threatening to become an embarrassment. She was eventually saved from fulfilling her social obligation by thoughtful neighbors who threw a going away party for Sophie McIntire when she relinquished her home to her son and left to spend her remaining days on earth in Florida, claiming the sunshine she felt was owed her after sixty odd years in a Northern Purgatory.

The festivities had been well under way when Mia arrived, sticking uncharacteristically close to her husband and as nervous as the seventeen-year-old girl she had been when she and Johnny McIntire had last met.

She was in no way reassured at her first sight of the slim, aristocratic looking gentleman the bosom companion of her childhood had become. He had—she could hardly believe her eyes—grown. The man was at least three inches taller than the boy had been, and that boy was by no means short. The dark hair of his youth was barely tinged with gray but had receded considerably from his forehead, no longer necessitating constant vigilance to keep it from falling into his eyes, eyes which were the same clear sea green that she had always secretly envied. He was dressed like a matinee idol, right down to the silk handkerchief in the pocket of his gray pinstriped suit.

He was bending over to give rapt attention to some yarn being related by Arnie Johnson, standing somewhat apart from the others. There were few present who hadn't heard Arnie's entire repertoire of stories as often as they cared to.

Mia glanced down at her own plaid Sears-Roebuck dress and pressed even closer to Nick. She was within a hair of making for the nearest exit when he raised his head and looked directly into her eyes. Recognition was followed by a slow smile, lighting up his still lean and boyish features, and he was across the room to her in a half dozen strides, leaving her no choice but to put out her hand and utter that gracious welcome, "You got different glasses."

"Yeah, the wire rims were starting to make me look too much like Woodrow Wilson."

Such were the first words of two who had begun as brother and sister and become closer still, now reunited after half a lifetime.

After that they had slipped into a casual friendship, or at least an unspoken truce. They saw each other fairly infrequently, and she, for her part, was cautious in avoiding references to the past. On those rare occasions that she did slip, her remarks generally received no response.

It was not especially difficult to distance the new John McIntire from the old. She needed to look long and deep at the charmingly urbane, self-assured, and humorous man to find anything of the lanky youth she had mourned and buried alongside her own girl-self so long ago. And looking long and deep was something she was not prepared to do. Just as it had been easier all those years ago to imagine that he lay dead on a muddy field in France, it was less complicated now to regard him as some distant relative of that long deceased friend, just a neighbor like all the others. And, thank God, she had not seen that three-piece suit again until yesterday's funeral where half those present had mistaken him for the undertaker.

She could hardly believe the way he had let himself be suckered into that constable job. He had seemed almost touchingly honored by the townspeople's proclaimed confidence in him. Well, she wasn't falling for it. There was just no way a man with his intelligence and background—an *intelligence background* for Pete's sake—could be so naive. He had to realize that nobody else in the township would have taken that office on a bet. Anybody who did show an interest would have been immediately suspected of some diabolical ulterior motive and soundly voted down. John *was* the perfect choice. He'd needed to be wheedled into it, and he hadn't been around long enough to have any axes to grind, although the miniature crime wave that curiously swept the township shortly after he pinned on his badge could have resulted in a few grudges in a less temperate man.

For all that his "ever so proper" ways made him the butt of countless jokes, she couldn't conceive that he would be the target of any real malice. He was, after all, the son of the revered Colin McIntire. And he became a bona fide darling of the older generation the minute he greeted one of them with *hyvaa paivaa* or *hur star det till*.

Still, he held himself back from what passed for the social life of St. Adele, preferring to spend his time wandering along the lakeshore or standing in some cold stream in hopes of hooking a fish. Mia was among those who expected that once he'd had his fill of woods and water he would move on to some more cosmopolitan setting, perhaps returning now and again for the occasional backwoods vacation.

John's wife had, on the other hand, fit easily into the community. Leonie's enthusiasm and extreme sense of duty to her fellow humans made her a favorite victim for every group that ever wanted a raffle ticket sold or a pie baked. Several months after their arrival she had driven off to an auction in Marquette and returned with some sort of ancient printing equipment. It was now set up in an upstairs room at the town hall, and, earlier in the year, Leonie had begun putting out a small bi-weekly newspaper.

The St. Adele Record, a lofty title for the four tabloid-sized pages, was an unqualified success. Filling those four pages necessitated that even the most mundane occurrence in the life of each of St. Adele Township's three-hundred-twenty residents be viewed as newsworthy, and Leonie faithfully reported each report card "A" and afternoon trip to Chandler with the same fervor she would have shown for the really big event, out-of-town visitors or a new car. The subjects of her stories were not always completely flattered by her interest, but so far she had not offended anyone to the point that they wouldn't be standing in line to purchase her next issue. It was Leonie's habit of topping off her long Wednesdays at the presses with an unescorted visit to the Waterfront Tavern for a restoring "pint," where she actually sat right up at the bar with the men, that really got people talking. For the most part it was a good-humored ribbing. The community would forgive, in an exotic foreigner, behavior they would never stand for in one of their own.

Mia was looking forward to reading Leonie's account of Nels Bertelsen's life and death. Maybe it would be a help in putting an end to his life in her own mind.

When John had told her that Nels was dead, before shock and sadness took over, Mia had experienced a moment of the most exquisite fear—the distinct feeling that this was only the first snapped thread in a raveling seam, the beginning of some downward slide into perils that she couldn't name. The vision had passed in an instant, but still, even yesterday's funeral had given her no sense of finality. She was beset with a feeling, almost a foreboding, that they had not heard the last of Nels Bertelsen, or of grief.

Even now, she shivered a little in her pool of warm sun and thought of her great-grandmother, Meogokwe, the ancient brown woman who'd given her her name—and possibly her life. That first Meogokwe, Mia's mother had said, had Powers, and Mia, by taking her name, might also be so blessed. She had never told Mia what those powers might be. Mia fervently hoped they involved arm wrestling. She'd as soon leave the sorcery to Lucy.

She gnawed her apple down to the seeds and stem, tossed them into the bushes, and opened her book. She had begun reading it several times, and had never gotten past "Mutiny."

She was not fated to do so today. After a few paragraphs she let her head fall back and closed her eyes. Within minutes the warmth of the sun and the lazy drone of insects drove all presentiments of evil from her mind and lulled her into a sound sleep.

She awakened with a start at the slam of a car door and the sound of footsteps crossing from the driveway. Nick already! Was it really possible that she had slept almost three hours?

After a close inspection of the grass for indications that the geese might have preceded him, Nick sat down with his back against the side of Mia's chair.

"So how was your day? Read any good postcards?" It was Mia's ritual greeting, and Nick gave his ritual response, "Anything you can get on a postcard ain't worth reading." He let his head sink back into her lap and closed his eyes. "Just another ordinary day—except that I hardly know what to do with myself after almost a week with no complaints from Old Man Bertelsen. That's going to take some getting used to."

Mia didn't respond, but ran her hand through his hair, twining the dark curls around her fingers and gazing over his head. The sight of a pine green late model sedan where Nick's unpretentious Dodge should be brought a clutch at her heart, but she kept her voice level. "Car in the shop?"

"Just getting the old bus spruced up a little."

It was another rite of spring, having the winter's collection of dents banged out, and one that it was necessary to conduct farther and farther afield in recent years. Nick had returned more than one loaner in a state requiring its owner's professional services.

"But speaking of the dear departed," he continued, "I did pick up the odd bit of information today. It seems that our esteemed constable has been galloping around the neighborhood asking no end of questions about Nels, and snooping into things generally. To top it off, David Slocum is missing."

"What do you mean, missing?"

"I mean *missing*, as in left home for God knows where, taken a powder, flown the coop."

"But he's taken off plenty of times before. Nobody seemed to think it was a big deal."

Nick sat up straighter, and Mia began mechanically kneading the back of his neck.

"Dorothy never called in the law before," he replied. "She must think it's a big deal."

Mia ceased her massage and let her hands rest on his shoulders. "By 'law' do you mean John McIntire?"

"That's what I heard from a reliable source whose phone Dorothy used…John McIntire, walking dictionary *and* Law West of the Huron. Quite the well-rounded guy."

Nick had been among those who had conspired to put the new constable through some pretty stiff paces, mostly, Mia suspected, to assess her own reaction. That reaction had been one of unfeigned indifference. John McIntire had proven long ago that he didn't need her to fight his battles for him.

"But what," she asked, running her hands back up into his hair, "do David Slocum's escapades have to do with Nels?"

"I don't know that they do. That's another story."

"So, tell it."

"Well, the word is," Nick informed her, "that when Johnny-boy skipped out on the funeral festivities he was poking around on Nels' boat and—get this—in the dump."

"And what does 'the word' have it that 'Johnny-boy' was looking for?"

"That, My Lovely, remains a mystery. But his car was in Nels'—or should I now say Lucy's?—yard when I went by today. And they say Guibard paid him a visit later."

Mia left off twisting Nick's hair and went to work on her own. "Those two had their heads together and were whispering like a couple of schoolgirls at the dinner yesterday. It was right after that John slipped out," she recalled. "I figured he was getting one of his headaches."

"If you ask me our 'British gentleman' *is* one great big headache." Nick yawned. "He got another of those packages today, the ones that come from the *United States Department of Defense*. I'd give my eye teeth to know what he's up to."

"Maybe it was a big box of money. His pension."

"Too heavy," Nick laughed. "But that's just it. If he's retired why's he getting...whatever it is that he's getting? He does get a check from them, too, now and then." Nick sprang to his feet in one movement and reached for her hand. "Come on, it's been a long day. Time for a nap."

Mia laughed. "I've already slept half the afternoon. I can't say I'm too tired. Which," she added, "is no doubt just what you were hoping to hear."

X

McIntire navigated the winding street that climbed up a gear-strippingly steep hill into the parking lot at the rear of the Flambeau county courthouse, a seventy-year-old structure situated high on a bluff overlooking Chandler's main street and the waters of Keweenah Bay. Before getting out of the car he pulled a small spiral-bound notebook from the glove compartment and recorded the date and the twenty-one miles he had driven from St. Adele.

The sheriff's outer office was narrow, cramped, and colorless, an appropriately somber setting for dealing with the darker side of Flambeau County life. A bank of file cabinets lined the wall opposite the entrance, and identical desks faced one another from the end walls. A heavily scratched oak table flanked by three straight-backed chairs occupied the center of the room. On the wall behind the desk on the right hung a very large map of the very small county. Before it Sheriff Pete Koski sat hunched over a second map, a red pencil in his hand.

Even sitting down, with his lower body obscured by a couple of hundred pounds of furniture, the sheriff was an imposing figure, uncannily resembling, as it was frequently said, a hefty John Wayne. He was not above exploiting this fortunate happenstance. The furrowed brow he often presented, especially nearing election time, was as much the result of the narrow western boots on his size sixteen feet as an expression of concern for the well being of the citizens of Flambeau County. It was his misfortune that Leonie, with her abiding passion for all things Western, couldn't vote.

He circled a small inland lake on the map and slid a folded copy of the *Chandler Monitor* casually over the spot. As if McIntire would have any interest in going after his lethargic walleyes. "Afternoon Mac," he said, "what's up? Cecil's been burning with curiosity ever since you called." He indicated the deputy's vacant chair. "I sent him out to buy paper clips. Be interesting to see how long it takes him to get back." When the sheriff laughed even the floor under McIntire's feet seemed to vibrate. "So what's the problem? The good folk of St. Adele giving you a hard time again?"

McIntire wondered what information the sheriff might be privy to that he was not, but decided that this was not the time to pursue it. He took the matchbox from his shirt pocket, slid the lid off, and placed it on the desk. Koski studied the contents intently, rolling the bees over with the point of his pencil. "This is very nice, John, but you're going to need a hornet and maybe a carpenter bee to make your collection complete." He shoved the box back across the desk. "What the hell is this? Bees are legal in this state, even in St. Adele."

McIntire sat down and detailed his suspicions, watching as the sheriff's expression grew more incredulous by the minute. But to his credit, Koski neither laughed outright nor escorted McIntire to the door. "It seems to me bees do tend to run around in groups," he said. "What's so odd about finding two of them together? A bee off on its own would be more out of the ordinary."

"Bees might join their chums to tiptoe through the tulips, but they don't generally pair up for shipboard cruises." McIntire hesitated as he noticed the merry light that sprang into Koski's eyes, a light he'd learned to recognize in his St. Adele neighbors. It was that word "chums" he supposed. He mentally added it to the growing list of vocabulary to exorcize from his brain, and continued, "and, as you so kindly pointed out, these don't even look like the same sort of bee. But they are. They're the same species, I mean—Three-Banded Italian honey bees. The big one is a drone, and drones don't generally go flying around at all. Before winter they'd be driven out of the hive and killed, and one or two might escape, but this time of year they should be living the high life as members of the queen's harem."

Koski grunted. McIntire took it to be an expression of mild interest and plunged ahead. "These bees were both on Nels' boat, *in* his clothes—each bee had staked out a claim in a different shirt. Guibard found one with Nels' body. The one that I found was in a shirt hanging on the wall. The sleeve was kind of bunched up so the bee couldn't get out, but it apparently managed to get *in* with no trouble. And don't forget Nels gave himself that shot, which had no effect whatsoever—except maybe to kill him all the faster. The vial that contained the adrenaline has conveniently disappeared."

The sheriff fitted the eraser of his pencil into the cleft in his chin. "So you think somebody tampered with Bertelsen's adrenaline and then sneaked on board his boat and put bees in his shirts? That's pretty far fetched, John. Do you have any idea who this dastardly villain might be?"

"'Dastardly villain'? Good Lord, Pete, where do you come up with these archaic terms? I don't know who the son-of-a-bitch could be, although…"

"Although?"

"A young man who worked in the Bertelsen orchards has gone missing. There's probably no connection, but regardless, we'll be needing your help locating him."

McIntire forgot about semantics and filled the sheriff in on the situation with David Slocum, including his run-in with Nels and the incident with Cindy Culver. Koski acknowledged that he was already acquainted with David, several of whose earlier exploits had caught the attention of the county authorities. He himself had once or twice, none too gently, reminded the young man that school attendance was compulsory for those under the age of seventeen. David had not been impressed, and sending a deputy on a fifty-mile round trip each morning to escort him to school had not been deemed efficient use of taxpayer funds. Koski was obviously still somewhat rankled by David's steadfast resistance to intimidation. He screwed the eraser more firmly into his chin.

"Well, it looks like we better try to track him down, if his ma's getting worried. I'll send a deputy to look around up in the hills. Be just like the dumb kid to run his car off the road or get mired down in a swamp somewhere. If he did, it could be a long time before anybody stumbles across him. Nobody goes out there this time of year...except those intrepid uranium prospectors. Meanwhile, I guess we can ask around. The older son's got a barber shop down the street, and maybe the girlfriend knows something."

At that moment the door swung open and Deputy Cecil Newman sailed in, pink-cheeked and panting. He dropped his paper bag onto the sheriff's desk with a clunk and turned his attention to the visitor. "Good afternoon, Mr. McIntire." He cleared his throat, breathed deeply, and began again in an octave more suited to his status. "I hope it isn't some trouble that's brought you to us?"

Koski rose to his full six feet, five inches—without his campaign boots. "We were just waiting for you to get back, Cecil, so we can leave the office. Mr. McIntire has some," he paused to give the word more emphasis, "*investigating* to do, and I do believe that I could use a haircut."

After dropping the sheriff at Al Slocum's barber shop, McIntire drove to the residence of Warner Godwin, the widowed attorney who had taken Cindy Culver under his wing, that she might do the same for his motherless daughter. It was located on the north side of town in Chandler's most prestigious neighborhood, an area where a small group of homes, loosely termed "mansions" by the locals, were clustered on a steep hillside overlooking the bay. The houses had been erected before the turn of the century by those few plunderers of the area's abundant natural resources who chose to actually live, at least for part of the year, among their vassals rather than in the more stimulating environments of Chicago or New York City.

The Godwin home was set high above the street and commanded a panoramic view of the water and the distant opposite shoreline. It was built in a Tudor brick and stucco style. McIntire felt a surge of wistfulness for the solid architecture of Britain—a sensation that swiftly evaporated as he recalled the dank and dreary interiors of most of those picture-postcard domiciles.

There was nothing remotely dreary about the interior of the Godwin home, or about the petite young lady who answered the door. She was dressed in the requisite rolled-up blue dungarees and a raspberry pink pullover fashioned of some fuzzy material, the sight of which set McIntire's nose to itching. The costume fit the remarkable ins and outs of her form as if she had been knit into it. Waves of blond hair fell to her shoulders, artfully arranged to sweep across her forehead and partially veil one of the sparkling hazel eyes— a sophisticated *femme fatale* coiffure incongruously paired with the cupid's-bow lips and dimpled cheeks of a Rubens angel. When McIntire identified himself, she extended both hands in front of her body, and with a soulful look exclaimed, "Alas, I've been found out! Slap the cuffs on me, I'll go quietly."

She chatted as she hung up his hat and bounced ahead of him through the hallway. Of course she knew who he was.

She had seen him in church lots of times last summer. Her mother used to wait tables for McIntire's father when he had the bar. She was so excited to meet someone who had actually lived in another country, especially a place like England. She had seen *Forever Amber* three times and intended to travel herself someday, and England was going to be one of her first stops.

McIntire forbore explaining that Hollywood's version of seventeenth century Britain might not bear much resemblance to present day reality. He followed her through a shadowy dining room, past a table littered with papers and stacks of envelopes, to an airy plant-filled room at the back of the house, where Cindy indicated that she'd be able to "keep an eye on Annie." Looking out through the French doors, McIntire saw a broad carpet of lawn and a small girl on her knees, peering intently into a shallow pool. A fat straw-colored braid on each side of her face stirred the water as she slowly swayed from side to side.

"She's trying to hypnotize the goldfish," Cindy explained. "I have to be ready to haul her out if she puts *herself* in a trance first. Now Mr. McIntire, please do sit down and tell me what I can do for you."

McIntire's mild amusement at her Home-ec class comportment turned to consternation when Cindy, rather than positioning herself in a spot advantageous to keeping Annie under surveillance, sat down close beside him on the small sofa, threw back her head to look directly into his eyes, and beamed expectantly.

McIntire cautiously put a little more distance between his own and Cindy's knees and adopted a stiffly formal manner. "Caring for a child and a house is a big responsibility. It must be very difficult for someone as young as you."

Cindy bestowed a smile of benign tolerance upon her guest. "At home I had *seven* kids to look after most of the time and farm work besides. Here I have my own room, every other weekend off, the bathroom is indoors, and I didn't wake up with snow on my bed even once last winter…and we *never* have porcupine for dinner." The childlike face took on an expression of pure adult avarice. "I'm going to have a house like this of my own someday."

McIntire looked at the polished floors and subdued glow of the cherry paneling. He wouldn't mind having a house like this himself. "It is a grand home," he agreed, "but it must be a lot of work to keep up."

"Oh, Mr. Godwin has a cleaning lady come in twice a week. He did that even when Mrs. Godwin was alive. Wasn't that sweet? Mrs. Godwin did all the decorating herself, Got the ideas from magazines, Mr. Godwin said. She had awfully good taste, don't you think? In clothes, too. Mr. Godwin gave me lots of her things. Can you believe she was exactly the same size as me?" Since Cindy appeared to be only marginally larger than her juvenile charge, McIntire did find that moderately difficult to believe. His skepticism must have shown on his face. Cindy displayed signs of jumping up to fetch some of the treasured objects to substantiate her case, and he decided it was time to get down to business.

"Miss Culver"—he switched to his "constable's here, the party's over" demeanor—"David Slocum has left home without telling anybody where he was going, and his mother is worried about him. Have you got any idea where he might be?"

If Cindy was embarrassed by McIntire's evident awareness of her past indiscretions, she didn't show it. "I haven't seen David in months," she said, "not since before I came here."

"Have you had any contact with him at all?" McIntire pressed. "Has he ever talked about leaving home, or about somewhere he might want to go?"

Cindy looked guilelessly into his eyes. "I haven't seen or heard from David since last October. How would I know where he's gone? He's not exactly Mr. Responsibility. I'm sure it's not the first time he hasn't come home."

McIntire met her gaze. "So I understand," he observed. "Did you ever hear David talk about Nels Bertelsen?"

She looked at him now with frank curiosity. "You mean the grouchy man that lives by the orchards? No, why would David talk about him?"

"Mr. Bertelsen died last week, didn't you know that?"

"No kidding? I haven't been home for a while. From what? He wasn't all *that* old."

"He died from being stung by a bee. He was allergic."

Cindy's eyes opened wide. "Holy cow! A bee? Are you sure?"

McIntire assured her that there was no doubt.

"That is the weirdest thing I ever heard...but what's it got to do with David Slocum?"

"Like I said, David is missing. Before he died, Mr. Bertelsen was very upset about something that happened when David was working on his place. I thought he might have mentioned it to you."

"But David didn't work for Nels Bertelsen. He worked for that old one-armed guy."

"Old guy," was it? Thirty-six days older than McIntire himself. He ceased to concern himself with the proximity of Cindy's knees. "Yes, he did work for Mr. Petworth," he told her, "but Mr. Petworth and Mr. Bertelsen were business partners. Mr. Petworth managed the orchards, so David worked there sometimes. Mr. Bertelsen yelled at David and tried to kick him off the place. Did David ever talk about it?"

"No, I don't remember that he ever did, but I haven't talked to David for a long time. I thought he just worked for Wylie." She gave a shudder. "That guy really gives me the creeps, the way he sort of hunches over...and that half an arm. When I was little, my dad worked for him sometimes, and Ma would make me take his lunch over. Once Wylie lifted me up onto the hay wagon, and he had a hook on his arm! It scared the bejeebers out of me. I had nightmares for weeks. All us kids used to work picking strawberries at his place, but if I saw him coming I'd head for cover."

McIntire took time out from his investigation to give a member of the younger generation a lesson in both history and compassion, presenting Cindy with an inspiring account of the famous fire, the bravery and resourcefulness of both rescuer and rescued, and their abiding friendship. She listened patiently to his tale—Colin McIntire himself couldn't have told it better—not squirming more than was to be expected. Once or twice his words actually seemed to elicit a slight flicker of interest. Particularly, McIntire thought, when he mentioned the dashing young doctor Mark Guibard who had been no less heroic than Nels himself in driving horse and sleigh through a night of heavy snow to reach the fallen boy, and how, despite being forever maimed, that boy had grown up to become a respected and prosperous gentleman, maybe even wealthier than Mr. Godwin himself.

Her attention was transient, however. Cindy's face soon assumed the thoughtful, distant expression of a child on the brink of death by boredom. McIntire brought her back to consciousness with a final question—was she absolutely sure that she had no idea where David might have gone? He received a tolerant sigh and a, "Yes, I'm sure."

He stood up and fixed his eyes sternly on hers. "If you do hear from him, you'll let me or the sheriff know, won't you?" She nodded emphatically, a motion that sent her carefully drooping wave of hair cascading across her face, obscuring her expression.

As McIntire left, he noticed that Annie had abandoned the fish, and, with the help of a large collection of dandelions, was busy creating interesting yellow stripes on her chubby brown legs.

A few minutes later he was sharing the back booth of the Superior Bakery and Coffee Shop with Pete Koski and half a rhubarb pie, which appeared to be the sheriff's standard order. David's brother hadn't seen or heard from him, Koski said. He'd heard David was gone, of course, from their mother, but he wasn't too worried.

"Al says the kid's taken off before, usually after some disagreement, but never for more than a couple of days. Did he have a fight with anybody this time, do you know?"

"Dorothy says not," McIntire answered. "She says he seemed perfectly normal when he went to work on Sunday. Did his brother know where David went when he disappeared in the past?"

Koski swallowed a forkful of pie before he spoke. "When he was a little shaver he would run off to the barn or into the woods and just sit tight. When he got older, Al thinks he did the same thing except that he could get farther with the car, and sleep in it, too. What did you find out from the girl? Is she anything like her mother? Now there's a looker. Eight kids she's got, too—almost makes you believe in the stork."

Sandra Culver was widely renowned for her comeliness, which, if her husband was to be believed, was surpassed only by her vicious temper. As Earl Culver was wont to put it, without much originality, "She's as pretty as a picture and as mean as a snake." Earl's tales of his spouse and her extraordinary ferocity had long been a major source of entertainment at the Waterfront Tavern.

"So I've heard," McIntire said, "but I've only seen Mrs. Culver when she's been out shoveling snow, bundled to the eyeballs, so I can't comment on the resemblance. Cindy's an attractive child. Doesn't appear to be your wholesome, girl-next-door type though. She's happy as a clam at Godwin's, not exactly pining away for home, and who can blame her? I'd be willing to bet that the infamous Hunters' Dance incident was part of an ingenious scheme to get herself 'sent away.' No doubt poor David never stood a chance. She denies having had any contact with him since she left St. Adele, which is, to put it bluntly, a lie." McIntire took the letters from an inner pocket of his jacket and handed them to the sheriff.

Koski examined each of the envelopes. "Humph…Have you read these?"

"Every word, but I didn't find a thing to give a clue as to where David could be. She writes mainly about how she intends to be rich someday, or, more to the point, marry a rich man. She's a movie fan. Maybe David went to seek his fortune in Hollywood. I have it on good authority that he's 'as cute as a bug's ear.'"

Koski extricated himself from the booth with some difficulty. "Okay if I take these?" He stuffed the letters into his shirt pocket. "And," he added with a heavy note of resignation in his voice, "I'll talk to your fishermen. If there's anything to your suspicions, one of them would be the likely culprit. Maybe Bertelsen was cutting in on somebody's fishing territory." His expression showed plainly that he was of the opinion that, if such was the case, homicide wouldn't be entirely out of line. "If he was killed intentionally, I very much doubt that there's going to be any kind of hard evidence to show it. Unless somebody was seen snooping around the boat, or the murderer confesses outright, we don't have a ghost of a chance of finding out what really happened. That dock is pretty isolated. There wouldn't of been anybody just passing by unless they were on the water. You might want to ask a few questions around the neighborhood…maybe the guilty party came home in the middle of the night covered with bee stings and smelling like fish." He turned toward the door. "But don't start seeing bogy men behind every tree. This ain't London, you know."

XI

It was past eight o'clock, but the sun was still high in the sky when McIntire strolled into the Thorsens' yard for the second time that week. If he was going to "ask a few questions," Nick Thorsen might be the best place to start. He was always up and on his way early in the morning and, more to the point, from what Mia had implied, he had been out late the night before Nels died, most likely at the Waterfront Tavern. That tavern was located on a road that led to just one other place—Nels Bertelsen's dock. If anyone was messing around the *Frelser* that night, Nick or his friends might have seen them either coming or going. Nick was also in a position to be kept abreast of local happenings on a daily basis. And he wasn't above spreading the news of those happenings. The mailman was one of Leonie's most faithful sources. He would be sure to know about any unusual altercations Nels Bertelsen might have had.

Nick was seated on the porch, his feet on the railing, with a tumbler in his hand. He didn't get up when McIntire approached, but called out, "Bring another glass, Meggie!" and used one toe to push a chair in McIntire's general direction.

Mia came out, smiled a restrained greeting, and poured a second he-man sized glass of a dark liquid that McIntire feared was homemade wine.

McIntire watched as she retreated to the kitchen, her lean figure silhouetted by the light streaming through the screen door. He was, as always, struck by the contrast between Mia Thorsen and her husband. If she had combed the far reaches of the earth with the object of uniting herself to her exact antithesis she couldn't have made a better job of it.

Nick was short and compact, with the dusky skin and snapping black eyes of a gypsy prince. Even in his present relaxed attitude, he seemed as bursting with energy as a tightly wound spring. McIntire felt as he might have in the presence of a colorful snake lazing in the sun—one that he knew could deliver a deadly strike without warning.

He sipped tentatively from the glass and barely controlled an audible gasp.

"Chokecherry, September vintage," Nick informed him. "Good nose, eh?"

"A veritable proboscis," McIntire replied and watched Nick's eyes roll heavenward. "I imagine in a pinch Mia could use it to strip paint."

Nick gave him a pitying look. "It's an acquired taste. So what brings you out after supper? No more bad news I hope."

McIntire removed an envelope from his pocket and tossed it on the table. "This should have gone to the Munsons."

Nick picked up the letter and stuck it in his own shirt pocket. "Sorry. But you didn't have to bring it over. You could have just put it back in your mailbox."

"That's what I *usually* do." It slipped out before McIntire could bite it off.

"You get your package okay? It wouldn't fit in the box so I had to just leave it on the post. It didn't say 'fragile' or anything."

As Lucy had pointed out, in his professional capacity, Nick appeared to have a single goal: getting the mail out of his own hands before the end of the day. Such concern for its subsequent well-being was uncharacteristic. The mailman was on a little fishing expedition of his own. Imagine Nick's interest if he was to "accidentally" damage one of those packages and see that the contents were written in Russian. McIntire wished for both their sakes that the material was something more intriguing than what it was—generally a couple of dry manuals describing the inner workings of some kind of engine.

"No, the package was fine, nothing fragile. But I did have some other matters I wanted to talk to you about."

"Ah, so this isn't just a neighborly visit."

Nick was not above indulging in his own bit of sarcasm. McIntire had to acknowledge that maybe he had it coming. Neighborly visits were admittedly not something he made a regular practice of.

"We're just tying up some loose ends—about Nels Bertelsen." McIntire saw, with dwindling confidence, the light of curiosity in Nick's eyes. There would be no chance of passing his questions off as idle chit-chat. This was not Lucy Delaney. "Nels died early in the morning, and I know you're up earlier than anybody else around here. I just wanted to find out if you noticed anything out of the ordinary on Friday morning or," he added, "late Thursday night. You know, anything or anybody unusual."

McIntire was conscious of a sudden cessation of the domestic sounds that had been emanating from the kitchen.

Nick brought his feet down off the railing. "Like what? A bee headed straight for the *Frelser* with blood in his eye? What, exactly, are you getting at?"

The screen door creaked open, and closed softly behind Mia. "John," she asked, in a slow, deliberate voice, "are you saying there's something suspicious about Nels' death?"

McIntire frantically plumbed the depths of his brain for some plausible sounding lie, but came up empty.

"I don't know," he finally admitted. "He had medication, but it didn't do a thing. He died within minutes. There were bees in not one, but *two*, shirts that he had left on the boat. And one of those bees was a drone, which would never even leave the hive on its own."

Nick stared at him, wide-eyed with incredulity. "Mac, I think you spent too much time in Jack the Ripper territory. Meggie, no more wine for the constable! You can't possibly be serious. Who could come up with such a lunatic scheme?"

"It's not so preposterous," McIntire argued. "Everybody knew about Nels' reaction to bee stings, and probably knew that Lucy made him change his fishy clothes before he came into the house. It'd be a simple matter to slip a couple of bees into his shirt."

"But," Mia pointed out, "it wouldn't have done a murderer much good to put a drone in his shirt. They don't sting anyway."

"Not everybody would know that, and whoever did it probably got the bees at night—they'd be quieter then—so maybe they didn't notice. They could have just opened up the hive, scraped a few bees into a box or something, and got out in a hurry."

"They wouldn't only need to plant the bees," Mia said. "They'd have to make sure the antidote didn't work, and Nels never let that stuff out of his sight." She flicked her dish towel across the seat of a dusty wicker chair and sat down. "Unless somebody only wanted to scare him, and it was just a fluke that the shot didn't take. Nels could be a little crotchety sometimes, but we were all pretty much used to him. Who would hate him bad enough to want to kill him?"

"That's a good question," McIntire agreed. "Did he have any, for lack of a better word, enemies, that you know of?"

Nick answered. "You know what a bull-headed old coot Nels was. He probably fought with everybody in the state at one time or another."

"You?" McIntire asked.

Nick gave out with a terse "Humph" and took a long swallow. "Everybody has complaints about the postal service." "No doubt," McIntire responded. This was not the way to get into the mailman's confidence. Somehow Nick always brought out his most uncivil side. "Anyway, if somebody intentionally put those bees on the boat, they would have had to do it sometime during the night or really early in the morning. *Did* you see anything unusual on Friday morning?"

"Nothing I can think of."

"What time do you go to work?"

"About six. Somebody has to get the mail from the early train. It comes about ten after. I take it back to the post office, and then if Elsie's got the store open she gives me coffee. If she's not up yet, I head back home for breakfast. Marie comes in on the dot of seven and sorts the mail."

Marie Goodrow must have held the position of postmaster, or, in this case, postmistress, since sometime shortly after the last of the dinosaurs turned up its toes.

"At about seven-thirty," Nick continued, "I get started on my route. But anybody that figured to do away with Nels would have to be out a lot earlier than that. Nels'd be setting out hooklines in the deep water this time of year. He'd probably have been on the lake by around four o'clock."

"Do you usually see anybody when you're driving to work?"

Nick swatted at a mosquito that hovered hopefully around his left ear. "You mean early, when I'm going to meet the train?" At McIntire's nod, he replied, "Not often, maybe somebody going fishing or hunting. Once in a while a passenger gets off the train, or somebody's waiting to get on. I see Lucy Delaney from time to time if I go back home between the time I meet the train and when I leave to do the deliveries. She walks along the tracks to town every day to pick up her mail, you know, summer or winter, rain or shine. Neither snow nor sleet nor dark of night can keep her from her appointed rounds, that's for sure. Doesn't trust me I guess.

But if she wanted to put Nels out of the way she could have done it at home, fed him some poison. Maybe she did. You don't suppose she's one of those con artists you read about that marry people and bump them off for their money, another Michigan Wildcat?"

"Another what?" Had McIntire missed something?

Mia laughed. "Mrs. Boston, the Michigan Wildcat. Chandler's notorious husband murderer. It was twelve or thirteen years ago. But Lucy'd be jumping the gun. She hasn't married anybody."

McIntire filed Mrs. Boston away as something to explore later and went back to the problem at hand. "Did you ever see Nels in the mornings?"

"Nah, he'd be long gone before I'm even out of the sack."

McIntire hesitated before asking, "What about David Slocum?"

"David Slocum? Why him in particular?" Nick eyed McIntire closely. "You're not saying that kid really *did* have something to do with this?"

The phrasing of this last question led McIntire to suspect that his revelations were not coming as a complete surprise after all.

"You know that David has disappeared?"

"I might have heard something about it."

"Did you see David Friday morning?" McIntire persisted.

"No."

"What about on your way home Thursday night?"

Nick looked at Mia, and drained his glass. "My comings and goings seem to be more well known than I thought." His glance flitted to McIntire's face and then back to the empty glass in his own hand. "No," he said. "I did not see David Slocum or any other sinister being lurking about the lakefront, or cramming his pockets full of bees—not Thursday night, not Friday morning, or any other morning!"

Nick appeared to be running out of patience, and McIntire was running out of questions. It seemed like a prudent time to take his leave. He stood up and handed his glass to Mia. "Leonie will be getting up a search party if I don't get moving. If you think of anything let me know. Thanks for the drink. 'Night, Mia."

As he drove off, McIntire wondered if he'd been foolish in voicing his suspicions so soon, especially to one who traveled over half the county and was not known for discretion. Well, it *is* suspicious, he concluded, and it's already late to be starting an investigation. For better or for worse, the cat was out of the bag now.

XII

The cat was indeed out of the bag and had prowled over a remarkably large area in record time.

Upon accompanying Leonie to church Sunday morning, McIntire wondered if St. Adele might have been visited by some sort of divine presence, bringing about an attack of mass piety among its residents. After the services he found himself surrounded by townspeople, some skeptical, some outraged, some eager to give advice, but all consumed by a curiosity that he was in no way able to satisfy. He disentangled himself as soon as courtesy permitted. Leaving Leonie to join that hotbed of civic responsibility, the Ladies Aid, at their meeting to plan the town's upcoming Independence Day festivities, he walked the quarter-mile home. There he wasted no time in pulling on two pairs of wool socks and struggling into hip boots. He donned his father's ancient hat, complete with a few bedraggled trout flies stuck in its brim, picked up his fly rod, and struck out along the path that ran past the unoccupied barn and into the woods.

As promised, Pete Koski had interviewed the Lindstroms as well as the two other teams of commercial fishermen based in Huron Bay. He had informed McIntire of his findings, or lack of them, the night before over bottled beer at the Waterfront Tavern.

"If any of them was up to any skullduggery the others would know about it, and I don't think they would protect a murderer in their midst," he had said. "Those guys are living in each other's pockets from four o'clock in the morning until way after dark. They fish pretty far out in the lake this time of year, and when they get back they still have to clean the fish and pack them in ice and get them into Chandler in time for the overnight train to Chicago. There's sure as hell no time in their day for sneaking off to harvest bugs. And they've all got families. They couldn't go roaming around in the middle of the night without somebody catching on, even if they did have the energy. It was all I could do just to keep old Simon awake long enough to answer my questions.

"And it doesn't sound like anybody had a real motive. None of them would admit to disliking Bertelsen. They just said he was kind of picky, and thought pretty much of himself with that big fancy tug, which, in my experience, is not something people generally get killed for. Unless," he'd ruminated, "it started out as a practical joke, in which case they might all have been in it together."

"What about Jonas Lindstrom?" McIntire had asked. "Nels might not have been easy for a kid to work with. Considering how he treated David..."

"Jonas didn't have any complaints. Well, Jonas didn't say much of anything, but he's worked for Bertelsen since he was twelve. They must have gotten along reasonably well. I don't suppose Nels could have afforded to take on a grown man for a partner."

At this point Koski had wandered off for a bout with the pinball machine, returning triumphant in a few minutes with two more bottles of Pabst.

"Bertelsen usually left Jonas to clean things up while he took the fish into town," he continued. "When he got back he'd take the kid home. Jonas says Nels always made sure the boat was shut up tight before they left, but he didn't lock it.

Anybody could have gotten in at night. Jonas himself was there alone every night for at least an hour or two. Sometimes he fell asleep before Nels got back, and Nels would just leave him there. He'd have had to be back by four o'clock or so the next morning anyway."

McIntire told him about his conversation with Nick Thorsen, mentioning that the mailman had been out late the night that Nels died.

"Yeah, I guess there was quite a winging in here that night, the Touminen twins' birthday. You hear?"

McIntire shook his head.

"Probably went on long after closing hours," Koski said, "but I'd be the last one to hear about that. Fritz says he was up mopping floors most of the night, and he didn't hear anybody drive by. But somebody sneaking onto Bertelsen's boat wouldn't be liable to advertise it—they'd have taken the back way. Otto Wilke says he heard some kind of commotion on the road in front of his place in the wee hours. His dogs went crazy, he says. When he looked out he didn't see anything but car lights moving away."

So it looked like another dead end. McIntire twisted the neck of his bottle with both hands, like he was wringing the neck of a chicken. The bottle stayed intact. He'd never been much of a hand at killing chickens either.

"Thanks for checking anyway," he told the sheriff, "and for not treating me like the hysteric that people around here seem to take me for. Damn! I just can't believe this is all coincidence...and he died so *fast*. He didn't look like somebody who'd spent fifteen minutes choking to death. It was murder. I know it, and I know we don't have a snowball's chance in hell of proving it."

The sheriff's expression didn't change except for a slight lift of his eyebrows. "Don't be so ready to throw in the towel. I did get a *little* something out of Jonas."

"What? Why didn't you say so? What was it?"

"A very small brown bottle. It had a rubber cork in the top. Jonas picked it up off the deck of the *Frelser*, he said. Just stuck it in his pocket and forgot all about it until I asked if he'd seen it."

"The medication! Was there anything in it? Could you tell what it was?"

"Keep your shirt on! You're starting to sound like Newman. It was about half full of some kind of liquid. That's all I can say. I didn't open it, so I don't know what color it was or anything. The bottle smelled sort of fishy, but I guess that's to be expected. Everything around Jonas Lindstrom smelled fishy."

"Guibard should be able to tell if it really is adrenaline."

"Guibard? Shit! Maybe we could just feed it to a chipmunk and see if it dies. This is the twentieth century, John. I've sent it to Lansing to be analyzed. And in answer to your next question, I don't know how long it'll take. It depends on how complicated the testing turns out to be."

"Actually, I was going to ask about fingerprints."

"There weren't any decent prints on it." The sheriff picked up his beer. "You might well be right, John," he acknowledged. "I gotta admit it sounds like those bees didn't get where they were by accident, and when we find out what Nels squirted into himself, we'll know for sure. But we still might not have any way of proving who did it." He had then drained his bottle, and with a bleak, "This place sure ain't the same without your old man," headed for the door.

McIntire had stayed where he was, thoughtfully sipping his beer, trying not to make unpatriotic comparisons with that brewed on the other side of the Atlantic. Too late, he noticed the impending approach of the sagacious Arnie Johnson and reconciled himself to spending the remainder of the evening receiving the benefit of some small part of Arnie's vast store of Useful Lore and Fascinating Information. He was rescued from this fate by the arrival of Wylie Petworth, fresh from demonstrating his prowess at darts to a pair of poorer but wiser young strangers—probably some of those uranium prospectors that Koski had mentioned. Wylie slid into the booth and wiped his stump of arm across the table, using the folded excess flannel of his sleeve to erase the damp circles left by Koski's bottle. He fixed a gloomy stare on McIntire's face. "Well, Mac, don't see you here too often. I imagine it's hard to see the old place in the hands of strangers, eh?"

In fact, McIntire's only vivid memories of "the old place" were of the hours he spent behind the bar, up to his elbows in a basin of soapy water, while his father, equally facile with tongue or fists, deftly orchestrated the evening's drama of conflict and catharsis with a cast of unpredictable loggers and miners. He felt no nostalgia for those days. Sitting back and being served by Fritz or Hilda Ellman was fine with him. But he did sense Colin McIntire's presence here in a way that he experienced in no other place.

"Any sign of Davy yet?" Wylie asked. "I could sure use that kid now. I haven't really had much get-up-and-go these last few days, myself. You don't suppose something really has happened to him?"

"Well, we haven't found his car, and there haven't been any accidents reported. Dorothy says he took your Buick into town Sunday morning."

"To pick up Paulson, yeah. But he got back okay. He could have gone to see that girl when he was there. Maybe this has something to do with her."

"Actually, I did talk to her. She claims not to have seen him since last fall."

"Well," Wylie responded, "she wouldn't be the first female to be less than candid where her love life is concerned."

"Unlike us forthright males, you mean?"

Wylie's smile was evanescent, and McIntire experienced a fleeting recollection of a flushed and laughing Ragna Petworth executing a brisk polka around the kitchen table in the arms of her red-haired husband.

Was it possible that Wylie still felt the pain of his mother's desertion? Was it even possible that her duplicity played a role in her son's present solitary state?

When you got right down to it, both Ragna and Roger Petworth had voluntarily abandoned their small son. His grandparents had barely lived long enough to see him fully grown. He had no family and few close friends. It was not surprising that he was taking Nels Bertelsen's death so hard.

McIntire had then signaled to Fritz and settled in for a long evening of reminiscing, an evening that left him with a heavy head, but for the first time since his return, a comfortable feeling of belonging.

He stepped over a reclining barbed wire fence. Ten minutes of fast walking later he was standing knee deep in a stream of icy water casting his line and watching the fly being carried rapidly back towards him.

Ten thousand years had passed since the creek in which he waded and the gorge through which it flowed had been left behind in the wake of retreating glacial ice. Stunted and twisted cedars projected at odd angles from the sides of the ravine, defying gravity and cutting off what sunlight might have otherwise penetrated here. Mosquitoes and blackflies battled for their share of any flesh McIntire had left exposed. He began a slow progression downstream, alternately casting and swatting as he trod cautiously on the slippery stones of the creek bed.

It was here that he felt that he had finally found that for which he had returned. Oh, not the fishing—there was plenty of that in Scotland—but for the sense of peace and… *completeness* that he experienced in these isolated pockets of wildness that had remained unchanged since his childhood and for an eon before. He stood nearly motionless in the mid-day twilight and flipped the fly through the air. No sound broke the silence save the gurgling rush of water over stone and the soft buzz of the line past his ear.

While still in England he had done his best to communicate this beauty and serenity to Leonie. She had listened patiently for hours while he rhapsodized on the splendor of his birthplace—the awesome power of Superior, that greatest of all inland lakes with icy waters clear as glass; the steep jagged cliffs overlooking streams and waterfalls filled with leaping trout; the forests with their sheltering groves of spruce and hemlock and cedar; and especially the great pines, hundreds of years old, that towered over the occasional house or barn where they had by some miracle of oversight not fallen prey to the voracious appetite of the mills. He told her about the Huron Mountains, dark and brooding hills where no human lived. He'd described the months of stillness, when all the land was muffled in white and in the mornings the lake steamed like a giant's cauldron until the final weeks of winter when it, too, was imprisoned in ice.

In an attempt to be perfectly fair, he had also cautioned her that winter came early and generally outstayed its welcome, bringing with it temperatures as low as forty below and snow to the rooftops. Despite his warnings, she had agreed to the move almost too readily, leaving McIntire grateful but with a niggling at his conscience that he had persuaded her into an action she would regret when actually faced with the solitude, forced inactivity, and bonechilling cold of a Northern Michigan winter.

He was only slightly off the mark. By the middle of January, John McIntire, child of the boreal forest, could feel his joints slowly freezing into immobility. He was sick to the core of shoveling snow and coal, and desperately bored. But he needed have no anxiety about Leonie's ability to create for herself an active social life anywhere on this earth, and probably elsewhere. She had joined every association and club in the county and, when she felt things getting slow, had started a few of her own. And she basked in the warmth of central heating, a luxury she had heretofore never known.

She was, however, singularly oppressed by what she called the pall that was cast by the shadows of the precious evergreens, in much the same way McIntire's father had been. She had openly rejoiced, as Colin would have, when a late fall windstorm laid claim to a forty-foot white spruce that stood near their kitchen door. She even went so far as to suggest that only luck had kept the tree from falling onto the house, and perhaps the remaining large conifers in the yard should be removed to prevent future disasters. McIntire had been secretly amused at this suggestion, but he took care not to let Leonie see it. He well understood that after spending the war years in London, his wife's fear of her home crashing down upon her was not something to belittle.

Leonie seldom talked about the past, but McIntire was convinced that the promise of escape from the memories of violence and tragedy wrought by two world wars, each of which had cost her a husband, was the major factor in her acquiescence to his plea that she leave her lifelong home, and her daughters and grandchildren, to return with him to Michigan—that and the opportunity of getting a little closer to Texas.

On their wedding day Leonie had said that she didn't give a damn about "love, honor or obey." She only wanted his oath, preferably in blood, that he wouldn't die anytime soon. So far he'd kept that promise, but he wasn't sure he had been completely honorable in his other dealings with her.

He had held up St. Adele as a peaceful refuge, suffused with the beauties of nature and untouched by the ways of the world. It was less than a year after their return that August Adams was found in his barn, his head beaten in with a manure shovel. That slaying was quickly solved but not so quickly forgotten. And now, Nels Bertelsen. It was beginning to look like the haven to which he had lured his bride harbored at least two murderers.

He was thoroughly convinced that the bees in Nels' clothing had been deliberately planted. Whether the actual intention was to kill the man or only to give him a healthy scare remained questionable. Nels' medication had earlier turned up missing. That was a strong argument for homicide. With any luck they'd know for sure when the fluid in the vial was analyzed.

Moreover, there could hardly be any doubt that the killer was someone from within the community. It was not likely that a stranger would come skulking into town and tuck a couple of bees into Bertelsen's shirts just on the off chance that he might be allergic. If he was murdered, it was by someone who knew his vulnerabilities and his habits, *and* who had access to his medication.

Stealing the adrenaline would have been simple. Nels wouldn't have been carrying it with him during the winter. Anyone could have walked into the house before Nels began locking the doors, and probably have found the medication in five minutes. Lucy had admitted that even after Nels put the locks on, she didn't always bother with them if he wasn't home.

Procuring the weapon would also have been a piece of cake. There was no dearth of bees in the neighborhood. They might have come from the hives in Bertelsen's own orchard, but plenty of other farmers kept bees, too. According to Jonas, Nels didn't keep the *Frelser* locked, so getting on board wouldn't have been a problem. But how were the bees kept quiet? He'd noticed the buzzing right away, even with the competing noise of the engine. Of course, it would still have been essentially the dead of night when Nels donned that fatal shirt. The bee could have been inactive until warmed by his body heat.

McIntire was jolted out of his contemplations by a sudden jerk on his line. He took his time landing the fish, a sleek rainbow trout. When it lay twitching in his net, glowing iridescent in the dappled light, he considered throwing it back, but rejected the idea. It would likely go over better than a chipped vase. He picked up a fist-sized stone and, grasping it firmly, rapped the fish smartly on the head. He then stowed it in his creel, picked up his rod, and worked his was back upstream toward home.

By the time he strolled into the yard, Leonie had also returned and was on her knees facing the final few survivors of the two dozen rose cuttings she had smuggled into the country in her luggage. She had planted them near the barnyard fence, well away from the heavily shaded yard.

"Praying?" McIntire inquired maliciously.

"A bit of manure here, a bit of prayer there, it can't hurt." She regarded the spindly stems with resignation. "At home they would be three times this size by now. Well, where there's life there's hope, they say."

"I myself fared quite well in my battle with mother nature." McIntire extended the trout with both hands, "For you, my black thumbed one."

"I'm overwhelmed," Leonie assured him, rising and brushing the dirt from her knees, "and I'd be even more impressed if you'd cleaned it first."

"How are the fourth of July plans going? I'm frankly amazed the ladies would allow a loyal subject of King George to be privy to their discussions."

"There was some question concerning my reasons for being so keen to celebrate the day, but I wield the power of the press, don't forget. I'm meant to do the publicity, and," she added morosely, "I'm on the washing up squad."

"It's good to know," McIntire said, "that even after almost two hundred years the Spirit of Seventy-six lives on."

"The spirit of the monarchy lives on, too. We bid you to gut that fish and put it on ice. I've made lasagna for today. It should be almost ready now."

McIntire picked up his rod and creel, and together they walked toward the house. "You may be an enemy agent," he told her, "but thank God you've learned to cook American."

XIII

Mia Thorsen strode down the driveway, crossed the gravel road, and stepped over the shallow ditch onto a well-worn path. She traversed an open area, rampant with wild rose and raspberry still glistening with the previous night's rain, and followed the trail into the woods. The going here was easy. The track was wide and the space below the canopy of straight-boled beech and sugar maple was open and light. The undergrowth was sparse, a carpet of low growing vines and wild flowers: wood anemone, clintonia, and, here and there, the delicate pink lady slipper.

Mia's feet, in canvas oxfords, were soon soaked, and each step on the previous year's decomposing leaves released a musky, sensuous scent, punctuated at intervals by the pungent odor of wild onion. She walked briskly in an attempt to generate some warmth in her limbs, and to avoid providing a stationary target for mosquitos. Occasionally she brushed away a spider's web that happened to be stretched at eye level across her path.

Presently the trail began to rise as it led up the sloping end of a narrow ridge. The angle at which it ascended grew steadily steeper over the course of several hundred yards and then abruptly leveled off when it reached the crest of the ridge. The trees grew closer together here, with the space between them taken over by bracken fern and thimbleberry growing thickly around table-sized stumps, fire-blackened and covered with moss. Mia bitterly regretted that the great pine forests had been leveled before she was born. Even when she was a child only a few of the behemoths had remained. In those days the hillsides around her home had been naked but for their severed feet, stark testimony to what had once been. Soon even those had disappeared, grubbed out with oxen and horses to create fields to feed a flourishing community. But here on this hillside, too steep to plow, eighty years after the trees had been cut, trimmed, and floated down to the bay, the stumps still remained, their roots defiantly planted in the earth, even in death providing food and shelter for a myriad of woodland plants and small creatures.

Mia stopped for a moment, as she always did, faced one of the rotting stumps, and screwed up her eyes until the image blurred. The tangle of undergrowth disappeared and she found herself standing on a carpet of needles in a cathedral of stately columns and softly filtered light. The air around her became still and warm, infused with a magical incense. All sound ceased, leaving only the soothing whisper of a light breeze threading its way through the canopy high above.

She shook herself from her trance. Someday, she promised herself, she would take a trip to Oregon or Washington, where trees even bigger than those that had grown here still stood.

She continued walking for a half-mile or more until the forest abruptly gave way to a weedy clearing overlooking a hillside blanketed with low growing evergreens. In the center of the clearing towered a structure of weathered wood and iron—a dilapidated ski jump. The trail passed directly in back of it and continued on along the ridge until it dropped into the lumber yard that marked the southeastern boundary of the town of St. Adele.

Mia, however, did not pursue this route but instead turned and walked down the hill to the front of the jump. Its timbers creaked as she mounted the short ladder that brought her up onto the slide. She sat for a minute on the damp boards and, leaning down, gave the sole of each shoe a brisk rub with the end of her sleeve. Then she pulled herself to her feet and began the climb. A wood railing ran along both sides, a solid wall of boards about four feet high. On the right side, the one next to the sliding surface, a few boards had fallen away, leaving gaping holes like the missing teeth in a jack-o-lantern, but the railing on the left was intact and continued to look reasonably reliable. Mia gripped it to steady herself, but prudently kept her weight centered over her feet. She avoided looking down over the edge. Wooden cleats were nailed up the incline to form steps and she counted carefully as she went. When she reached thirty-two she took an extra long stride, skipping number thirty-three. Sometime during the winter, a nail had worked through, causing one end of that foothold to come loose. When she stepped on it earlier that spring, it had slipped and sent her scrambling to clutch the rail with both hands. There was no real danger; her slide was quickly arrested by the cleat below, but it was unsettling all the same.

When she reached the platform at the top of the jump she kept her eyes on her feet and her back to the railing while she inhaled three deep breaths. Then she turned and felt the familiar clutch deep in her breast at the first look down from the dizzying height. Only after that initial split-second of terror had passed was she able to relax and take in the vista presented to her.

Looking straight down she could see only the tops of the small balsams that had grown up weedlike around the base of the jump. The area along the length of the slide was cleared in a wide swath extending down through the pine and spruce on the hillside and into the tangled growth of cedar and tamarack in the marshy area below. In past winters a makeshift road had been plowed through the swamp for the convenience of those young men who were given to demonstrating their virility by hurtling down the slide and flinging themselves off the end. The recent war had watered down the urge for such exploits, and its aftermath had seen a mass exodus of St. Adele's young people. The jump had been unused for close to a decade, accounting for its present state of disrepair.

With her back to this landing area, Mia could see only the forested hills stretching in yellow-green billows of maple, birch, and beech, striated with the deeper color of the groves of conifers. Here and there a massive rocky outcropping thrust an ebony shadow above the trees.

Turning a little to her right, she could look over the treetops to the small cluster of buildings that made up the village of St. Adele on the shore of the bay some half-mile distant. A little nearer, just outside of town, was the open area still referred to as the "lumber yard," even though the sawmill had been gone for years, and the timber stacked there now was only waiting to be trucked away to be ground up for paper pulp.

Off to the northeast was the open lake, its foreground a smooth sheet of pewter under the heavily overcast sky. The invasion of clouds was not yet complete, and a thin band of buttery yellow marked the horizon. Far out on the water two boats crawled toward the west, trailing ribbons of silver like slugs on a garden path. It was a scene tranquil and timeless, but one that Mia knew could change in minutes to an unleashing of the powers of hell.

If Nels Bertelsen had to lose his life so soon it should have been in a fight with the lake, Mia thought. He must have hated dying the way he did, knowing he had been bested by an insect. But then again, she reminded herself, it might not have been the insect at all. If John was right, it was some enemy that Nels maybe didn't even know he had. Or, if he had suspected, didn't know who it was. She recalled Nels' recent behavior. He had always been cautious, but in the last few months he had become increasingly paranoid and downright belligerent. His attack on David Slocum was only one of a handful of similar incidents involving a half-dozen people, including her own husband. Maybe he hadn't been completely irrational after all. Maybe somebody was out to get him and he knew it. Well, he had always been a complainer, people could hardly be blamed for not taking his accusations too seriously.

The sound of a train whistle brought Mia out of her reverie. She looked toward the railroad crossing at the lumber yard. From her vantage point, she could just make out the figure of her husband, pacing while he waited to exchange mailbags with the brakeman. His car was nowhere to be seen, most likely hidden by one of the long piles of pulpwood. The train must be late. She was glad that the scene was out of earshot. The whistle blew again and the train chugged into view.

On most mornings the engineer slowed just enough for the brakeman to throw off his bag and grab the one Nick would toss to him, but this morning the train was apparently coming to a complete stop. That could only mean some heavier cargo to be deposited, or a passenger. Mia watched with interest as the train once again pulled away, leaving a lone figure standing near the tracks. Even seen from this distance, the new arrival was clearly female and youthful, and Mia wondered if Nick would break his self-imposed rule and offer her a lift the few hundred yards into town. Nick, however, had already disappeared. Mia was surprised to see that, instead of taking the road into St. Adele, the woman shouldered her small bag and struck out, with a childlike bounce in her step, on the path that led in her own direction.

The trail branched off in a few places to provide quicker routes, nowadays seldom used, between the town and various homes, but Mia could think of no one who might be expecting a visitor. Although maybe the women hadn't been met at the train because she was *not* expected. Before she came near enough for recognition, she entered the wooded area and was lost from sight.

Mia was about to descend from her tower when a voice broke the stillness, high pitched and feminine, rapid speech ending in a squeal of laughter. It was followed by the lower tones of a male. Someone had met the woman after all. Mia retreated to the platform and sat down to conceal herself in case one of the pair should look up as they passed under. Not that there was anything so odd about climbing the ski jump at six o'clock in the morning, but she would just as soon keep her habits to herself. She pulled the collar of her jacket up around her neck, shivered, and waited.

The voices marked the steady approach of the couple, with the girl speaking in a continuous stream, getting an occasional brief response from her companion. Mia could not make out the words.

After a brief period of silence, she raised herself cautiously and cast a wary eye over the railing. Seeing no one, she turned to leave her hiding place once more, when a stifled giggle sounded from directly beneath her. The two had obviously sought the privacy of the sheltered area under the base of the jump. Kids, Mia guessed, and nearly groaned aloud at the mating habits of the modern adolescent. She then smiled at her short memory. Things hadn't been so very different thirty years before, and probably thirty-thousand years before that. But at this time of the morning! And the ground must be soaked. She leaned back against the damp boards, mindful of the creaking—not that the little darlings would be likely to notice—and tried not to listen too closely to the scuffles, whimpers and panting that emanated from below.

Through their exertions the two must have worked up a hearty appetite for breakfast, for in a surprisingly short time she again heard footsteps scurrying off into the woods, and then all was silence. Just the same, she waited a few minutes before venturing out of her aerie and making her way down the incline.

Going down was slower work than climbing up. She walked sideways to grip each cleat, counting backwards this time to avoid the loose board. Now and again she had considered fixing it. It would be easy enough to bring along a hammer and a couple of nails, but somehow it always seemed too much like tainting pleasure with business.

She exhaled a long breath when her feet were at last firmly planted on solid ground, and trudged, with slightly wobbly knees, up the hillside to reach the path. As she passed the base of the jump, a small shiny object lying in the wet grass caught her eye, and she stooped to retrieve it. A lipstick. She looked at the bottom. *Passion's Flame.* Must be good stuff, she surmised. She placed it on one of the structure's cross braces in case its owner should return to claim it. In doing so, she noticed a neatly folded handkerchief and a white canvas shoe, similar to the ones she was wearing, lying in the grass farther under the jump. Mia brushed aside the balsams, ducked under the timbers, and bent to pick up the shoe.

On rising, she found herself staring directly into the glazed and sightless eyes of its owner. Cindy Culver lay like a cast-off doll, crumpled against one of the massive timbers. Mia froze, arrested in her half-erect position, transfixed by the horror of the scene—a child's dress-up game turned to mayhem: the halo of golden waves surrounding the cherubic face, horribly bruised and swollen under its layer of inexpertly applied make-up; the head hanging limply to one side, pillowed on a shoulder robed in grown-up silk from which an open leather bag dangled, its contents spilling into the weeds; legs in shredded nylon stockings, scraped raw and bleeding; and the tiny feet, side by side, one encased in a canvas tennis oxford, the other with the stocking torn away, exposing the most brilliant of crimson gracing the nails of its chubby white toes.

After what seemed like a lifetime, Mia tore her eyes away from the grotesque tableau, clutched the mate to that shoe to her chest, scrambled through the bushes, and ran back down the trail the way she had come.

XIV

Mia had run only a few hundred yards before she was forced to slow to a walk. Wheezing with every stride, she strove to clear her head and hear her own thoughts over the roar of the blood pounding in her ears.

If she went home and called the sheriff, it would be an hour or more before he could get there. John McIntire would be quicker, but calling the constable from her house was out of the question. The sound of the McIntires' 'two shorts and a long' at this time of the morning would send every one of the six curious parties on their line scrambling for the phone. The news would spread exponentially until it reached the Culvers themselves, probably in about fifteen minutes. If they had expected Cindy to be on the morning train they wouldn't have to guess twice at the identity of the victim. It was no way to find out your daughter had gotten killed.

She took the path that branched toward McIntire's house. It was not much farther than her own home, but the trail was overgrown from lack of use, and at one point she temporarily lost it. Concentrating on finding her way had a calming effect, and by the time she pounded on the McIntires' kitchen door, the racing of her pulse had slowed and her breathing had returned to near normal. But once inside she began to shake uncontrollably and could only extend the shoe to the robed and rumpled constable. It was several minutes before she was able to give a marginally coherent account of what she had seen.

McIntire roused his wife, who appeared in pincurls and turban, wrapped a coral-colored afghan about Mia's quivering shoulders, and put a kettle of water on the stove preparatory to the brewing of her remedy for every calamity.

He then put through a call to Mark Guibard. The doctor answered brusquely after a dozen rings. McIntire informed him only that there had been a death and asked him to come as quickly as possible to the old ski jump, and to please alert the sheriff's department. Neither the doctor nor Koski had to deal with the infamous party lines. Jeannie Goodrow, who had the job of overnight operator, could generally be relied upon to be reasonably discreet. Nevertheless, McIntire wasn't about to name any names or send the word murder hurtling out over the phone lines.

He dressed in seconds, and, with, "You stay here 'til I get back!" to Mia, was out the door.

The trip to the railroad crossing at St. Adele and along the path to the jump took only a few minutes, but the doctor was already standing in the clearing wringing water from the cuffs of his trousers when McIntire came puffing up the trail.

"I hope this business of dragging me out of bed in the middle of the night isn't going to get to be a habit. I retired to get away from this kind of shit." Guibard ran his fingers through his uncombed hair, adding to his already uncharacteristically disheveled appearance. "I couldn't get hold of Koski. Best I could do was that kid. He's on his way. What the devil's going on here anyway?"

Quickly, without allowing himself to think about what he would find there, McIntire walked around the trees to the underside of the jump. He saw a tangle of wet grass and weeds, but no evidence of either Cindy Culver or any of her worldly goods. He turned, nearly trampling the doctor who'd followed on his heels.

"Mia Thorsen just came to my house. She was the next thing to hysterical, said she saw Cindy Culver here this morning, dead. Strangled, by the sound of things." He filled Guibard in on the sketchy information he had gotten out of Mia.

"Well, there's nobody here now. You don't suppose Mia was mistaken, the girl was just asleep or something? What the hell was *Mia* doing out here at this time of the morning?"

McIntire hadn't thought about that. "She didn't say," he answered. "But Mia's not the fanciful type. She was positive that Cindy was dead." McIntire looked at the broken and flattened ferns. "You can see somebody has been here. Oh-ho! Look at this!" Several streaks of red decorated one of the concrete footings that anchored the jump to the earth. "This look like blood to you?"

The doctor peered closely at the stains. "That it does, John." He touched a finger to the edge of the blotch. "And recent—it hasn't dried much yet."

McIntire began searching through the matted weeds. "There's no question about it being recent. It rained pitchforks and paper devils last night."

"Did it? I didn't notice. Over the years I've learned to sleep soundly when I have the chance." The doctor looked up at the leaden skies. "But it won't be long before it's coming down again. I'd better get a sample of this while I can. I'll have to risk another of Koski's lectures about not touching a thing until he gives the okay." He picked up his bag. "By all rights, he should be the one waiting for the go-ahead from *me.*"

McIntire looked at his watch. "I just hope he gets here soon." What could possibly have happened to the body, if it was a body? Maybe Cindy *had* only been unconscious and had come to and wandered off. Please let it be true! In fact, he hardly dared hope that the girl was alive. Mia's description had been graphic and had not left much doubt. Even if she was still living, it was unlikely that anyone could get up and walk away with such injuries. Another possibility—that Mia might have interrupted the murderer and been observed by him—was unthinkable.

Guibard crouched over the bloodstains. "If you want to wait here for Koski," McIntire told him, "I'll have a look down in the swamp. If I wanted to hide a body that's where I'd go."

"Maybe Mia was mistaken, and the girl just got up and walked off under her own steam." Guibard echoed his own prayers. "Shouldn't we check with her family and see if she made it home before we get carried away?"

McIntire pushed aside the thought of informing Cindy's parents of Mia's discovery. "We better just wait for Koski," he said. "Anyway, if Cindy was on this path, she wasn't headed home."

He traversed the cleared swath that extended down the precipitous slope, looking for signs that someone else had recently passed this way. He saw none. At the bottom, where the incline leveled off, the open area was dotted with tufts of swamp grass and decomposing stumps amid pools of turbid water. It was bordered on three sides by the desolate cedar swamps. He continued around the edges of the clearing, but saw no indication that anyone else had walked there recently.

He peered into the tangle of vegetation. It would indeed be a perfect spot to conceal a body, but transporting it into that no-man's-land would be arduous, bordering on impossible. It was as if all the detritus of Michigan's forests had been dumped here to slide downhill and rot into the ooze. Living trees, their roots entwined with the downed trunks of their ancestors, twisted over the soggy ground, creating an all but impenetrable barrier. Not a single foot-sized space of solid earth presented itself for the convenience of anyone passing through.

Clutching at the spindly branches of tamarack trees to steady himself, McIntire stepped from pulpy, moss-covered log to slimy exposed root and scrambled a few yards into the thicket before admitting defeat.

As he retraced his steps back to the clearing, he heard voices that he hoped meant that Pete Koski had arrived. He climbed back up the hill as quickly as his fifty-year-old lungs would allow to be greeted by boy deputy Cecil Newman.

"Uncle Pete takes Mondays off," Newman explained in his piping adolescent voice. "He'll be bass fishin' somewhere. He's real secretive about his spots. So what's the story here?"

The deputy listened while McIntire told him, his baby's bottom cheeks growing more pallid by degrees. "How long ago did this happen?"

"Around six-thirty or thereabouts." McIntire consulted his watch. "It's almost seven-forty now so it's been over an hour."

"Quite a lot over an hour!" Newman's voice rose to a squeak. "Why in hell didn't you say that it was homicide? I thought some moron had fallen off the jump. Now you're saying murder! We could have gotten some people out, set up some roadblocks. That body could be in Wisconsin by now! Where's the witness?"

McIntire knew that his reasons for not being more specific on the telephone constituted a pitiful excuse for his short-sightedness and he didn't try to mask it. "She's at my house," he replied. "My wife is with her," he added. No need to appear even more incompetent than the pubescent deputy already took him to be. After all, he could hardly have known the body would be gone.

"Well, why don't you get back there and see what she can remember? I'll send somebody to talk to her as soon as I can. Call Pete's wife, and she'll get a deputy to shag him in. She's the only one will know where he is, and she'll be cagey about telling, so you have to make damn sure she knows it's an emergency." He turned to Guibard. "Can you stay while I get my equipment from the car?" He followed McIntire down the path and sprinted past him, but not before turning back to the doctor one more time. "And don't touch anything!"

XV

By nine-thirty Sheriff Koski himself was on the scene, along with his three deputies and a swarm of volunteer searchers. Among these were Earl and Sandra Culver and two of their older children. They stood apart from the others, a stonefaced clique cloaked in the armor of impassivity. An assortment of hunting dogs had also been pressed into service. Most of these were unleashed and circled one another suspiciously, occasionally expressing their confusion at this off-season call to work with a quick, fierce battle. Koski's own German shepherd, Geronimo, sat aloof at his side, superciliously ignoring the antics of his less experienced cousins.

The searchers had been held off while the sheriff took the time to examine the scene and make a quick circuit of the area in order to give Geronimo the opportunity to pick up the trail of anyone who might have gone off into the woods. It was a futile exercise. At some time that morning either Mia, McIntire, Cecil Newman, or the doctor—who had come in on a shorter path leading from an unused gravel pit—had taken each of the trails leading to the ski jump.

Koski walked over to where McIntire stood under a dripping poplar. "You absolutely sure this wasn't just some figment of that woman's imagination?"

"Positive," McIntire said. "And there was the blood. I take it you didn't find any sign of her then?"

"No. And once this bunch gets done trampling around out there, we won't."

"But you're gonna let them go?"

"I got no choice. She could be lying out there somewhere." He turned and bellowed, "Okay, people, listen!"

He lost no time in dividing the volunteers into groups and detailing areas to be searched. They would concentrate on the tract of land on which they stood and the roads that encircled it. Those searching the woods were instructed to stay in a line, remaining close enough to touch fingertips with the person on either side. An injured girl couldn't have gotten far, but in dense underbrush someone would almost have to trip over her before she would be found. The sheriff huddled briefly with the Culvers for a few private words then whistled to his dog. The two of them trotted down the hillside—Geronimo with his nose to the grass where McIntire had walked that morning—and plunged into the swamp. A contingent of about a dozen men, with Wylie Petworth in the lead, followed him.

McIntire, having neither a rugged appearance nor a fully operational dog, had been assigned to the group whose task it was to walk the surrounding roads, looking for signs that one of the numerous trails and primitive tracks entering the woods had recently been used, or that a vehicle had been concealed. The area, like most of the Upper Peninsula, was honeycombed with abandoned railroad grades and logging roads. They were seldom used in summer, when the abundant insect life and the lack of a season for killing anything legally kept most people out of the woods. If a car had been driven on one of them that morning it should be readily evident.

The threatening rain had not yet materialized, but neither had the sun appeared to dry the effects of the previous night's downpour or eliminate the morning chill.

By midafternoon the roads and the woods that covered the area around the jump and down both sides of the ridge had been thoroughly explored with no results other than a general consensus that the population of partridge was definitely on an upswing. A complete search of the swamps and adjacent slough areas could take days.

When McIntire returned home he found a yard full of vehicles and wet, weary volunteers, human and canine. Leonie was handing out sandwiches, without regard to species of the recipient, from a table set up near the front porch. She poured McIntire a cup of steaming, inky black coffee from an enormous enameled pot and handed him an open bottle of brandy. He added a healthy dollop to his cup and attempted a smile. "So you've finally figured out that tea has its limits. How's Mia?"

"She's inside with the sheriff." Leonie threw half a tuna on rye to a mud-encrusted spaniel. "She's trying to convince herself she just dreamed the whole thing."

"Afraid not. We know for sure that Cindy Culver was on that train this morning, and she hasn't turned up. Have Earl and Sandra been here?"

"Just long enough to eat and send one of the boys home to see to the younger children. They wanted to see Mia, but I told them the sheriff wasn't letting her talk to anybody. It's not true, but I don't think she could have faced Sandra today. They went back out again. Nobody could stop them."

"They're probably better off doing something," he assured her. "As long as somebody else doesn't get lost. Those woods are like a jungle. I doubt that she's there anyway. It would take a couple of hours to get far enough into the swamp to conceal a body, and anybody gone that long would be missed." At Leonie's questioning look, he conceded, "I don't believe for a minute that child is still alive. Mia was right. Cindy Culver is dead, and nine chances out of ten the body was carried out to the road. If I'd been doing my job, we could have gotten out early, and there might have been a chance at catching whoever did it."

"Oh John, don't be an ass. You couldn't know she'd be taken away, and anyway, the murderer had time to be long gone before Mia even got to our house."

McIntire shrugged and walked up the steps. He was nearly mowed down by Lucy Delaney backing out the screen door with a tray of sandwiches balanced on one arm and a devil's food cake on the other. He made a quick dive for the cake and caught it just before it would have become an unaccustomed delicacy for a pair of vulturous Labrador retrievers. Lucy clutched at his arm with her now free left hand.

"The sheriff wants to talk to me," she whispered. "Does he think this has something do with Nels? Do you reckon he thinks that David Slocum killed them both?"

Lucy's words probably reflected the unspoken thoughts of the majority of those present, but McIntire wasn't prepared to admit that such a possibility had occurred to him as well.

"He probably just wants to know if you saw anybody this morning," he replied noncommitally.

"Well I didn't! Why does everybody seem to think I have nothing better to do than spend the mornings spying on my neighbors?" Lucy snapped. She reclaimed her cake and swept down the steps to the lawn, leaving a startled McIntire staring at her broad back.

He found the sheriff and Mia in the downstairs bedroom where his parents had once slept and which Leonie had converted into the "library." Mia appeared spent. Her shoulders sagged, and her face had taken on a hue hardly differentiated from the misty gray of her hair, but she had regained her composure and was just completing her story when McIntire entered.

Koski motioned to him to sit down and continued to prod Mia's memory. "Tell me one more time, what was she wearing?"

Mia put her elbows on her knees and rested her forehead in her hands for a long moment. When she spoke, it was in the robot-like voice of one who had repeated the same words many times. "She had a coat on, a long sort of a raincoat. It was half pulled off, and underneath she was wearing a dress. It was a dressy type material, silk or something that looked like silk. It was a bright turquoise color and had beads around the neckline. Her clothes were pulled every which way and wet from the grass. She had on nylon stockings—they were all ripped up—and canvas tennis shoes. One tennis shoe." Her voice dropped so she could barely be heard. "She had her toenails painted."

"What else do you remember seeing on the ground besides the other shoe?"

"The handbag was lying in the grass, but the strap was still around her arm. It was flat so you could tell it was empty or close to it. It was good sized, a tan color, made of a kind of soft leather, expensive, I should think. There was another shoe—I mean a different kind, not the mate to this one." She indicated the canvas oxford on the coffee table. "More dressy, a sort of high-heeled sandal. White, too." She closed her eyes and pressed the tips of her fingers against her forehead. "A handkerchief, a gold colored compact, and a silk scarf, turquoise like the dress. It was folded up. That's all I remember....No," she added suddenly. "There was a book."

"I don't suppose you noticed the title?" Koski asked.

"Not that kind of book," Mia explained. "It was a little book, like for addresses. No, bigger, about yay...." She made a rectangle with her thumbs and forefingers. "A date book or diary maybe. I really can't remember anymore. Can't I go now? Nick will be home soon."

"In a minute," Koski assured her. "Do you want some coffee or something to eat?"

Mia shook her head. "Leonie's already poured me full of tea."

"Are you sure," the sheriff continued, "that you didn't hear anything Cindy or the person with her said?"

"I couldn't make out any of it. It was just two voices."

"But you're sure one was male?"

"It was a low voice. It sounded like a man to me. But I might have just assumed it would be a man that Cindy was meeting." Mia was silent for awhile. "The way she giggled…it must have been a man."

"And it must have been someone she knew," Koski said.

McIntire entered the conversation for the first time. "Don't be too sure. I suspect Cindy Culver could get on giggling terms in no time at all."

He didn't know if the shock that registered on the faces of Mia and the sheriff was occasioned by his irreverence toward the dead or by the abrupt entrance of a wild-eyed Nick Thorsen.

The appearance of her husband brought about a remarkable transformation in Mia. The haggard lines of her face were replaced by a thin smile of resigned determination. She got to her feet, lifted her narrow shoulders, put her arm around Nick's waist, and led him out the door.

The sheriff also stood up, closed the door on the Thorsens' retreating backs, and beckoned McIntire to his side. "More good news, John," he said, "I got the results back on the stuff in that vial."

McIntire knew he could wait until Christmas for Koski to tell him those results without his asking. He was beginning to understand the frustrations suffered by Cecil Newman. "What was it?"

"Nicotine, enough to drop a horse."

His expectations had not prepared him for the shock he felt at hearing the truth. He reached back to the nearby desk for support. "You mean from tobacco? The killer could have made it from cigarettes or something?"

"He could have, I suppose, but he didn't. It was an insecticide, nicotine sulphate, forty percent nicotine. Extremely toxic and extremely common. Probably most of the farmers and half the gardeners around here have some. We'll need to get an order to exhume the body." He gave a John Wayne-sized sigh. "I might as well send these people home. The state police will be here in the morning. They'll be in heaven when they find out we've got two murders to play with. We'll be getting as much respect as Detroit...Oh, and they're bringing in Florida Mowsers."

McIntire stared at him. "What the hell are they, some sort of a weapon? What are they planning to do with 'em?"

"It's not a what, it's a who. He's a tracker—or not so much a tracker as a finder. He's got dogs that could sniff out a grain of salt in the Sahara desert. If that girl's lying out in the woods somewhere, he'll find her...and I'd damn well like to get to her before the crows and turkey buzzards do."

XVI

McIntire was up early the next morning, after a night spent in long hours of wakefulness relieved only by a fitful sleep plagued with visions of Cindy Culver's angel face staring, cold and ghastly, from a slime covered pool. The rain that had remained entrapped in the clouds all the previous day had been unleashed around sundown and had fallen steadily throughout the night, no doubt effectively washing away any physical evidence that might have led to Cindy or her killer. About the time the first fissure in the darkness showed at the windows, McIntire had begun mentally compiling a list of all known information concerning the deaths of both Cindy Culver and Nels Bertelsen.

He was now seated at the kitchen table committing his list to paper, a neatly printed column for each of the deceased. Reducing the violent deaths of his neighbors to a tidy chart of black on white temporarily alleviated some of the sickness and horror he felt, and he entered into the task with the same zeal with which he attacked the Sunday crossword. After assessing the results, he used the side of the butter dish as a straight edge to draw a heavy line connecting information included in both columns, to wit: the early morning hours of the deaths and a relationship to David Slocum.

Possibly an association with Warner Godwin, too. Lucy had mentioned the lawyer as one of the few people, along with the "Indian chief," Charlie Wall, that Nels got along with. He could have been Nels' attorney. Here McIntire drew a dotted line.

He had taken a fresh sheet of paper and was heavily involved in making a second list, this one detailing the personality characteristics of both victims, when a thunderous knocking nearly jolted him out of his skin and sent him scrambling for the door. A red-eyed Sheriff Koski leaned against the jamb.

"Sorry," he said. "I thought you'd still be in bed. Hope I didn't wake up your wife."

"Oh, no chance of that. Yesterday was the first time I've seen Leonie up before ten since our wedding day. It's not likely to happen two mornings in a row. What can I do for you?"

Koski had come with a request that McIntire join him in interviewing the Culver family.

The Culvers lived at the terminus of a dead-end road in a house that had started life some sixty-five years earlier as two modest log cabins. They were now united at right angles to make a single, no less modest, home. It was built in the Finnish mode—the logs planed square, with tightly fitting dovetailed corners. The entry was sheltered by an awning style roof supported by rough-hewn posts, which made a sort of porch across the front and around one side of the structure. The entire conglomeration was covered with patched asphalt roofing in various shades ranging from a dusky red to black. Spreading limbs of a maple overshadowed the house, and a tangle of lilac bordered the path to the ramshackle privy.

All in all, the dwelling would have presented a charmingly picturesque scene if the rope strung between two nearby birch trees, draped with forlornly dripping diapers and undershirts, hadn't proclaimed that this was no rustic hunting lodge but a year-round home to a family of ten—now nine.

McIntire followed the sheriff across the cracked concrete slab that made up the floor of the porch, through an obstacle course of three-wheeled wagons and armless dolls, past a wringer washer, to the front door. The washing machine appeared to serve as a symbol of either social status or optimism; no electrical lines entered the cottage.

Even in her present state, Sandra Culver, shed of her heavy outerwear of the day before, was, without question, the most exquisite woman McIntire had ever seen, on or off the silver screen. He lagged behind the sheriff and tried not to gawk at the honey-colored skin and the short waves of hair that fit her perfectly shaped head like a helmet of molten bronze and ended in charmingly captivating curls at the nape of her neck. She was dressed in a rumpled too-large shirt and faded baggy shorts, exposing suntanned legs that made Betty Grable look like an underfed stork by comparison. The full lips were set in a hard line and the deep amber eyes…if the eyes are the window to the soul, Sandra Culver's shades were drawn. She mumbled a terse, "How do you do?" and shook McIntire's hand. He was relieved that the situation precluded further social pleasantries.

Sandra stood near a wooden table littered with bowls of various colors and sizes, most half filled with milk in which overlooked Cheerios floated soggily. She was surrounded by seven sober-faced children, testimony that her legendary fierce disposition softened at least a little from time to time. They ranged in age from the boy of about sixteen, whom McIntire recognized from yesterday's search, to the toddler brother in his arms. At a word from their mother the entire flock scattered and disappeared like chicks fleeing the shadow of a hawk. Sandra led the two men into the living room.

It was dim, with a ceiling so low that McIntire felt it would ruffle the hair on the top of his head, had there been anything much to ruffle. The floor was covered in a blue-patterned linoleum with worn black ridges delineating the uneven boards underneath. It sloped precipitously towards a wood burning heater fashioned from a fifty-five gallon oil drum. The stove was a cold and dormant hulk now, belying its ability to transform itself into a lethal red-hot demon. McIntire absently rubbed his forearm where it still bore the scars of his own childhood barrel stove encounter and stepped forward to shake hands with Earl Culver, who had just emerged from the narrow stairwell at the far end of the room.

Earl was not a large man, but he had the muscular arms and barrel chest of one who spent his winters skidding logs out of the woods to sell for pulpwood. It was obvious that the morose aspect that he habitually presented for the amusement of his friends as accompaniment to his pitiful tales of spousal persecution had born no resemblance to genuine suffering. His thin face was a study of anguish and helpless dismay. He was dressed in a double layer of flannel shirts and bib overalls faded almost white at the knees, and carried a pair of cracked leather boots and a newspaper.

"We'd like to ask a few questions," the sheriff stated without preamble. "We'll try not to take up too much time."

"I don't have much time." Earl crossed to the window and spoke with his back to the room. "I need to go look for my little girl, and you should be doing the same."

Koski ignored this and deftly herded both of the bereaved parents to a lumpy davenport, where they obediently sat down at opposite ends. He and McIntire took the only other chairs in the room. McIntire tried in vain to picture the entire Culver clan gathered here on a frosty winter's evening.

Earl extracted a single sheet from the newspaper and proceeded to fold it precisely in half, but was checked in his project by a cough and a frown from his wife.

"Were you expecting your daughter to be on that train yesterday morning?" Koski began. McIntire wondered if he should have had his notebook with him. The sheriff didn't appear to intend to write anything down; he had brought no equipment to do so.

"Of course not. You already know that." Sandra's Culver's tone of voice was in keeping with her reputation. "If we had known she was coming, Earl would have gone to pick her up. We live six miles from town. She wasn't walking toward home, anyway. She was obviously going somewhere else, to see somebody else."

"Had she ever done that before?"

"Done what?"

"Come back to St. Adele to see someone outside of her family?"

Sandra looked at Earl, but continued to do the responding. "No. Why would she?"

"I don't know," Koski answered. "I wish I knew why she did it yesterday. But," he questioned, "could she have met somebody here—or somewhere else—in the past without you necessarily knowing about it? Did Warner Godwin let you know whenever Cindy left his home?"

Earl's eyes narrowed. "What are you trying to say?"

"I'm only trying to find out why your daughter was on that train yesterday morning, and," he added, "who knew that she would be on it. Now, tell me about Cindy's work schedule. Did she get regular time off?"

"She was off Thursday afternoons and every other weekend," Sandra replied.

"Was she off this past weekend?"

Earl and Sandra looked at each other. Sandra hesitated before answering. "I'm not sure. She didn't always come home on weekends. She liked to stay in Chandler where her friends are. You know how it is with young girls."

"I surely do," the sheriff acknowledged glumly. "Did Mr. Godwin let you know when Cindy was leaving his house? For overnight, I mean. Do you know for sure that when she didn't come home on her weekends off, that she stayed at Godwin's?"

Earl made a sudden move to rise to his feet, but Sandra slid closer and put a hand on his arm.

"If Cindy was coming home she sent a letter or a postcard," she said. "Other than that we don't—didn't hear too much from her. She liked being in town. Her work at Godwin's wasn't hard and she had plenty of free time."

"Too damn much free time." Earl didn't look at his wife, but his voice boiled over with accusation. "I knew we should have brought her back home for the summer. Who knows what kind of ideas she picked up in town?" He folded the newspaper into a thick pad, gave it a thunk with his fist, and stuffed it into one of the worn boots.

McIntire considered that it was supposedly Cindy's "ideas," and her propensity for acting on them, that had gotten her sent to town in the first place. He cleared his throat. "Whatever happened to Cindy happened *here*, not in Chandler." Three sets of perplexed eyes turned to him. "I mean," he explained, "that she wouldn't have had to come back here to meet somebody from Chandler. She must have been with someone from St. Adele."

Sandra Culver turned to him with ice in her eyes and vitriol in her voice. "Don't beat around the bush, we know what happened to Cindy, and we know who did it. Now you get out of here and find that boy, and make the son-of-a-bitch tell you what he did with my baby!" Tears at last began to well up into her eyes, and she turned away. "It rained so hard last night…"

XVII

Koski drove directly from his meeting with the Culvers to Warner Godwin's office in Chandler. He made no mention of dropping McIntire at his house. He seemed to have almost forgotten the constable's presence, and that someone would eventually have to drive him back to St. Adele. McIntire didn't remind him. He really wasn't quite sure why the sheriff had sought out his company that morning. It couldn't be that he thought McIntire would be of help in getting information out of Earl and Sandra. Koski knew that he wasn't well acquainted with the Culvers. And although the pair didn't have a lot to say, when they did speak it was in perfectly understandable English.

Koski might have read his thoughts. "I find it's a good idea to have two people in on an interview, and we're spread pretty thin right now. You don't mind?"

McIntire assured him that he didn't mind.

"Just to have another person to listen. You don't need to ask anything."

McIntire assured him that he'd keep his mouth shut.

Godwin's offices occupied a single-story wood frame building just a half-block from the waterfront. McIntire remembered it as Tony's Cigar and Tobacco Shop. Before they went inside, Koski paused to make a slow circle around the jaunty Jeep wagon parked near the door, squinting as he examined the rugged tires and running an admiring hand over the gleaming wood paneling.

The attorney's receptionist announced their arrival ceremoniously and escorted them into the inner sanctum with a reverence that might have been more in keeping with an audience in the Oval Office.

Warner Godwin was round. From his naked balloon-shaped head balanced on his orbital torso to his circular spectacles perched on his ball of a nose, he was a collection of perfect spheres. In his black three piece suit, he resembled nothing so much as a snowman bridegroom, or maybe, "how to draw a bear starting with circles."

He stood to reach across his desk, an imposing lawyerly affair incongruous in the tiny room with its dingy mint-green walls and flowered curtains covering a window looking onto the street.

The handshake was firm, and his voice had a deep timbre not at all in keeping with his comic-page appearance.

"I don't have a great deal of time. I have to be in court in half an hour," were the first, but by no means the last, words out of his mouth. "Has she been found?" he asked anxiously, and continued without waiting for a reply, "I haven't told my daughter yet. She was crazy about Cindy. I don't know how she'll take it, first…her mother and now this. You're sure she's really dead? Not just run off, or been…taken somewhere?"

He had a disconcerting tendency to pause in mid-phrase, a practice which might well have been a survival skill, since he seldom stopped long enough between sentences to draw breath, or to allow anyone else to get a word in.

"Was Cindy the kind of girl that might have run off?" Koski asked.

Godwin appeared to give this question some thought before answering. "Who knows these days?"

"Did she ask you for permission to leave yesterday morning?"

"Oh yes," Godwin assured him. "I took her to the train myself. It's not far from the house, but you have to be there by about five to get the early train, so I gave her a ride. She said that an aunt from Milwaukee was visiting her family and she wanted to see her. Not true I suppose? I didn't mind letting her go. She stayed most weekends, and hasn't asked for extra time off before. Annie spent the day…with some neighbors. She's there today too. They have a child her age so it works out well for everybody. She's used to being left with sitters. Her mother worked, too, sometimes."

Koski laboriously dragged the train of conversation back onto the track. "Didn't you wonder why Cindy was so dressed up, just to take the train home? It's possible that she was wearing a dress that belonged to your late wife. Had she done that before, worn your wife's clothes when you were around?"

For the first time Godwin seemed at a loss for words, but recovered quickly enough. "I didn't see what she was wearing. I mean she had a coat on. It was forty degrees, for God's sake. She had on high-heeled shoes. I noticed that because it made her taller. You say she was wearing Nina's clothes? When she died?"

"You did give her some of your wife's belongings?"

"Yes." His billiard ball forehead crinkled slightly. "Yes, I did. Last winter. I decided to start off the new year by clearing out some of the old reminders. But they were much too old for her. I didn't really think they were anything a young girl would care for. I thought maybe she would pass them on to her mother. The family is very poor, you know. Well, with all those kids, who wouldn't be?"

"Where did you go after you dropped Cindy at the train? Back home to bed?"

"No. I had a dentist appointment at ten-thirty in Marquette. I left right away and I didn't get back until…early in the afternoon. I'm sure my girl told you that yesterday."

The man was awe-inspiring; he answered Koski's next question without even waiting for it to be asked. "Of course I didn't take my daughter to the neighbors that time of the morning. We have a system. If Annie gets up and no one is home, she knows to have a bowl of cereal and go straight to the Butlers'. They're only next door, and Annie is very dependable. Mrs. Butler was expecting her. She'd check if she wasn't at her house by seven-thirty or so."

"What time did Cindy say she would return?" McIntire's breaking of his vow of silence brought with it the element of surprise, enabling him to catch Godwin off guard and jump in.

"By the afternoon train. It gets in about six-thirty. It's about a ten minute walk from the station, so I wouldn't have expected her until about six-forty-five. Of course I heard that she was missing long before that, so I wasn't expecting her at all. I just told Annie that Cindy had to stay away a little longer. I expect I'll have to tell her tonight that Cindy isn't coming back, and maybe get the Jarvi girl in to look after her. She baby-sat before I...hired Cindy, but of course she didn't stay evenings, and I do need to work evenings quite often. I have an office at home, but you still can't expect a five-year-old to fend for herself every night while Dad's upstairs writing briefs, now can you?"

"No, you sure can't," Koski agreed hastily. "Now, if you would just answer a few more quick questions we'll be on our way. Has Cindy seen or communicated with David Slocum that you know of?"

"David?...oh, you mean the young man that Earl was so...no, unless he gave an alias, he never came to the house. Of course he could have telephoned when I wasn't home."

"Couldn't he have *visited* when you weren't home?" McIntire asked.

"Not without my hearing about it later. Annie's not one for keeping secrets."

"So," Koski observed, "she could probably tell us the names of some of Cindy's other friends, who she ran around with, where she went, things like that?"

A flush crept up Godwin's chipmunk cheeks. "I hope you won't be wanting to question my daughter, Pete. She's just a child, and she's had more than her share of tragedy. No. No, I'm afraid I can't allow that. If you—"

"We'll try not to upset her, but a girl is missing and we have to get all the information that we can. Now I wanted to ask a few questions about Nels Bertelsen's estate and then we'll be off. You were his attorney, weren't you?"

Godwin displayed no curiosity about the implied connection between Cindy Culver and Nels Bertelsen. "Odd that you should mention Nels. As you see, I was just looking at some of his records. Mr. Petworth sent them over, but I'm afraid I'm going to need some help." The ledgers that McIntire had seen in Wylie's kitchen were stacked on one side of the desk. Godwin drew the top one off, opened it, and pointed to the lines on the yellowed page, still as sharp and legible as the day they were written—in Norwegian. He chuckled and pushed a button to summon his gray-haired "girl," who promptly responded with the Nels Bertelsen file. McIntire idly picked up the ledger. Its brittle pages exuded a scent of mold and India ink.

Godwin patted the folder in front of him, Nels Bertelsen's life reduced to a two-inch pile of papers. "What would you like to know? I'll tell you what I can, but of course you realize that some information is confidential."

"Did Bertelsen leave a will?" the sheriff asked.

"Yes," was the attorney's uncharacteristically terse reply.

"And what were the terms of that will?"

Godwin didn't hesitate. "He left everything to Lucille Delaney."

McIntire smiled. "That will be a relief to her. She's been fretting about being thrown out into the street since the minute she heard he was dead."

The startled look on Godwin's dumpling face was impossible to miss.

Koski leaned forward. "Do you think," he asked, "that Lucy knew she would inherit?"

Godwin seemed about to deny any such opinion, but then made a subtle adjustment to a gold cufflink and admitted, "She was with Nels when he signed the will, right here in this office."

"Just how much is 'everything'?" the sheriff asked.

"Approximately less than nothing. Nels borrowed money against the home and orchards to have that boat built and set up his fishing business. Fishing hasn't been too great the last couple years. He was just breaking even, managing to keep up payments, but lately it's the income from the orchards that's been keeping the fishing business afloat—in a manner of speaking—and that can't last much longer. Competition from the western states is just too great. If it was anybody but Wylie Petworth handling the fruit business it would have gone to pot right after the war. He was more or less doing it as a favor to Nels. There's no guarantee he'll want to keep it up with Nels gone.

"Lucy might be able to sell the boat and nets, but the way things are she isn't likely to get anywhere near what Nels paid for them. So unless she's got another sugar daddy waiting in the wings, she could very well end up out in the cold anyway. Somehow I can't picture her netting herring. And of course the will has to go through probate before Lucy will be awarded anything. There could be other claims against the estate."

McIntire looked at the opening page of the ledger and read the inscription that began the family saga that had reached its finale with Nels Bertelsen's death. The venture into the apple business had apparently been financed by a bequest to Christina Bertelsen from her mother. When Sigrid passed away in that little village on the Norwegian Sea, she had given her daughter the means to begin a new life. She had also set in motion the chain of events that had eventually led to the extinction of the entire family—at least in the United States.

"So," Koski was saying, "we're going to need to have a look at Miss Culver's room."

"The door's open. Annie's still at the Butlers', so just go in." Godwin stood up. "I hope you get your man soon. Although if it drags on long enough I might have the satisfaction of nailing the bastard myself. I've filed for county attorney, you know."

XVIII

Cindy's bedroom was one of four on the second floor. High-ceilinged and approximately half the size of a high school gym, it was furnished with heavy mahogany and strewn with the paraphernalia of budding womanhood. Koski strode to the tall windows and yanked open the curtains, but McIntire hesitated. He felt a tightness in his throat as he stood in the doorway, his gaze shifting from Clark Gable smiling intimately from his place on the yellow-sprigged wallpaper to the pink cotton pajamas that lay crumpled on the unmade bed.

The sheriff looked up from rummaging through the drawers of a mirrored dressing table. "Come on John, don't go squeamish on me now. We've got a big job to do here. God, have you ever seen so much junk?" He frowned at a half-full pack of Pall Malls secreted in the bottom of a box of stationery. "Is this what I have to look forward to with Marcie?" He shoved in the drawer and turned to removing a collection of snapshots that had been Scotch-taped to the mirror. "We can try to find out who these kids are. That's a start. Maybe there's a school yearbook around here."

McIntire began a systematic search of the closets and wardrobe. They were packed with clothing. Most were the suits and dresses of a more mature woman. No doubt the legacy from the ill-fated Nina Godwin.

"Leonie would kill for clothes like these," he observed.

"Well, that's a thought. Cindy done in for her second-hand wardrobe." Koski lifted up the mattress with a grunt. "Blackmailed by My Lover's Son!" and "My Minister's Wife Stole My Husband!" screamed up at him from the cover of a well-thumbed copy of *True Story*. He lifted the magazine gingerly by its corner, examined closely the prime example of voluptuous femininity that graced its cover, and flipped through its pages. "That does it. I'm locking Marcie up 'til she's twenty-one."

McIntire's musings that having Sheriff Koski for a father would do more than any locked door to keep a girl and her would-be suitors treading a straight and narrow path were terminated by the discovery of a miniature chest tucked under folded blankets in the bottom to the wardrobe. He removed it and swept aside assorted pots and jars to place it on the dressing table. It was made of polished walnut with a stylized design of three-lobed leaves and vines carved around the edge of its lid. A small heart-shaped padlock was attached to its clasp, a lock that was no match for Pete Koski and a manicure kit. The box was lined in cedar, and contained three lace handkerchiefs, a string of what looked to be genuine pearls, and four leather-bound diaries. They were also locked but took even less time to open than the chest.

The frontispiece of each read *Nina Everett Godwin*. Entries began the week of Nina's marriage to Warner and ended December thirty-first, 1948.

"When did Nina Godwin die?" McIntire asked.

"A little over a year ago—middle of May."

"So unless she quit writing, we're missing the first five months of 1949." McIntire thought for a minute. "Didn't Mia mention a book with Cindy's stuff?"

The springs of the bed issued a protesting shriek as Koski sat down. "Now what," he wondered, "could have been in Nina Godwin's diary to send Cindy charging off to St. Adele with it? And," he added, "get her killed in the process?"

The search was hastily completed, and the door to Cindy's chamber taped shut. The two men left, driving from the heights of the bluff down into the town and uphill once again to the sheriff's office, where they were greeted by a flustered Deputy Newman and two impatient state investigators. The detectives were uncannily alike in appearance, both small men with thin, humorless faces, oozing confidence from every pore.

They listened without comment while Koski imparted what paltry information he possessed concerning the death. They asked no questions. The one on the left jangled his car keys. "If you could just lead us to the scene."

With a glance at their perfectly creased trousers and spit-shined oxfords, the sheriff nodded.

Once outdoors, they were joined by what appeared to be the shriveled husk of a human being, a bent and wizened man whose face, under his railroader's cap, had the topography of a raisin and whose slightest movement unleashed a curious effluvium of unwashed flesh and licorice. Florida Mowsers. He held the tethers of a pair of bloodhounds, each having a similarly corrugated visage and a lugubrious aspect suggestive of having seen much of life.

After brief introductions, the entire troop set out.

When dropping McIntire at his home, Koski handed him two of the diaries. "We might as well read these before we mention them to the state boys. They're not likely to get much out of them, not being local people. If they don't say anything important we can just slip them back to Warner."

The house was quiet. McIntire found a note from Leonie informing him that she had gone to the Culvers' to help with the children. He settled in to read the innermost thoughts of Nina Godwin.

The entries were short, and McIntire completed the reading of the first volume while eating a lunch of sandwiches left from the previous day's impromptu gathering. The journal contained nothing of obvious significance, mainly tales of home decorating and morning sickness. The second covered the year 1948, and was the most recent save the one that Cindy likely had in her possession when she died. McIntire rapidly scanned the first few pages, then began to read with more attention. After a short time, he closed the book and sat methodically tapping its leather binding. Finally, with a sigh, he pushed his chair back from the table and stuffed the diary into his pants pocket. He donned a pair of rubber overshoes, stepped out the kitchen door, crossed the wet grass, and walked briskly toward the Thorsens' house, taking the reverse of the route that Mia had used the previous morning.

XIX

Mia was just leaving the workshop when he arrived. Purple half-moons showed under her eyes, eyes that were encircled by the red tracks of the safety goggles now pushed up onto her forehead. She did not look entirely pleased to see him. "Just have a seat for a minute while I wash up, and I'll make some coffee." She wrenched off the goggles and attempted to smooth her hair behind her ears. "On second thought," she decided, "you can make yourself useful by getting me some fresh water." She disappeared into the house and emerged a moment later to thrust a galvanized pail into his hand. "You know where it is."

The pumphouse was as cellar-like and clammy as McIntire remembered, but he was relieved to find that the old hand pump had been replaced with an electric powered model. The Thorsens were slowly but surely creeping into the twentieth century.

When he got back to the house she was already measuring coffee into the pot. He surveyed the room where he had spent a major part of his waking hours during his first six years of life. It was, like all such things are likely to be, much smaller than he remembered. It was hard to imagine that this kitchen was once the center of life for ten adults and their various progeny. The long table where the group had gathered three times a day was gone. The space it had required was now occupied by one less than half its size. That left room for a massive cupboard crowded with all manner of kitchen gadgets the purposes of which McIntire could not begin to guess. A modern gas range had usurped the position of the yellow enameled wood cookstove, but a small pot-bellied coal heater stood beside it. Missing, too, was the distinctive odor, a montage of new wood, varnishes, paint thinners, and mysterious glues, that had permeated every room in the house when Eban Vogel had done his work in the side room.

McIntire set the bucket down with a thump and a splash. "You should have married me, Mia," he ventured. "I'd have given you indoor plumbing."

"If I wanted indoor plumbing I'd get it myself." Her hand shook slightly as she dipped water into the pot, and a small puddle formed on the counter. "Of course I never *carry* the water myself if I can possibly talk somebody else into doing it." She held a match to the gas burner until it ignited with a poof, then busied herself with cups.

McIntire took a deep breath and looked intently at his hands. "Well, why didn't you?" he asked.

She kept her back turned to him as she replied airily. "Oh, you know how it is. We talk about it from to time, but we never seem to get around to actually doing it. It's only been a few years since we got electricity in this neck of the woods, you know."

"You know what I'm talking about."

She pulled out a chair and sat down without looking at him. "I don't remember that you ever asked me to marry you."

McIntire smiled. "Well, I guess you've got me there. It's true, I didn't. You asked me, though. Twice as I recall. You asked me when we were six and again when we were fourteen, and I said yes both times, so you can't get out of it that easy."

Mia leapt up to turn down the flame under the sputtering coffee pot. When she turned around she faced him squarely. "And were you expecting me to wait thirty years?"

"I don't think a few months would have been too much to ask. I had hardly gotten off that boat in Liverpool before Ma wrote that you were engaged to the mailman." It amazed him that the bitterness was still there, and that it showed so plainly in his voice.

He waited while she spent an inordinate length of time transferring the cups from the counter to the table and once again sat down. "It wasn't that soon, and you know it," she finally said. "But from the day you left, I knew I'd never see you again. I thought it would be because you were killed, but I knew you wouldn't come home…and I was right. God, you never even *wrote*."

"I'd have come back if I'd had anything to come home to."

"Oh, no! It wasn't my fault you stayed away, and don't you dare try to pin it on me. Your mother would never forgive me!"

"We were babies together and we grew up together. We were meant to always be together." Even to himself, McIntire sounded like a mulish child.

Her response was slow in coming, and was in the manner of a tolerant adult to a obstreperous child. "John," she said. "We didn't grow up together. We were *growing* up, and then the war came, and all of a sudden you were a man. I was still a kid, but you were a soldier on your way clear across the world to kill people."

McIntire sputtered, but she ignored him and went on. "In those days before you left, you were a different person, cold and tough…and frightening."

"I was a terrified seventeen-year-old boy!" McIntire exploded. "I wasn't tough, I was scared out of my wits. I don't know what I dreaded more, facing the Germans or facing my father when he found out I'd enlisted."

"I understand that now, but back then I didn't, and that's exactly what I mean. I was just a dumb kid." She stood up and poured the coffee. "I was scared, too, you know, and not very brave. You can't have forgotten how I depended on you for everything. Good grief, I could hardly make a move without you to give me a shove. After you left things were unbearable. It was like losing half of myself. I—"

Her tone had grown intense, pleading, almost, and she halted suddenly, looking away. When she began to speak again, it was once more as the patient lecturer.

"Going back to school that fall was a nightmare. I didn't have a single friend there. Even Wylie was gone away to that farm school or whatever it was. People acted like Papa was the Kaiser's right hand man. *Papa*, who worshiped the U.S. flag. Don't you remember how he raised hell with people who wouldn't speak 'American'?"

McIntire remembered it well, remembered that he himself, even at age four, knew that one stuck to English when Papa Vogel was within earshot.

"And then they started remembering that Mama was nothing but a dirty Indian. Say what you will about your father, but he was the only person in this town who would even say hello if he met us on the street. You can't imagine how lonely it was. When Sandy Karvonen was killed, and then that kid from Chandler died in the training camp, the whole community came together—the whole country really— but we were shut out. And I knew I'd never see you again. I *knew* it. I didn't have the courage to admit that you wouldn't come back to me, so I pretended that you were dead too."

She was silent again for a time, then shook her head in wonder. "You know, after a while, I think I really believed it. I even found a white rock and put it back under the trees in the cemetery for your headstone. Sometimes I would come and put flowers on it…but then somebody found it and threw it away." A bleak smile played across her face. "They probably thought some kid was besmirching the sanctity of the cemetery by burying a dead bird."

"Mia…" She gestured him to be silent.

"Then Nick came along, delivering the mail on a *motor-cycle*, of all things. None of us had ever even seen one before. He was handsome, and exciting, and fun. He showed absolutely no sign of ever growing up. And furthermore, he wasn't going to end up drafted and buried somewhere in France. Carrying mail was too important.

"It all happened so fast. Every girl around was after him. Of course he didn't have a whole bunch of competition left. But he liked me best, and he made me laugh, and you never wrote.

"After Mama caught flu and died, Papa was so angry. He wouldn't have a funeral. He said it would only give people a chance to turn up their noses at her one last time. So it was just him and me and Reverend Jordan at the graveyard. Once Mama was gone he hardly ever stuck his head out of his shop. It got too sad being alone…so I married Nick."

McIntire went back to studying his hands. "What did he say when he found out you weren't a virgin?"

Mia looked up in amazement, and then burst into laughter. "I see you haven't turned into the *complete* British gentleman after all!" She appeared to give the question serious consideration.

"To tell the truth, it never entered my mind to think about it. Of course I didn't know what a virgin was until long after I wasn't one. You mean he could tell?" She laughed again. "I guess he must have been too drunk to notice."

"You mean even then—?"

"What? Oh, no, he wasn't always a drinker. It was only after we lost the babies that he really started."

"Ma told me you had a miscarriage. I'm sorry."

"Sophie *would* say that."

"You mean it wasn't true?"

"I didn't have any miscarriages," she said. "I bore three live children, two boys and a girl. The first two never really breathed. The third lived for almost four days."

"Oh, God, Mia, I'm sorry. I didn't know. How awful for you."

"After she was born I was really sick. Childbed fever, they called it. By the time I got better she'd already been baptized—Nicole Ramona—and buried. They told me she looked like Mama, but I don't know. I held her and I nursed her and dressed her, but I don't know a thing about her. The fever took my memory away." She gripped her cup with both hands and stared into it. "It's the not remembering that's the hardest part. It's like she never really *was*, never really existed. Nick and Papa, and even the doctor and the priest—they all had her for a little while, but I, *me*, the one who gave her what life she had, might as well never have had her at all." The cup clinked sharply against the saucer as she set it down on the table. "Forgetting was a blessing, they tell me."

McIntire searched for words, but nothing came, and Mia continued.

"After that I couldn't try again. Maybe I should have. I was my mother's fourth child, and the only one to live. But I didn't have any Indian granny to run away to." At the strident honking of the geese, Mia leaned across the table to look out the window, then sat back with a shrug. "Well, anyway, Mama always told me that I had gotten my life from her grand-mother, and maybe she had something there. She lost two more after I was born, you know."

McIntire's mind was invaded by a rush of buried memories: whispering, shushings, Mama Vogel absent from the kitchen, and Mia's father, seen through the foggy upstairs window, his long beard sparkling with frost, digging in a circle of lantern light. He looked out the window toward the lightning-scarred pine at the edge of the yard.

Mia followed his gaze. "There are five little bodies under that tree," she told him. "My parents lived in Chicago when they lost the two who would have been my older brothers. My Nicole was the only one to hang on long enough to make it to the cemetery. We might have been a large family. Think how different things would have been if even some of them had lived." A hint of moisture glistened on her colorless eyelashes. "I'm grateful for one thing. At least Mama wasn't here to see her grandchildren die, too."

McIntire reached toward her, but a stiffening of her shoulders warned him away.

"How ever did you bear it, Mia? How can you bear it even now?"

Mia twisted her long braid around her fingers. "When my little girl died and I was so sick, and delirious, I suppose, from the fever, I dreamed that I would climb to the top of the ski jump and fly off. As soon as I could stand up, I dragged myself out of bed and headed for that jump. I could barely walk, let alone climb, but I got myself to the top, dead set on flying off into eternity. I don't know where I even found the courage to climb up. The jump was new then so it was in a lot better shape, but you know how I've always been about heights. Anyway, I sure didn't have the guts to jump off.

"I went every morning for almost a month, every day thinking that this would be the day. Then Nick got sick and I needed to take care of him round the clock. After that I gave it up. I figured the jump would always be there. I still go up every now and then, just to reassure myself."

"Mia—"

"Sorry, I don't mean to be morbid. It's comforting…and a great view…or it was until yesterday."

She suddenly sat back in her chair, ceased tugging on the braid and flipped it over her shoulder. "So things turned out for the best after all, as far as you're concerned. If I wasn't such a coward, I might not have married the first man that came along. I might have waited for you—and you *might* have come back. But then if I wasn't a coward, I also would have taken that leap. Those could be your babies under that tree, and you'd have a wife alongside them."

McIntire opened his mouth to protest, but she put out her hand and touched his cheek. "It's been lonely without you, John. I'm glad you're back."

Before he could respond, she said, "She came this morning—Sandra. I know I should have talked to her yesterday, but I just couldn't. I probably wouldn't have opened the door today but she caught me in the studio. I told her Cindy looked like she was asleep. She told me I was a liar." She wrapped her sweater over her chest and held it. "I never felt such hate. It's like she thinks if I hadn't been there to see it, it wouldn't have happened."

"She has to hate somebody. Right now you're the one that's handy."

"I guess so," Mia responded with a sigh. She stood up to refill the coffee cups. "Pete Koski was here last night."

McIntire was surprised that the sheriff hadn't mentioned it that morning. "I suppose he thought you might remember something more. Were you able to tell him anything new?"

"He didn't come to see me," Mia answered. "He was talking to Nick. He asked him a lot of questions about yesterday morning, made him go through every move he'd made and what he'd seen. He asked about his feud with Nels, too."

"Feud?"

"Well, maybe feud is too strong a word. Mutual antagonism, then."

"I thought that situation existed between Nick and a good share of his clientele—and between Nels and everybody in town for that matter," McIntire said. "Was this particular dispute something out of the ordinary?"

"Not really, and it was quite awhile ago. Nels had a big mongrel dog that felt the same way about Nick that most dogs do. Talk about mutual antagonism! I don't know why Nick has such a thing about dogs. It's not like he has to get out of his car on his route. Maybe it's a holdover from his motorcycle days. Anyway, Nels' Truman would lie in wait for Nick every morning and chase his car a half-mile down the road. Well, one day Nels found the dog dead in the ditch, and he figured Nick had hit it—on purpose—which he might have. At least he probably didn't try very hard to avoid it. Nels called old Walleye, but he said that if the dog was chasing cars there wasn't anything he could do about it. Then Nels threatened to get Nick fired for drinking on the job. He actually tried to get the neighbors to sign a complaint, but he didn't have many takers."

"How *does* your husband manage to keep his job?" McIntire asked. "I mean, you have to admit, Mia, he can be a little… difficult, and, even if you can overlook that, he isn't overly conscientious about putting the mail in the right box. We got two postcards from the Ringdahls' daughter in Denver last week."

"Mary Ellen? How's she doing?"

"Just dandy. She climbed Pike's Peak, and she got her hair cut. Tell her mother if you see her."

Mia's quick burst of laughter sounded reassuringly ordinary. "Nick's been carrying the mail for longer than most people can remember. He was only sixteen when he started. In those days it was no easy job. He had that motorcycle in the summertime, but once the snow fell he had to slog through the drifts with a horse and sled like everybody else, and he couldn't wait around for the plow. He brought the mail out from Chandler then, and it sometimes took two days to make the trip. He might be kind of eccentric but he gives people something to talk about. No two ways about it, my husband is something of a legend in his own time."

"He is a topic of conversation now and then, I'll give you that."

"Even through the Thirties Nick was just about the only link some people had with the outside world. He was always willing to bring out little necessities for anybody that couldn't make it into town. So they're willing to overlook some inconvenience in the U.S. mail. And then, too," she smiled, "Nick has always been quite a favorite with the ladies."

"Still, isn't he just a little afraid of losing his job? There is a limit to what people will put up with, especially the ones who've moved here recently and care more about getting their mail on time than they do about the local legends."

"You're the only one who's moved here in the last fifteen years," Mia laughed, "and now you're starting to sound like Sheriff Koski."

"Ah, that reminds me." McIntire produced Nina Godwin's diary from his pocket.

"That's it! That's the book! Where did you find it?"

McIntire related the story of the search of Cindy's room. "But they aren't Cindy's diaries," he informed her. "They're Nina Godwin's. They must have been in with some stuff that Warner gave to Cindy last winter. How well did you know Nina? Weren't you sort of related to her?"

"'Sort of' is about it. We're second cousins, or first cousins once removed, something like that, on Papa's side. Since Papa's family drummed him out of the clan when he married Mama, I hardly knew her, and I only have a nodding acquaintance with Warner. I wasn't invited to the wedding…I went to her funeral though. You don't need an invitation for that."

"What exactly happened to Nina Godwin?" McIntire asked. "It must have been shortly before we came here."

"Well, there's no mystery there," Mia responded. "She hit a deer and ran her car off the cliff along the shore just north of Chandler…deer, bees, Walleye and that pig…what do you suppose we've done to bring the wrath of Mother Nature down upon us?"

"Any number of things, I don't doubt," McIntire replied. "I was hoping you knew Mrs. Godwin well enough to give me some insight. Her writing is a bit cryptic. Could you look at it anyway? Maybe it will help to see it from a woman's point of view."

Mia smiled sweetly. "Well of course, I was issued the universal standard female brain at birth, so I'm sure I can enlighten you." She reached eagerly for the book. "Besides, wild horses couldn't keep me from reading this. Does Warner know you have it? Never mind, of course he doesn't…which would make it awkward to ask someone who really *did* know the Godwins to read it."

They sat in silence while Mia slowly turned the pages.

"I see what you mean by cryptic," she finally said. "Who is this Nordic god she keeps mentioning? Somehow I can't picture Warner in that role."

"No, it becomes pretty clear when you read on that it's definitely not Warner, but who? There's not a clue. It could be almost anybody."

Mia looked up from her reading and gave an unladylike snort. "Next time you take a walk around Chandler clean your glasses. It could be *nobody*. Nordic god! Nina must have had some imagination. Maybe she got a double dose of the 'female point of view,' or maybe she should have gotten away from those books and out into the real world more."

"Books?"

"She ran the Chandler library. Didn't you know?"

"No, I didn't," McIntire admitted. "But from the activities she hints at in her journals, I don't get the idea that she was any stranger to the realities of life."

"Oh yeah?" Mia turned a few more pages, then looked up sharply. "Do you actually think that something Nina wrote in her diary could be connected to Cindy's death?"

"It must have at least had something to do with the reason she came to St. Adele Monday morning. I can't believe she brought the diary with her just to have some reading material to pass the time on the train. Cindy was ambitious, not to say greedy. And," he suddenly remembered, "she had a story dealing with blackmail hidden under her mattress."

"So you figure," Mia's voice dripped with disbelief, "that this guy of Nina's was somebody from St. Adele, and Cindy was trying to blackmail him, and got killed for it? Pardon me, but have you dusted your brain lately? The idea of Nina Godwin having a fling with one of our local yokels is ludicrous. And blackmail isn't an emergency situation. Cindy could have waited for her regular day off. What's more, the blackmailee could have just taken the book from her...well, unless he knew there were more diaries. Even if he did, he'd have no need to kill Cindy because of his affair with somebody who's been dead more than a year, and didn't name names anyway." She flipped through the pages. "Was Cindy Culver smart enough to figure out who this guy is?"

"When we can't, I suppose you mean? We don't know what was in the fifth journal, or in the two that Pete has," McIntire insisted.

"But you're guessing that Cindy had the diaries for quite a long time. What could have happened in the past few days to send her scurrying back here?"

"That's a good question. She must have decided to take the trip shortly before she left, but it couldn't have been a spur of the moment thing, exactly. The killer had to have known she was coming. She must have arranged to meet him in advance."

"Not by phone," Mia stated.

"Not likely," McIntire agreed.

"I guess that leaves the mail." Mia spoke hesitantly.

"Not necessarily. She could have contacted him in person. Maybe she saw him somewhere in Chandler, or maybe there was a third party involved."

"Pete Koski asked if Nick had noticed any mail on his route that might have been from Cindy in the few days before she died," Mia said. "Nick said he hadn't. Well," she elaborated, "he said he didn't have time to spend playing any damn guessing games with people's mail. Which is not strictly true, there's nothing he likes better."

McIntire studied the sludge in the bottom of his cup. "However she arranged it, you're right, there had to have been something that happened recently to cause her to act on information she'd had for a long time."

"Like David taking off?"

"Maybe, but what could David's disappearing act possibly have to do with Nina Godwin's exploits?"

"Maybe Cindy was trying to talk David into going into cahoots with her on the blackmail scheme. Or just possibly," Mia continued innocently, "the catalyst was a visit from the aristocratic John McIntire. She *was* headed straight for your house, you know. Maybe Nina's library was a front for smuggling toilet paper out of Canada, and Cindy was coming to give you the dirt—so to speak."

"You don't suppose she *was* coming to see..." McIntire shoved his glasses back on his forehead. "No." He spoke decisively. "If Cindy discovered that somebody had committed a crime, she could have gone to the sheriff. She wouldn't have had to go to the trouble to get on the train at the crack of dawn."

"John!" Mia's laughter lit up her face for just a moment before, as usual, being choked off like a tap. "But you're right about one thing. This is the sheriff's business. Maybe you should just leave it to him."

"What?"

"You've always been the...curious sort," Mia answered, "but maybe this is something that should be handled by the professionals."

"Curious am I? Well if that's the way you feel, I expect I'll just have to take that diary and go."

Mia clutched the small volume to her chest.

"I thought so. Well, you can do your civic duty by reading the *Memoirs of a Deceitful Wife*, and I'll exercise my curiosity and my legs by walking around the roads one more time." He rose from his chair. "Let me know if you come up with anything. Or notice any Greek gods skulking about in the bushes."

"Nordic," Mia corrected.

XX

McIntire enjoyed walking, a pastime that was raised to an art form in Britain but viewed with extreme suspicion here in his native environs. He strode out of Mia's driveway and steeled himself to the knowledge that any passing motorist would be insistent on stuffing him into the car and hauling him somewhere. Anywhere. Oh for autumn, when he could stick a shotgun under his arm and walk in peace. "Odd," he had told Leonie, "how if you're on foot and not out to kill something, you're looked upon as some kind of psycho." McIntire felt some measure of camaraderie with Lucy and the comment her habitual morning treks provoked.

Leonie herself was not particularly sympathetic. As a woman well into middle age whose favored form of transportation was a sleek black bicycle, she had endured her own share of ridicule.

He tramped methodically along the side of the road. The sun was only now beginning to break through after the two nights of rain. Puddles steamed gently and beads of water glistened on the ferns that choked the shallow ditches.

He felt little hope of finding anything helpful. The tracks of any vehicle left on the side of the road or pulled off into the woods would probably have been obliterated by the downpour. Any traces of such activities that did remain could easily have been left by yesterday's searchers. Still, he advanced slowly and peered intently into the roadside bushes. Looking for what? he asked himself, a fragment of turquoise silk? A muddy tennis shoe? Long blond hairs caught on a wild rose bush? Maybe a neon sign reading *This Way to the Killer*?

He sighed and stepped up his pace a bit as he approached the county gravel pit, then stopped in mid-stride when he caught a movement behind the brush that screened its entrance. As he furiously weighed the benefits of concealing himself in the bushes at the side of the road against the potential discomfort of entering the ten inches of water in which they stood, a doe stepped daintily out into the open. She noticed the foreign presence at once and kept her eyes fixed on him as she walked with measured and deliberate steps across the road. When she reached the opposite side, she stopped and waited, as motionless as McIntire himself, while two tiny spotted fawns, all ears and legs, imitated her jerky promenade across the wet gravel. When the entire family was united, the watchful mother gave a snort and stamped her foot, and they disappeared into the woods with a flash of white.

McIntire went into the gravel pit. It was a large area, hidden from the road by a heavy growth of alder and choke-cherry. You could park a freight train in here, he thought, and no one would be the wiser. If the killer had concealed a vehicle when he went to meet Cindy, this was the likely place. It gave privacy and easy access to the quickest route to the ski jump area. That easy access had led Guibard and several of the searchers to park here, so even yesterday morning there hadn't been much chance of identifying tracks left by any one individual. The pit had been thoroughly searched the day before, and most likely had already received the attention of Mowser's sad-eyed bloodhounds. Nonetheless, McIntire made a slow circuit of the area. Gravel had not actually been excavated from the spot for several years, but the poor soil held plant growth back to a few anemic-looking grasses. The resulting open space, shielded as it was from prying eyes, afforded a perfect spot for adolescent boys to sit huddled around a fire, valiantly ignoring the smoke in their faces while they drank warm beer and practiced the lies that would serve them so well in their adult social interactions, or for pubescent couples who were too unimaginative to seek out the more picturesque spots overlooking the lake. Well, as far as romantic locales went you could hardly beat the actual lakeshore itself, with its pale sand beaches. *There is a rapture on the lonely shore.* True enough, McIntire recalled.

He hadn't responded to Mia's repeated comments that she had received no letters from him after his departure. It was a long time ago, and he wasn't absolutely sure himself of his reasons for not writing. Maybe it was partly rooted in an unconscious desire to keep his old life completely separated from the new, to freeze it in time until he again found a use for it.

What he had said was true; he had been terrified of going overseas, although by the time he left he knew he would be unlikely to ever find himself involved in actual battle. It was something of a fluke that he had gone at all. He had only been a few days at the training camp in Battle Creek when those in charge discovered that his eyesight was such that he would have a tough time distinguishing a German soldier from a fence post without walking up and giving it a kick. He would have been summarily packed off for home if he hadn't made certain that they also learned that he could communicate fluently in Swedish, Norwegian, and Finnish, and passably in Italian and German. More importantly he could read and write those languages. When he shipped out he knew that he would spend the war translating doughboy mail for army censors.

Still, he was going to a war zone and he was scared, but outweighing the fear was the exhilarating sense of freedom he felt at escaping his father's constant bitter disappointment and, to be honest, Mia's smothering dependency. That wasn't quite fair, he knew. He had been every bit as reliant on her. They had taken care of each other.

Ironically, it was that very intimacy that contributed to his distancing himself from her. It was with profound shock that he had learned, shortly after his arrival at Camp Custer, that the novel and oddly comforting games that he and Mia had devised together were not unique; that a young woman who indulged in those activities was not highly thought of; and moreover, according to the pamphlets and posters on the barracks wall, such pursuits could drive you insane and even kill you. He could smile about it now, but at the time his newly acquired knowledge had given him more than one sleepless night.

None of this, he knew, was any more than another way of saying that he had been a selfish child who left his dearest friend stranded in a lonely and hostile wilderness. He had no right to gripe if she had managed to find her own way out. He was forced to admit that his thoughts of Mia had been infrequent until Sophie's letter had arrived informing him of her impending marriage. The pain he felt at that announcement had been filed away along with the rest of his early life and had intruded little on the ensuing decades. Mia said that she had felt lost when he left, that half of herself had gone. Strangely, during those years, when times were darkest, deep within his being he'd found solace in the knowledge that half his own self still remained at home.

As McIntire left the gravel pit and continued his peregrinations, he pondered Mia's inference that his own visit to Cindy might have led to her sudden trip to St. Adele. Of course Mia was only joking when she said that Cindy might have been coming to give him information. Although why would that be so strange? After all, Pete Koski and his crew could be pretty intimidating to a young girl. McIntire tried, and failed, to picture an intimidated Cindy Culver.

Could it have been something he said that brought her to St. Adele and her death? They had talked about David. If she had really known nothing of David's disappearance, maybe hearing that he was missing could have been the catalyst, as Mia had put it, but why, he couldn't imagine.

They had also discussed David's confrontation with Nels Bertelsen and Nels' death. McIntire had supposed that Cindy knew Nels had died, but he now realized that he had no real reason to think so. Cindy hadn't been home. She probably didn't read the papers, and, unless her employer had mentioned it to her, she easily might not have known about it. She had seemed genuinely unaware both that Nels was dead and that David worked in his orchards. But how could those two facts possibly be connected to Nina Godwin?

You couldn't get much more "Nordic" than Nels Bertelsen. No, that was absurd in the extreme—Lucy *and* Nina Godwin?

Maybe Cindy had discovered something that had nothing to do with Nina's indiscretions. Warner Godwin had handled Nels' legal affairs. He had mentioned working in an office in his home. Cindy probably wasn't above doing a bit of exploring. Maybe she found out about some legal or financial dealings. Maybe the diary *was* just for reading material on the train. None of that made sense. There wasn't apt to be anything in Nels' attorney's file that would be understood by a young girl, let alone interest her. If it contained something that implicated a killer—something so blatant that even Cindy could recognize it—why hadn't Godwin himself come forward?

So Cindy could have been coming to St. Adele with what she felt was a juicy bit of information for someone. But who? Who would she expect to be interested in Nina Godwin's affairs, or Nels Bertelsen's?

McIntire resolutely turned onto the road that led to the late fisherman's home.

His knock at the door went unanswered, but the sound of running water brought him around the side of the greenhouse. Here he discovered Wylie Petworth turning a garden hose on a dozen or so young trees that occupied the bed of a pickup truck.

"Didn't those things get enough to drink last night?"

Wylie smiled broadly and dropped the hose at his feet. "Well, no, they didn't," he said, "but they've just about had their fill now." He went to the side of the building and turned off the tap. "They need a good soaking before they go in the ground. Look at these babies. Cortlands. Good for eating, good for pies, and they'll keep all winter. Old Man Bertelsen never dreamed of anything like it."

McIntire considered the spindly twigs that emerged from the bulbous, burlap-encased roots. They looked like overgrown onions gone bad. "If you say so, Wylie. Anyway, I'm glad to see you're more your old self."

"Well, life goes on, as they say, and Nels lived a pretty long one compared to that poor child who died yesterday." From his demeanor, McIntire assumed that the impending exhumation of Nels Bertelsen's body had not yet become common knowledge. That situation wouldn't last long. Leonie's paper would be out the following afternoon and the *Chandler Monitor* the day after. They would take care of the few who already hadn't gotten the news by grapevine, party line, or Waterfront Tavern line.

McIntire averted his eyes as Wylie deftly rolled the hose into a spiral with his single hand and hung it on its bracket. "If she *is* dead," Wylie added. "Find any sign of her yet?"

"Not a thing," McIntire responded. "The tracker came this morning. He wants everybody else to stay out of the woods for now so his dogs don't get confused by all the scent, and so the scent of the girl or the killer doesn't get any more messed up, I guess."

"It's sort of late for that isn't it? The woods was crawling with people yesterday, and wouldn't the rain have washed away the scent anyway?"

"According to Koski, rain helps if it's not too heavy, settles the scent down. He seems to think that the trees would have protected it from being completely washed away. I doubt that it matters much. It's my guess she was taken away in a car," McIntire said. "Otherwise she'd have been found yesterday. I imagine," he went on, "you were up and about early yesterday, since your hired hand has flown the coop. Did you notice anybody drive by?"

"I was not only up. I was out. I brought these trees over from my place about…" Wylie scratched the back of his head, pushing his cap down over his eyes. "Oh, I'd say seven or seven-thirty. Didn't see a soul, though, except the Lovely Lucy on her daily pilgrimage. I even offered her a ride into town, but she turned me down flat."

"Turned you down? That doesn't sound like Lucy. Did she say why?"

"No she didn't, maybe my Five Day Deodorant was expired, eh?" Wylie laughed. "She just said it was such a nice day that she'd as soon walk, and she didn't want to take me out of my way. I didn't argue with her. She seemed to be her usual jolly self, said there was a fresh pot of coffee on the stove, and I should help myself. Then she continued on her merry way." He sat down on the damp tailgate of the truck. "Odd though, I wasn't here more than five minutes or so when she came hot-footing it back."

"Maybe she forgot something. A letter to Cary Grant. Did she leave again?"

"I didn't notice. I was working in the greenhouse. Otto Wilke was coming to help me plant the trees. He got the call about the girl just as he was leaving home, so he picked me up and we took off."

McIntire looked toward the house. "I wonder where Lucy is now?"

"Well, Mac, I can help you there. An hour or so ago she came out the door dressed to a fare-thee-well and—believe it or not—took off in Nels' precious De Soto, headed for the Big Town."

"She drove?"

"Like a pro."

"I swear, that woman is just a bottomless fount of surprises."

"Well, could be that's what kept Nels interested. God knows there must have been something more than meets the eye. That is one homely woman!" Wylie observed.

"Maybe Nels wouldn't let her drive the car when he had anything to say about it."

Wylie rose from his seat. "Generosity never was one of Nels' faults. He was too tight to drive it himself except in the direst of emergencies. Not to mention that he was afraid of getting a spot or two of mud on it. I hope wherever he is now he couldn't see the way Lucy spun those tires." He closed the tailgate with a satisfying thunk. "You know, Mac," he went on, "I'm having a hard time seeing you as the Great Detective. I mean, I know that you worked in intelligence, and I guess you always were a little...I don't want to say nosy, but..."

"Curious," McIntire corrected. "Curious and downright enraged, and with plenty of time on my hands."

"Well, if you're looking for a way to keep yourself occupied," Wylie patted the nearest burlap wrapped root ball. "I am short a hired man, and these little beauties need to go into the ground. Handling a shovel isn't one of my talents."

McIntire halted in the middle of his understanding nod and laughed aloud. "You used to pull that one on me when we were fifteen years old and Miss Van Opelt wanted the snow shoveled off the path to the girl's outhouse. I fell for it every time, too, until I got to wondering how you always managed to come up with plenty of worms when you wanted to go fishing."

He left Wylie caressing his trees and executed a quick retreat across the yard. He slowed as he passed by the house. Boxlike and unadorned, it crouched stoically in the center of its open field, where once it had been shielded from the elements by a newly planted grove of evergreens. The structure itself had changed little since Ole Bertelsen built it. Its fake brick siding curled slightly at the edges, but the white painted window trim and green shingles looked as crisp as when the entire family of fiercely independent Bertelsens had lived there. Independent, that was, where the rest of the world was concerned. The four of them were as like to one another as the proverbial peas in a pod, with their corn-silk hair and cheeks with the blush of the fruit they cultivated. They were also as one in their single-minded dedication to the task they had set for themselves, a task they attacked with a vigor and tenacity at odds with their jocund appearances. They were gone now, every one of them, and the sadness of it struck McIntire for the first time. Gone, with no one to reap the benefits of the dream for which they had toiled so hard. No one except Lucille Delaney.

The grass in the barren yard had been recently trimmed, but a few dandelions that had dared to rear their heads had been allowed to grow.

McIntire reached his home only minutes ahead of Leonie, whose arrival was accompanied by the spattering of gravel and a flurry of Barred Rock hens stampeding for cover. The slam of the car door was followed by the announcement that David Slocum had been run to earth and was now being held in the Flambeau county jail.

"I've just come from the court house." Leonie smiled serenely. "For once we'll get the jump on the *Monitor*."

"So what's happened? Do they know where David was? Has he been charged?"

"Not yet," Leonie informed him. "The game warden found him in an abandoned camp back in the mountains. He was half starved and his car was a mile away, stuck in the mud and out of petrol. He wasn't there all the time he's been missing though. They checked the place last week. The warden only went back because he smelled smoke. David was trying to cook some kind of wild game. A marsh hare, the deputy called it."

Marsh hare? What the hell...? "Oh, for the love of Mike! That's a muskrat, Leonie, and muskrats and their like are not usually considered game animals, at least not around here. Gamey, very possibly, but not game." McIntire recalled Cindy Culver's reference to her family's occasional dinner fare, and hoped that he spoke the truth.

"So where was David the rest of the time? What did he give as his reason for leaving?"

Leonie looked him with wide eyes. "For heaven's sake, John, I didn't question him myself! I only know what I could squeeze out of that deputy. And now," she said decisively, "I've got to get back straight away and write this up so I can *roll those presses*." She was off again in a whirl of spinning tires and chicken feathers.

McIntire continued to sit morosely on the front steps while the shadows deepened and the trilling of spring peepers grew from the first tentative notes to a symphony. The chickens began to abandon their industrious scratching and, one by one, wandered in to roost. Kelpie roused herself from her spot on the porch and waddled to him, toenails clicking softly on the floorboards. She turned her rheumy eyes to his face expectantly. He picked up the arthritic animal and carried her down the steps to set her in the yard so that she might amble off to perform her nightly rounds.

"David," McIntire puzzled. It seemed so obvious, and yet somehow illogical. Yes, he had cause to be angry with Nels, but Nels wasn't killed in a fit of anger. Surely he was just an ornery old geezer to David, no different from a half-dozen others, probably. If David was the kind of kid given to plotting the deaths of those who gave him a hard time, Nels Bertelsen would hardly have been the first to go. Maybe the sheriff only suspected David of *Cindy's* murder, but why? That would rule out the theory that Cindy was killed to keep her from blabbing something she knew about Nels' death, and what other motive could David possibly have? And where could Nina's diary fit in?

Dusk had now settled heavily around the house and outbuildings. McIntire crossed the yard to latch the hen house door against plundering foxes and stood for a time looking out toward the overgrown pastures at the rear of the barn. There the sun still cast rusty slanting rays on the knee high grasses. Flocks of finches flew twittering from thistle to burdock. A jacksnipe executed its warbling dive, while farther away, near the river, the booming voice of a bittern announced the approach of night.

He turned back to the house, which was already cloaked in deep shadow. Maybe Leonie was right. Maybe a few of the trees should go.

XXI

The McIntires shared an early breakfast the following morning, a rare circumstance supposedly precipitated by Leonie's eagerness to see her paper in the hands of its readers with no undue delay. In contrast to her exuberance on the previous evening, however, Leonie appeared subdued and in no particular hurry to be off. She ate slowly and indifferently, totally lacking the zeal with which she ordinarily attacked even the most mundane of tasks. When she picked up knife and fork and began cutting her toast into minuscule triangles, McIntire put down his cup and demanded, "What *is* the matter? You're acting like you have a date with the dentist instead of your big chance to scoop the *Monitor*."

Leonie poked at the toast with the tip of her knife. "I'm starting to feel just a teensy bit ghoulish," she said. "I would hardly have believed it of myself. I'd just walked in the door when Dorothy Slocum called from the Lindstroms' to let you know what happened. The words were hardly out of her mouth when I was off that phone and in the car. I almost beat the sheriff back to town."

"That's what a good reporter does."

"Is it? Well, maybe it is, but a good neighbor might have had a few words of comfort for a mother whose son has been missing for over a week and finally turns up only to be hauled off to the lockup. My first thought was how fast I could get the details and spread the news."

McIntire patted her hand. "Don't feel bad. The news is going to spread regardless, embroidered with all sorts of details, no doubt. You might say you're doing the family a service by printing only established facts and," he emphasized, "reporting them in an *unbiased* manner."

Leonie looked up sharply. "You don't think he's guilty, do you?"

"Guilty of what?" McIntire asked. "Killing Cindy, or Nels, or both? I don't know, Leonie, both of these murders took a bunch of advanced planning. Someone had to have gotten to Nels' adrenaline and replaced it with the insecticide, someone who knew that bug spray would be lethal. He had to have planted bees in strategic places, who knows how many times before Nels eventually got stung? He had to lure Cindy onto that train and into the woods, and figure out how to spirit away her body without being seen. That doesn't sound like David Slocum to me."

"You've never met David," Leonie reminded him.

McIntire felt some surprise when he realized that this was true. "But think of everything we know about him," he argued. "He was a good worker, but only so long as Wylie told him exactly what to do. He allowed Cindy Culver to use him as a dupe to get her out of the family penal colony and into the lap of luxury. He ended up stranded out in the bush. Eating muskrat! Good Lord! He might have starved to death if he hadn't been pinched first. Little Davy just doesn't seem like someone given to a lot of thinking ahead." He appropriated Leonie's untouched bacon and went on. "He really didn't have any strong motive for killing Nels that we know of, and if he didn't kill Nels, why would he have killed Cindy? She was about the only friend he had…and I sure as hell can't believe David Slocum figures in Nina Godwin's diaries."

"Yes," Leonie agreed, "that does seem improbable."

"It was Nels' paranoia—his idea that somebody was out to get him—that caused him to get so belligerent toward David in the first place. Nels had no complaints about David until after the medication turned up missing, and he started finding evidence that someone was going into his house and outbuildings. I mean, this business started *before* Nels put David on his shit list, and that list was a pretty long one. Nels Bertelsen was never an easy-going sort of guy. He could have built up quite a stockpile of enemies over the years. But if he did, I wasn't around to hear about it, and when I try to get information out of anybody that *has* been here, I just get the old Nels-would-be-Nels song and dance. I don't believe that everyone was so tolerant of Nels' contrariness as they make out to be."

"Well, you promised to go visit his stepmother. Maybe she can help you out."

"Ah, my dear, how would I manage to keep track of my social obligations without you?"

Leonie put down her fork. "You know, John, if you'd put yourself out a bit to take care of those social obligations on your own, you might find the witnesses to be more candid."

"What's that supposed to mean?"

"May I speak frankly?"

"You generally do."

"Well, you can't just horn your way in and expect people to spill everything they know to a…to an interloper."

"Interloper? I was born here!"

"You're as much a newcomer in this community as I am. Matter of fact—pardon my bluntness—you're worse than a newcomer. You're a snooty outsider who puts yourself above them."

"Leonie, how can you say that? Snooty? Above them?" More like the prissy buffoon too far beneath them to take seriously.

"Are you denying that you feel superior? No, never mind. Whether it's true or not is irrelevant, but try to see yourself from the point of view of the people here. You left as soon as you could get out the door and didn't keep up any kind of contact. And now you come waltzing back, with a new car and plenty of money, which as far as they can see you do no work to earn. You take over your father's house, although when he was alive you wouldn't give him the time of day. And the first time you condescend to seek out any of your neighbors, it's to snoop."

"If they didn't want me to snoop they shouldn't have talked me into being constable." That Leonie, of all people, should turn on him like this...it was, as a *real* Yooper would say, "one hell of a note. And you know damn well that election was one big practical joke. If the joke backfired, well...." He gave up. It was something Leonie would never understand, and he wasn't sure he wanted her to.

"I'm sorry if I hurt your feelings. It's just...if you socialized a bit more...." She looked into his eyes. "I don't like seeing you so lonely."

Lonely? Was he lonely? McIntire didn't know. He'd never been the gregarious type. "I simply don't have much in common with most of the men here," he said. "I can't spit tobacco worth a damn."

Leonie laughed and popped one of the bits of toast into her mouth. "You could learn."

"*You* could, Leonie. I'm not so sure about me. But maybe I will go see Laurie Post. We can commiserate. She was an interloper for better than twenty years, and she always was good company." He swallowed the last of his orange juice. "Here's a real scoop for you, Lucy was seen yesterday morning, by a reliable witness, *driving* in the direction of Chandler."

Leonie stood up. "Well, goody for her. I guess if I'm going to be seen *pedaling* in the direction of St. Adele, I'd better get moving. I should be home shortly after noon, but there is a Ladies' Aid meeting later this morning to make the final arrangements for the Fourth of July, so who knows? Try to find something constructive to do whilst I'm gone, outside of badgering the neighbors. The grass could use some attention." She kissed him on his thinning hairline and left by the kitchen door.

Leonie obviously made a distinction between "socializing" and "badgering." But badgering the neighbors was exactly what McIntire had in mind, and, to that end, he drove off in the car, which Leonie had so generously left for him, and, with some strategic planning and lucky guessing, intercepted Lucy Delaney just at the point where she would have left the road and continued her hike home along the railroad tracks.

His offer of a ride was readily accepted despite the warmth of the sun and the short distance she had left to travel. Lucy must be partial to walking in cold, damp weather. Maybe Wylie's deodorant *was* failing him. It must be tricky to get in under his right arm. Lucy settled her broad bottom comfortably on the seat and smiled at McIntire as Rapunzel might have done at her liberator. Even driving at an undertaker's pace, McIntire barely had time to inquire after her health and receive a scrupulously detailed response before they reached the end of their journey. He accepted the offer of coffee nearly as eagerly as she had the one of transportation. Lucy heaved herself out of the car with a grunt and glanced toward the orchards. "Looks like the boy's back."

McIntire looked up the hillside and saw a lean figure silhouetted against the morning sun, not far from Wylie's pickup with its load of young trees. Lucy waved vigorously but got no response. She led McIntire to the house but, like Mia had done, stopped him at the door and requested that he earn his keep by fetching her a bucket of fresh water.

Lucy's coffee was strong and was accompanied by an impressive array of cookies, rolls, and cup cakes. McIntire chose a cinnamon roll and slathered it with butter. "Do you think David is behind these deaths?" he asked. There was no point in beating about the bush with Lucy.

"David's always been sweet as pie to me. He especially likes my peanut butter cookies," she said complacently. "But I reckon murderers can be nice as any other folks when they're not going about their business of killing people. If they weren't we wouldn't have no trouble catching them now, would we? If the sheriff thought David was a murderer, I don't suppose he would have let him go."

"How did you find out David had been arrested?"

"Well, I didn't hear it rubbernecking on the telephone like some!" Lucy's umbrella of hair bounced with indignation. "What good is the phone if a body can't have a private conversation, I ask you? No, I heard it from Sheriff Pete Koski himself. I went in to town to see Mr. Godwin about Nels' property, and I dropped in at the sheriff's office just to see if he had found anything out yet. He kept me there, pestering me with questions for forty-five minutes, the same questions he asked me on Monday: Did Nels have enemies? How did we get along? Do I know what happened to the medicine Nels lost last winter? Who took the trash to the dump before Nels' funeral? I don't know what all! My head was fairly spinning. Then, after all that, he said they'd made an arrest. I asked if it was David, and he didn't say no. So if he thinks David did it, why was he giving me the third degree? And now David's out already—and right here on Nels' own property!"

She sank back into her chair as if exhausted by her lengthy oration, and McIntire did the same, stretching his legs to their full length. "I hope Mr. Godwin was helpful about your situation and all," he said companionably.

"He said the will would be held up because Nels died under suspicious circumstances. That's why I went straight to the sheriff. Nels left everything to me, you know. Now the sheriff's acting like I'm another Mrs. Boston, *and* he says the state police will probably be talking to me, too."

"I can see it must be difficult, having the responsibility of keeping all this up," McIntire waved his hand in a circular motion, "without any income. Have you thought any about taking up fishing?" His attempt at levity was met with a steely glare that reminded him that "bad manners bring bad luck," and cut him off in mid-chuckle. He sat up straight. "I mean," he said, "you might consider hiring someone to run the operation."

Lucy lowered her hackles and once more became her confiding self. "Fact is, Nels wasn't doing so well this season anyway. He was thinking about letting Jonas go and trying to handle it all himself. Well, that was just plumb crazy! A boat that size should have a crew of four or five. But he was barely taking in enough to keep us alive and make the payments. Warner"—no more "Mr. Godwin," McIntire noted—"is being just as kind as he can be. He says I don't have to worry none about paying on the loan until the estate is settled. And he told me that Nels and him were working on some other financial plans, and that we can get together," she smiled meaningfully, "to talk about it when the rest of this mess is straightened out."

"Did he say what the plans were?"

"Oh, he's not at liberty to discuss things until I'm declared Nels' legal heir, and that could be months—years even, if anybody raises a fuss—as I'm sure many would like to do! I guess he'll get it through the courts as quick as he can. After all, I imagine he wants his money, too."

"No doubt, but the longer it drags on, the bigger his fee will be in the end."

"Oh, I didn't mean the attorney's fees. I was talking about the money Nels owed him. He loaned Nels the money for the fishing rig, you know."

McIntire hadn't known, and he would bet Pete Koski didn't know either. It might not be the world's best kept secret, but he was sure Godwin hadn't mentioned it that day in his office.

He had appeared confident in his statements that Lucy would not end up with much of anything when Nels' estate was settled. Was it because he was going to acquire the lion's share himself? It would be interesting to know about those other financial plans he was dangling before her. McIntire forced his attention back on Lucy's stream of conversation.

"...can stay in this house, and I have a little money put by, so I shouldn't have to go to the county. I'd sell myself on the streets of Hurley, Wisconsin before I'd go on relief."

Was this an allusion to a lurid past? She munched a cookie, her aspect less that of prostitute or poisoner than a placid Holstein.

"Wylie's offered to help out. I suppose he felt it was the least he could do, being Nels' partner. Of course I wouldn't accept it...he has been awfully attentive to me since Nels died, offering to drive me places, doing little chores around the place." She leaned toward him with her elbows on the table. "You don't suppose he's after this property himself, do you? That he might think he could get it *one way or another?*" she added with a definite smirk.

Wylie might as well join the club, McIntire thought. Warner and Wylie, a battle for Lucy's affections between Flambeau County's two most eligible bachelors. He could hardly wait.

McIntire allowed as how a single woman always had to be wary of being taken advantage of, and asked, "Miss Delaney, when the neighbors were here after Nels died, who *did* take your trash to the dump?"

Lucy threw up her hands. "Not you, too! I'll tell you the same thing I told Sheriff Koski—three times—I *don't know.* Almost everybody in the neighborhood came by for a least a short time that weekend to help out. Even our Mad Mailman stopped for a few minutes on Saturday."

"What about David? You mentioned that he was a big help the day before Nels was buried."

"David picked up the Paulsons at the train station in Chandler and brought them here. Then he stayed to help out, but to be honest he mostly just hung around listening to that old duffer tell war stories. After Wylie took the Paulsons back to his place—they spent the night there—I guess David left. Wylie must have driven over here in his pickup truck, and he would have taken his company home in the car, so David probably drove the pickup back, and he might have hauled the trash to the dump, but I don't know. I had other things to think about."

Before leaving, McIntire walked up the hill with the intention of introducing himself to the prime suspect. As he approached, David stabbed his spade into the earth and picked up one of the saplings to plop it into its permanent home. He was thin and muscular, a sullenly handsome youth. "Cute" didn't seem to be the most apt description, but then McIntire had not actually seen a bug's ear. A wave of dark hair fell across his forehead and concealed his eyes as he bent to his task, which he continued to do while McIntire valiantly attempted to engage him in conversation.

"It's a good day to be working outside."

David produced a pocket knife and reached into the hole to slash at the burlap that enveloped the tree roots. "I guess so," he said to the tree.

"I imagine Wylie works you pretty hard," was McIntire's next brilliant observation.

"I'm a good worker." He began scooping soil into the hole, using the point of the spade to pack each new addition carefully around the roots.

"I know, Wylie told me that."

The halting of a shovel full of earth poised over the hole indicated a glimmer of interest, and McIntire leapt on it. "He says you're a hard worker, the best he's ever had."

David flung the hair back from his face with a flip of his head and looked directly at his visitor. His eyes were a clear gray, and communicated an attitude of cool indifference. "He likes me," he said simply.

McIntire fought the urge to squirm under the youth's penetrating stare. "Cindy liked you too," he said. "You must feel terrible about what happened to her."

David turned back to his work, and once again the hair veiled his expression. "It's not my fault if they can't find her. I don't know where she is." He stomped heavily to pack the earth around the spindly trunk.

"Do you think she might be still alive?"

"The sheriff said she was by the ski jump, but now they can't find her. Maybe she took off somewhere. Dead people don't move."

McIntire pictured a nine-year-old David keeping his vigil beside the unmoving body of his father. He spoke more softly. "But they can *be* moved."

The boy again turned his disconcerting gaze on his visitor. "I have to plant the rest of these trees now," he said.

McIntire accepted his dismissal and walked away. The short conversation, if it could be called that, left him feeling oddly discomfited. It was difficult to tell if David's attitude reflected insolence, furtiveness, grief, or simple indifference. Maybe it was plain old shock. After all, he had supposedly just spent a week lost in the bush, not to mention a day with Pete Koski being more or less accused of the murder of one of his few friends. David could hardly be blamed for not being eager to pass the time of day with a prying stranger. Still, McIntire hadn't gotten the impression that David's antagonism, if that's what it was, was directed at him personally. On the contrary, David's demeanor seemed distinctly impersonal. He glanced back as the slender youth dragged another tree from the bed of the truck. There was something about David that had an unsettling ring of familiarity.

XXII

After leaving David, McIntire checked his watch, his gas gauge, and possibly his good sense and, rather than turning north on Nels' Orchard Road, headed south on the even more primitive route that would take him to the main thorough-fares and eventually north along the peninsula and inland to Painesdale and the home of Laurie Post. He had not much hope that it would be a fruitful venture, but at any rate, the hour-long drive through the countryside would afford a welcome respite from the anguish occasioned by the events of the past weeks. McIntire relished driving almost as much as he did walking. He had seldom found the opportunity in Europe and had never before owned a car. The purchase of the blue Studebaker Champion the previous summer had been one of the high points of his life.

As he traveled between trees with limbs arching to meet overhead, a great blue heron that had been standing in the narrow roadway took wing. For several minutes it continued to fly, silent and spectral, at eye level in front of the car, leading him onward through the tunnel of green shadows, until it finally rose off over the treetops abandoning him to find his own way. McIntire had an impulse to turn back and try to convince Leonie to accompany him on the trip, but by the time she was finished with her newspaper and her Glorious Fourth preparations the day would probably be shot.

He also regretted that he had not taken time to call to let Laurie know to expect him. He had no one but himself to blame when, after receiving directions to her house from the youthful attendant at the filling station, he found that she was not at home.

He was just turning away from her door when a white clad Laurie appeared from around the corner, walking briskly in her nurse's shoes. Here in the outdoors, McIntire could see that she was even more diminutive than she had appeared within the confines of the church, and more ancient. She must already have reached middle age when she first entered the Bertelsen household. He lost what optimism he had that she would be able to give him any useful information.

She regarded him curiously until she was only a few feet from where he stood. Then she smiled, exposing teeth that appeared to be mostly original equipment, and sprang forward to clutch at his arm. "Well, John, how nice. I've been hoping you'd come, but I have to admit I didn't really expect it."

McIntire patted the bony hand. "I should have called first, but I just happened to be in town. I hope this isn't a bad time."

She flung open the front door of her narrow mining-company house and urged him inside with the quick, jerky movements of an energetic mouse. "There couldn't be a better time. I've just finished my shopping, and I'm on the late shift this week, so I don't have to be at work until four o'clock." She deposited a brown paper bag on a chair by the door and unpinned her hat. "You're surprised to find me still working, aren't you? Probably surprised to find me still alive!" She cackled merrily and, after seating him in the living room and being assured that his mother and Leonie were in excellent health, scurried off to the kitchen, giving McIntire ample time to scrutinize his surroundings.

The room did not at all conform to his notion of the parlor of an elderly spinster, if Laurie could be called that.

The early afternoon sun produced foreshortened rectangles of light on the faded oak floor and revealed furnishings that consisted of not much more than a sofa and chair covered in fawn colored corduroy with a low table placed between them. Those positions that one could have reasonably expected to be occupied by a montage of mementos and family photos were taken up by a staggering array of green plants. No fussy little-old-lady violets or geraniums but masses of philodendron, diffenbachia, and tropical ferns spilled from pots and baskets, twined over the windows, and created patterns of soft shadow on the chalk-white walls. Simplicity and serenity reigned.

McIntire was on his feet, surreptitiously glancing about, searching in vain for some reminder of Laurie's life with Ole Bertelsen, when she returned with a tray. She lowered it to the table with a rattle of cups and a slosh of milk from the pitcher.

"Is this what you wanted?" She spoke abruptly, and McIntire had no ready response other than to gaze in astonishment. She stared back for the briefest of moments before saying with a little sigh, "Oh dear, I just get so used to asking. Carrying trays is mostly what I do these days. I don't see as well as I used to. But it's good to keep busy." McIntire was baffled by this statement until he realized that she was referring to her employment. She sat down on the edge of the sofa. "Anyway, I hope this is all right. I thought you might prefer tea. Sorry, but I'm fresh out of crumpets, whatever they are. Have a cookie."

"Tea is just fine," McIntire lied, then added truthfully, "and I don't much care for crumpets. You have a lovely home."

"Oh, thank you, John." She poured them each a cup of the anemic looking liquid and added a hefty spoon of sugar to her own. "It's a bit spartan, I know, but by the time I bought this place there didn't seem to be any reason to begin acquiring a lot of junk. Travel light through this life, I say.

You'll leave less baggage for others to contend with when you're gone." She leaned forward to peer with cataract-clouded eyes into McIntire's face. "You don't resemble your father much," she observed. "And not just in appearance, I suspect."

McIntire braced himself for the glowing eulogy that generally accompanied any mention of the late Colin McIntire, but Laurie's remarks went off in another direction. "I haven't seen you since you were a boy," she said, "except—where was it?—oh yes, the funeral." She picked up a Hydrox cookie and separated the two halves. "Nels' funeral was the first time I've been back in St. Adele since Ole died. Being there again brought back so much that I thought I'd forgotten, memories of Nels and the others I left behind, too." She nibbled at the cookie. "Maybe we have something in common."

McIntire agreed that maybe they did. "I did my best to keep memories of home alive all the time I was away," he told her. It was a rude awakening when I came back and found out how little the St. Adele I had concocted in my mind resembled the real thing."

"Well, I guess we're not that much alike after all," Laurie responded. "The day I left, I made up my mind to never give the good folk of St. Adele another thought." She chuckled and brushed a few crumbs from her lap. "But I sometimes feel maybe it was wrong of me to just get up and take off the way I did. Not everybody in St. Adele treated me like a leper. Maybe I was a little too ready to see accusation in every sideways glance. I really didn't give anyone much of a chance to be friendly even if they had wanted to be."

"Still," McIntire sympathized, "it must have taken a lot of courage to stay on after Tina Bertelsen was gone."

"Courage? I don't know about that. I didn't have anywhere else to go, and I didn't care much about what anybody thought. Still don't. Maybe that's the wrong way to be, too. Folks don't care much what I think either…" Laurie's voice trailed off, and she frowned slightly before going on. When she did continue, McIntire was relieved to see that he'd have no struggle to induce her to open up. "It was harder for Ole," she said, "and, of course, Nels, than it was for me. After all, those people were their friends and neighbors. It was especially bad for the boy, being at the age he was, only sixteen or so. But regardless of the gossip, I don't think he would have wanted me to leave, do you?"

"I'm positive that he wouldn't have."

"Poor Tina was never able to be much of a mother to him. I hoped to make things a little better." Laurie's hand fluttered out like a tiny paw to pick up her cup, then returned it to the saucer without drinking. "We never quite know for sure how the things we do will affect others, do we? Nels had already lost a brother years before, and then his sister died the way she did—it was her appendix, you know, and they were just too stubborn to get any help for her until it was too late—and his mother goes off her rocker over it. The next thing you know she's gone, too, and"—she gave a self-deprecating smile—"Pa's got some doxy in her place. He had a lot on his plate for sure, and I have to shoulder some of the blame for his problems. I'm sure he took more than his share of grief on my account…all kinds of teasing and torment… and then there was that tragedy with the younger boy."

At McIntire's questioning look she explained, "The one who lost his arm."

"Wylie Petworth," McIntire said helpfully.

"Yes, Wylie. Funny name. They were good friends, don't you know? Wylie was just a little tad, but he followed Nels around like a puppy. Well, he'd lost both his parents, and he looked up to Nels. Even before all the troubles, Nels didn't have a lot of friends. I think his quick temper kind of led other young people to keep their distance." At McIntire's nod she continued. "But it didn't seem to bother Wylie. He was a tough little nut, I'll say that for him, always so chipper, and wasn't afraid of anything. Maybe it would have been better for him if he had been."

Like a lot of older people, Laurie might be getting fuzzy where the here and now was concerned, but she seemed to be able to relate stories of the past without missing a beat. Still, this last comment was perplexing.

"Why do you say that?"

"For all that they spent so much time together, that boy did tend to get Nels stirred up."

"Well, like you say, Nels wasn't hard to stir up. But even so," McIntire said, "he and Wylie always stayed good friends. Nels cared enough to risk his own neck to drag Wylie out of that fire."

"Oh my yes! And a good thing that he did."

McIntire couldn't argue with that. "And Wylie's toughness gave him the fortitude to cope pretty well with his injury. That must have been terrifying for a young boy."

Laurie sat back and closed her eyes for a minute, as if making a supreme effort to dredge deeply into her store of memories—or perhaps taking a minute to relish the anticipation of telling her story. "It was dreadful! They'd been fishing through the ice on the bay. They went almost every day after they'd got home from school and done their chores. They had that warming shack on the shore. After the explosion and the fire, Nels managed to come to his senses enough to get Wylie out and away from the shack. He left him lying in the woods and ran all the way home to get help. Ole was off in Chandler, so I had to go—being a nurse, I'd have gone anyway, but Ole would have been a help..."

Her voice grew faint, and McIntire nodded encouragingly.

"We took the team through the woods. When we got there the shack was roaring like an inferno and the dead trees around it had caught fire, too." Laurie leaned forward and pressed her hands to her chest. "It was like a scene from hell!— flames leaping all around and that poor boy screaming like a banshee. We wrestled him into the sled, and Nels held him down so I could rip his sleeve away and pack what was left of his arm with snow. Sorry they're storebought."

Where had that come from? "Storebought?"

She shoved the Hydrox his way. "You're still way too skinny. I hate making cookies. Fussing over all those little blobs of dough. I used to work all morning, and Ole and Nels would polish off the whole batch in a half hour. If I wanted any I'd have to hide them. Now I just buy whatever I want, and I have them all to myself." She moved the plate closer. "Eat."

McIntire obediently took one, and only one, cookie. "You were telling me, Miss Post, about putting Wylie in the sled. Did you take him all the way to Chandler?"

"Just to the hotel in St. Adele. They had a phone there." She swung back into her story. "I'll never forget that trip if I live to be a hundred. Nels drove along the lake on the ice. There was no road then. It was pitch dark and snowing like crazy, the horses slipping and stumbling over big chunks of ice, and Wylie screaming and swearing at me every step of the way. Called me names I never dreamed a thirteen-year-old boy would know. I hadn't heard some of those words myself, and I was raised in a lumber camp." Her throaty chuckle became a sigh. "Well, that was a long time ago, and luckily young men have a forgiving nature—or short memories."

"But after it was all over he must have realized his pain wasn't your fault."

Laurie looked curiously at him, the confused frown reappearing.

"No, of course it wasn't *my* fault...well, not directly, anyway. And it sure wasn't my fault if bed seventeen got cornflakes instead of oatmeal yesterday. I just carry the trays, I don't put the stuff on them!" This minor outburst was followed by an expression of dismay, then a self-conscious giggle. "Oh dear, I'm sorry. I'm afraid I get off the track sometimes. What was it?"

"You took Wylie to St. Adele, and…"

"Oh yes, the boy in the fire. So that young doctor came out from Chandler, twenty miles through the storm. My wasn't he just the handsomest man? Anyway, he did what he could. The next morning he put the boy in his sled and took him over to that little lumber town on Keweenah Bay. The water was open there. They got him to the hospital in Houghton by boat. That's where they amputated his arm."

"It was thanks to Nels and you that Wylie didn't lose more than his arm. And lucky that no one else was hurt."

"Nels' hands were burned, too, and they were rubbed raw from driving the horses, but he wouldn't let the doctor touch them."

"Why ever not?"

Laurie threw up her hands. "Who knows? I think mostly he was too stubborn to admit that he needed help, but then, he still sort of blamed Guibard for his sister's dying. Anyway I took care of his burns myself. I was a nurse after all. I still am, regardless of what some people might think!"

She seemed poised on the brink of another disturbing trek into the confusing present, and McIntire hastily raked up a story from the deep past.

"What was it that you said about Nels losing a brother, too? I don't remember hearing about that."

"Oh, it was before they came here—the reason that they came here really. They were living in Minnesota then, on the North Shore, or in Duluth, I suppose, in the winter. They spent the fishing season on Isle Royale. It was early spring and Ole and his older son—Lars was his name—made a run to the fishing grounds around the Apostle Islands when the south shore fishermen were still iced in. A storm came up and Lars was swept right out of the boat. There wasn't a thing Ole could do. The boy sank like a rock and never came up again. Ole probably would have died himself if he hadn't been rescued by a freighter."

"The Bertelsens sure had more than their share of bad luck."

"It got worse." Laurie spoke just above a whisper, causing McIntire to wonder if he should check behind the ferns for secret agents. "Tina was pregnant at the time, and she went into labor early, shock maybe. They ended up losing that child, too—stillborn."

And the Mrs. Bertelsen that McIntire knew had always seemed so cheerful, at least to his child's mind.

"Then Tina's mother died and she inherited a little money," Laurie went on. "She badgered Ole until he gave up fishing for farming, so that's how they wound up here."

"Yeah, I guess you couldn't grow many apples on the North Shore."

"Apples? Oh that's right, that's what it was. Well, there are probably better places to do it than St. Adele township, too, but some of the emigrants from Tina's district in Norway had settled here, so she felt more at home."

"She didn't speak much English," McIntire recalled. "I used to enjoy talking to her, or listening to her, I should say. She talked mostly about her early life in Norway. I imagine she was lonely and missed her home." Or maybe she simply hadn't wanted to think about more recent events. "She never mentioned meeting anybody around here that she knew in the old country. She said she was the only one in her family to leave Norway, except for her grandfather, but that was before she was born, so she never knew him, and he was long dead."

Laurie nodded. "Her grandfather was a wanderer, traveled all over the world. After Tina's grandmother died he found himself a new wife and left Norway for good. Tina's mother was a married woman herself by that time so she stayed behind. Maybe Tina inherited the old man's wanderlust. She came here to marry Ole more or less sight unseen. They had met once or twice as children, but really only knew each other through letters."

The original mail order bride.

Laurie held the pot in both hands as she refilled their cups with the now lukewarm tea. "Not everybody found a better life here in the Promised Land. Tina Bertelsen just wasn't cut out for happiness, I think. Ole said she was always a little...different. She could do the work of three men for weeks, hardly stopping to eat or sleep, then all of a sudden it would be like she just didn't care. She wouldn't even get out of bed for days at a time. Finally one morning she'd just hop up and start in where she left off, like nothing ever happened."

All the Bertelsens had worked like horses. McIntire couldn't see that it was odd if Christina had needed a little time off.

"When Julie died she really went to pieces. Ole didn't dare leave her alone for a minute. So he got me in, and we'd take turns staying with her around the clock. She never seemed to need to sleep. She was strong as a bull. And crafty. Anything she got her hands on, she could use as a weapon."

"A weapon? Are you saying that Christina Bertelsen was—"

"Vicious! I fell asleep on my watch once—and believe me only once! When I woke up she was standing over me with a broken lamp chimney in her hand. Ole wasn't home. I screamed bloody murder, and when Nels came running in she went after him instead. He was just a skinny kid, hardly a match for her, but he managed to wrestle her down and get the broken glass away. She cut her hand to ribbons, and Nels ended up with a nasty gash on his shoulder."

McIntire found himself without words. He could only stare until Laurie continued. "Oh, hers was a tragic case all right, and I'm sure it left its mark on her son. Having a father 'living in sin' was the lightest of the crosses he had to bear."

It certainly had left its mark, literally as well as figuratively. McIntire remembered the thin blue scar he had seen on Nels' body.

"If you don't mind my asking," he said gently, "why didn't you and Ole Bertelsen get married?"

Laurie again regarded him with another puzzled wrinkling of her brow. "Mainly because bigamy is illegal."

"I mean after Tina died, why didn't you marry Ole then? Not," he added, "that it's any of my business."

Laurie put down her cup and cleared her throat. "John, Christina Bertelsen isn't dead. Her mind may have left her thirty-five years ago, but her backside is still warming a chair at the state hospital in Newberry."

XXIII

For once McIntire failed to be distracted by the awesome beauty of the landscape as he wound his way home over the forested hills and along the western shores of Keweenah Bay.

Christina Bertelsen imprisoned these past thirty-six years in an asylum for the incurably insane! And the man she had crossed the ocean to marry let all the world think she was dead. Had Ole actually lied? Had he *said* that his wife had died? McIntire didn't know. His own mother might remember. Given the Scandinavian predilection for bearing one's misfortunes in silence and, at least on the surface, respecting the right of others to do the same, it was just possible that no one had directly asked Ole about the fate of his wife. Ole would have been the last one to volunteer any information. It hardly mattered now. Tina's life had been effectively taken away. She must be a tough old bird, to have survived so long in one of those places. Mental hospitals were bad enough in this "enlightened age." He didn't want to think what it must have been like in 1914, especially for a woman, a woman deemed violent.

Violent! Tina Bertelsen? He could hardly conceive of it. The Mrs. Bertelsen he remembered was robust and apple-cheeked, with a fat braid down her back like Mia's. In contrast to the rest of her family, she had been loquacious, and seemed delighted to converse with "Yonny" McIntire in her native language. She'd spent hours relating legends of trolls and elf-maidens as well as real-life tales of the fishing village where she grew up, all the while with her hands moving rapidly as her tongue as she flew from one task to the next. He wondered if she found anyone she could talk with in the asylum. Did Ole ever visit? Did Nels? Or did he think that his mother was dead, too? How could they have done such a thing?

Most disheartening of all was the knowledge that Laurie Post had stood by and allowed such an...*enormity* to take place. Laurie unselfishly sacrificing her good name to rebuild a home for two grievously bereaved men? Hardly. Try Laurie coolly and cruelly stepping into Tina's shoes the minute she had been yanked out of them—before, even—and Laurie sharing Ole Bertelsen's bed while his wife, the mother of his children, lay shackled to a narrow cot in a mental ward. Hell, the ever-competent Laurie could well have been the instigator of this outrage. It was she who was providing Tina's supposed medical care, she who presented that seductive aura of strength and serenity. Ole would have listened to her advice. Any wonder that she had spent her life with Ole—what were her words?—"seeing accusation in every sideways glance"? And how had she financed the purchase of that cozy little cottage if she had really left Ole's house taking nothing more than the clothing she'd come with?

He had left Laurie as soon as he could break away without excessive discourtesy, forgetting about the original purpose of his visit: the gleaning of information from the old woman concerning anything from Nels' past that might have contributed to his death.

Nothing she had said gave any insight as to who might have wanted Nels dead, although her revelations may have pointed out someone who would definitely have wanted him to stay alive, at least long enough to outlive his mother. With Tina still alive, Nels' estate could amount to even less than

Warner Godwin had predicted. If Ole Bertelsen had died without a will, maybe a good share of the property he owned had gone to his surviving spouse. Maybe even all of it. It was conceivable that Nels owned nothing at all. Even that albatross of a boat might not really be his. If Lucy Delaney knew that Tina was still living, she might well be concerned for her own security in spite of Nels' will. She surely wouldn't have wanted Nels out of the way yet—*if* she knew about Tina.

Lucy was no fool, but, strangely, could the same be said for Warner Godwin? Would he, an *attorney* for God's sake, loan Nels money, taking his home and business as collateral without first making sure that Nels actually had title to that property? Maybe if Nels had been appointed his mother's guardian it wouldn't matter. Maybe he could encumber her assets any way he chose. And what about those "other financial plans" Godwin had been supposedly making on Nels' behalf, that he "was not at liberty to discuss"?—or was he just not at liberty to do anything about them until the old lady snuffed it?

The legal questions were mind-boggling, and who better to answer them than Nels' own attorney? Well, Godwin was looking for a translator and, according to popular opinion, McIntire needed a job.

XXIV

He was back in his yard, pushing the lawn mower over the sparse grass, alternately trying to dispel the vision of a gaunt and hollow-eyed Tina Bertelsen lashed to a chair and wondering what information Pete Koski might have extracted from the uncommunicative David, when the sheriff himself drove up. He emerged stiffly from the car and leaned against the rear fender, kneading the back of his neck, while he waited for McIntire to approach.

Mowsers and company, he said, had turned up Cindy's coat, wadded into a ball and crammed inside a cavity under a burnt-out pine stump, just off the trail between the ski jump and the gravel pit.

They didn't find any other sign of her, although there had been so many people in the woods during the search that the dogs hardly knew where to start. It looked like McIntire could be right, she'd probably been taken away in a car that had been parked in the pit. The area around the old slate quarries and railroad cut had been thoroughly searched, also with no results. Now the tracker had joined forces with the sheriff's department, and, with the aid of the game wardens, they were turning their attention to the more remote hills and the lakeshore.

"If we find anything," Koski concluded, "it'll be just dumb luck. There are thousands of acres of woods out there—not to mention hundreds of miles of nice soft sand. We might have a better chance of finding her if she was buried along the shore. Once a few waves washed over, you could walk right on the grave and never know it was there, but the dogs could sniff it out with no trouble."

"You know," McIntire said, "if the murderer was somebody from this community, and it *must* have been, I don't see how he could have taken the body very far. The news of Cindy's disappearance was all over the neighborhood within a couple of hours, and every able-bodied man who wasn't away somewhere working was helping with the search. If anybody was gone for the length of time it would take to bury a body, or to haul it way back into the mountains, it would have been noticed."

"Unless he just hid the body somewhere, stuffed it in the trunk of his car, maybe, until after the search started. It would have been easy to duck out for a few hours in that confusion, and if he came back tired and covered with mud all the better."

"Yeah, I guess that's true," McIntire conceded. "And on the other hand, if this alleged perpetrator was *already* missing…"

"That's what I stopped to tell you, I've let the kid go. We're hanging on to his car, so if he tries to take off again he won't get far, but see if you can keep an eye on him anyway, will you?"

"So you're still thinking he did it?"

"Shit, if I was really sure of that I wouldn't have let him go. I thought maybe the dogs could tell if the body'd been in his car, but if they know they're not saying. Our Davy's a weird one though, cool as a cucumber when we questioned him. Even the state guys couldn't get him flustered. He didn't seem to be overly upset about his girlfriend's death, either, just sat there with that hangdog look of his and kept saying—quote—'It ain't my fault.' I figure if we let him go and keep a close watch on him he might do something to tip his hand, lead us to the body or make some slip of the tongue."

He began to massage his lower back. "We managed to get a few words with Godwin's daughter. Warner sat right there of course, so we couldn't try out our new set of thumb-screws. I don't know what the hell he thought we were going to do to the kid. Anyway, Annie—that's her name—says Cindy got a letter on Saturday, and she thinks it was from her boyfriend. She said Cindy was all happy and 'danced her around the room.'"

"The letter wasn't in her bedroom."

"She could have had it with her. But you know we didn't find *any* letters in her room. David swears up and down that he never wrote to Cindy, and, according to Annie, Cindy hadn't gotten any letters at all before Saturday."

"Maybe that accounts for her being so excited. Did Annie actually say the letter was from David?"

"No," the sheriff answered. "She just said she thought it must be from her boyfriend because Cindy was laughing and dancing around."

"So whoever wrote that letter could have arranged to meet Cindy on Monday morning and killed her, and who else but another kid would set up a meeting in the woods?"

Koski squinted into the sun. "Unless Cindy expected to be met at the train. She was pretty gussied up for a jaunt into the bushes. Maybe she just started walking because nobody showed up. But then," he reconsidered, "according to Mrs. Thorsen she didn't wait any time at all, and she was wearing those tennis shoes, carrying her good shoes in the bag. It looks like she expected to be walking. You've got something there. It is hard to imagine a grown man, or woman, arranging a rendezvous at a ski jump."

"But if the letter was from David he was taking a big chance that it wouldn't be found later."

"I guess," the sheriff agreed. "But maybe he asked her to destroy it for some reason, or made sure she'd bring it along, put a map or some directions in it. And then again, maybe

David didn't write the letter, at all. If the writer thought the handwriting couldn't be traced, he, or possibly she, wouldn't care if it was found or not. Maybe it was typed. The fact of the matter is," he concluded with an exasperated sigh, "we don't really know for sure that the letter had anything to do with Cindy's murder."

"...or if there really was a letter."

"Oh, I think she got a letter all right. So far Annie Godwin is the only person I've talked to in this investigation that I'd say was telling the truth, and even she seemed to be holding back a little."

"Speaking of holding back, here's another tidbit to further erode your faith in human nature." McIntire told him what he had learned about Warner Godwin and the loan Nels had gotten for the purchase of the *Frelser*.

"It looks like I'll have to have another little chat with Lawyer Godwin." Koski stood up straighter and transferred his rubbing to the seat of his pants. "Lord, if anybody'd told me twenty years ago that I'd be spending ninety percent of my time behind the wheel of a car, I'd have gone into the hardware business with my old man. Arnie Johnson tells me if you sleep with a dog you'll never get arthritis." He glanced fondly at Geronimo stretched out on the back seat. "I don't think Marian would go for it. Anyway, keep tabs on our young Dan'l Boone. He won't get far on foot. Come to find out he's never had a driver's license, either."

He pulled open the car door and turned back to McIntire. "We've got an order from your," he hesitated and sighed, "Justice, to exhume Bertelsen's body." McIntire smiled outright at Koski's grudging mention of Myrtle Van Opelt, St. Adele's long-time school teacher, now retired but continuing to wield her considerable power as Justice of the Peace.

He gave a sad shake of his head before going on. "For tissue samples, but it probably won't be done 'til next week sometime. Guibard says once we get him out of the ground he can get things done in a few hours, but the samples have to go to Lansing, and they won't be in any rush. And by the way," he added, "was there anything worthwhile in Mrs. Godwin's diaries? The ones I have are mainly about baby teeth and curtains."

In McIntire's preoccupation with Christina Bertelsen, he had temporarily forgotten Nina Godwin and her transgressions. Now he informed the sheriff that at least one of the journals indicated that Nina had indulged in activities that might constitute grounds for blackmail. He steeled himself against the sheriff's reaction when he heard that the crucial volume was in the possession of Mia Thorsen. "Nina Godwin was Mia's cousin, I thought she might be able to get more out of them than I could."

"…and did she?"

"I haven't heard from her, so I'd guess not. It turned out that she never really knew Nina that well. Their families were estranged."

"Well, I'm going to need to turn the diary over to the state police. This won't be getting us into Warner's good graces. Having his baby sitter murdered wasn't exactly a bang-up way to kick off an election campaign. If it turns out that it had something to do with his dead wife, he can kiss any chance at that county prosecutor's office goodbye."

McIntire marveled at Koski's calm acceptance of his blithely passing out evidence to the neighbors, and also at the sheriff's apparent lack of curiosity as to exactly what Mrs. Godwin had done for entertainment between bouts of decorating and child rearing.

"Pete," he ventured, "Nina Godwin was involved with another man. She's dead. Is Warner going to have to find out?"

The sheriff shrugged. "We took the diaries from Godwin's house. They'll have to be returned to him eventually. If it turns out that Cindy was killed because of something she knew about Nina, it'll all come out." McIntire's expression must have been as bleak as his thoughts. Koski looked at him with something close to sympathy. "Murder's generally not a barrel of laughs, John, except in the movies.

"When you pick up the diary," he went on, "maybe you could have another go at your infamous mailman, being that you're a friend of the family. He was pretty closemouthed with me. He might have noticed if David ever mailed any letters. Find out exactly what he saw the morning Cindy was killed. According to your post master, he was late getting back with the mailbag from the train on Monday and came in looking like an unmade bed. She figured he'd been out on a tear the night before. I wonder if his wife actually saw him drive back into town after he picked up the mail. I don't suppose she'd tell *me* if she didn't, but maybe you could find out." Koski grimaced as he stuffed himself into the car and pressed the starter.

"Say 'hello' to Leonie. Maybe she should be handling this investigation. She sure pinned Cecil to the wall yesterday."

McIntire watched until the sheriff drove out of sight. The prospect of "having another go" at Nick Thorsen was not a particularly agreeable one. He was finding that he had little stomach left for the whole dreary mess. Murder was indeed not a barrel of laughs.

Leonie should have been home hours ago. The plotting of the great Independence Day Extravaganza must have hit a snag. Maybe they'd decided that this was not the best time for a celebration.

Poor Leonie. She'd spent the better part of her life dealing with the problems wrought by sudden death, and he'd dragged her away from her home and children to give her more of the same. When she had extracted from him the promise that if, after two years, she wanted to return to England, he would comply without question, he'd had no doubts. She was guaranteed to fall in love with his homeland. Now he wasn't so sure that he wouldn't be the first to pack his bags.

Instead of spending thirty years idealizing a North Woods Utopia, he'd have done well to remember why he left in the first place. No…that wouldn't have made a difference. It hadn't been any presence of evil lurking under the idyllic surface that had driven him away, although from what he'd learned lately, he wouldn't have had to dig far to find just that. There was really only one reason that he'd turned expatriate—Colin McIntire. He'd let his father drive him away from the home and the woman he loved. Well, it wasn't going to happen again. He wasn't a seventeen-year-old boy anymore. This time he would stand up to the slimy bastard who threatened to douse his homefires. It was a comforting, if melodramatic, thought, but first he would have to figure out who that slimy bastard was.

XXV

Another evening had come, and McIntire once again found himself seated with Nick and Mia Thorsen and the ever-present wine bottle. Nick's face was rosy in the twilight and his hair was twisted into damp ringlets—fresh from his Wednesday night sauna. McIntire felt a surge of optimism that his host might have steamed himself into a more mellow frame of mind than was customary. He was disappointed.

"I hope you're not here to play detective again." Nick handed McIntire a hefty glassful of the wine. "Mia's had about all she can handle, and frankly, so have I."

"Actually, the sheriff did want me to get some more information, but I guess he could come and ask you himself."

Nick gave a short bark of laughter. "You're getting better at this. Okay, you win. We wouldn't want to inconvenience Pete Koski. Fire away. But I've said it all a thousand times." When Mia stood up he waved to her to remain where she was. "I'll get you started: I didn't see anybody on my way to work. I saw the Culver girl get off the train, but I didn't see what she did then."

"Did you think it was odd that there was no one there to meet her?"

"I didn't think about it one way or the other. I didn't know where she was going. It's only a quick walk into town."

"Did you recognize her?"

Nick took a long drink and refilled his glass. "I didn't pay any attention to her. If I had, I guess I might have known who she was. I don't really remember if it registered or not."

"She was a pretty attractive girl. Most men would have taken at least a little notice."

Nick held his glass up to the slanting rays of the sun. "Maybe so."

"But you didn't offer her a ride into town?"

"No, I didn't. I couldn't have anyway. When I got back to the car, it had a flat tire."

This was something new. "Did you change it right then?"

"No, I drove the whole route on the rim." He rolled his eyes, and added a restrained groan for good measure. "Yes, I changed the tire."

"How long did that take?"

"Twenty minutes, I suppose. Maybe longer. I had a hard time getting the lug nuts off, and I had to pump up the spare some." He pulled a cigarette from a pack of Camels and tapped the end lightly on the table before making an elaborate, drawn-out production of the ignition process.

"So you were about twenty minutes late getting back with the mailbag?"

"I said it could have been longer. It probably *was* more than twenty minutes because the train was late in the first place. I'm sure Marie could tell you to the second, since you're so interested."

Something in Nick's demeanor told McIntire that it just might be time to turn the subject to a less touchy area.

"I know that you probably don't look too closely at people's mail"—that hadn't come out exactly the way McIntire intended, but he ploughed ahead—"but did you notice if anybody around here got mail that could have come from Cindy Culver in the few days before she died?"

"A blackmail note, you mean? No, I didn't. Here's a real eye-opener for you, there's always a chance I might not recognize Cindy Culver's handwriting if I saw it, and I doubt that she was in the habit of including her name and return address on her extortion notes."

"What about from Warner Godwin?" Mia put in. At their curious looks, she explained, "If Cindy wanted to conceal the source of her letter, and also make darn sure that she would grab someone's attention, she could have mailed her note in one of Warner's business envelopes."

"*Did* you notice any letters on Godwin's stationery?" McIntire asked.

"Damn near everybody in the county got a friendly little message from Warner Godwin last week. Letting each and every one of us know that he's ready to take up the sword in our behalf. He's running for county attorney, remember."

McIntire did remember. He remembered receiving his own "friendly message," and he also remembered the piles of papers and envelopes on the table in Godwin's dining room. Cindy could easily have slipped a note into any one of them. Maybe she was smarter than they had given her credit for.

"The morning of the murder did you see anybody else on the road, other than Cindy herself?"

"Not a soul." He paused before adding, "Well, Guibard came roaring by like a bat out of hell, I suppose on his way to the scene of the crime. Though he always drives like he's going to a fire."

"Not Lucy Delaney?"

"Nah, she usually doesn't show up until after Marie gets in to the post office—right after, that is. She waits with bated breath while Marie sorts the morning mail. She wasn't in the post office on Monday when I got there, and the only time we meet *en route* is if I go home for breakfast after I pick up the mail from the train. Sometimes I pass her when I'm on my way back in."

"But she couldn't have known you'd be late getting in with the mail from the train on Monday. She should have gotten there about the same time you did."

"That is odd. Maybe she's clairvoyant. They say she does have strange powers."

"Has she ever said why she comes in to pick up her mail instead of waiting for it to be delivered?"

"Has anybody ever asked her?" He didn't wait for an answer. "Maybe she doesn't trust me to get it to her. Maybe she thinks I'll read her post cards, or she didn't want Nels to find out about those love letters she gets from Gary Cooper."

"Does she get a lot of mail?" McIntire supposed it wouldn't do to ask for specifics. "I suppose she picked up Nels' mail too."

"Johnny-boy, now I *am* shocked! The U.S. mails are a sacred trust! Marie sorts it in total privacy. I see only those messages I am duly authorized to deliver—that does *not* include letters addressed to Lucille Delaney—and Lucy gets the mail that has her name on it, and that's it. You can count on that."

"But since Nels died…"

"It gets marked 'deceased' and returned. Marie's not going to turn anybody's mail over to their floozy."

"So you still delivered Nels' mail when he was alive."

"Certainly."

"Even after you had your 'falling out'?"

"People can't fire their mailman like he was a gardener or something."

"But Nels did try to get you fired."

"Yeah, so I stocked his boat with bees. If that didn't work I was planning to put scorpions in his mailbox."

McIntire decided to abandon this line of inquiry also. He was rapidly running out of topics. "The night before Nels died there were a lot of people at the beer joint. Did anything unusual happen?"

"Like what?"

"Just anything that seemed curious. Did anybody leave early, or disappear for awhile and come back later?" McIntire recalled the sheriff's mention of a "commotion" on the road near Otto Wilke's house. "Did anything out of the ordinary happen on your way home?"

Nick stubbed out his cigarette on the table and flicked it over the railing. "Okay, listen good because I'm going to say this for the last time. On the night before that ornery bugger died, I went to the Waterfront, I had a couple of beers. I forgot to keep tabs on who stepped out to the can, and I came home. That's it." He stood up with a sudden motion that sent his chair skidding across the floor boards. "Like I said before, I've had about all of this I can take. I'm going to bed. Some of us have to work for a living." The screen door slammed shut behind him, leaving his wife and McIntire sharing an embarrassed silence.

"He gets tired," Mia finally said. She looked at McIntire's still-full glass and smiled sympathetically. "Drink up, it'll put hair on your chest."

They sat in darkness, watching fireflies winking in the tall grass at the edge of the garden. The call of a loon cut through the stillness, followed by the faint echo of an answer from a far-off mate. Mia pulled the collar of her flannel shirt closer around her neck. "That sound always gives me the willies, even if it is my namesake."

"Namesake?"

"Yeah, or maybe I'm its namesake, I never could figure which was which. However it goes, Charlie Wall tells me that's what my name means. Meogokwe is loon, or more specifically, Loon Woman."

"No kidding?" McIntire gave in to the smile that forced its way to his lips. "Mia, do you mean to tell me…?"

"Yes, John. You don't have to say it—Potowatami for 'loon' and Vogel in German means 'bird,' and thank God nobody figured that out when I was a kid! Can you imagine—'Old Loony Bird'? 'Bird brain' was bad enough."

"Did your mother know that's what it meant?"

"Oh, I don't think so. She wasn't even quite sure how to pronounce her grandmother's name. The way the Indians said it, it had some clicky sounds, she said. She was always changing her mind about how we should spell it, so when I started school it was easier to stick with plain Mia. But Charlie says it means loon. Keep it under your hat."

"Your secret is safe with me. I'm a professional, remember."

"I'd hardly be likely to forget! You must know that everybody around here is dying to know what sort of cloak and dagger intrigues you've been involved in over the years." She hesitated, as if on the verge of pursuing the subject further, then just asked, "And were you also a professional at *uncovering* secrets?"

"As much as I hate to disappoint you, I have to admit that I really didn't do much of either keeping *or* discovering secrets. Like Will Rogers, all I knew was what I read in the papers. Mostly I just kept up on what was being reported in the European press." It was a variation of the response he always gave when questioned about his military career.

"Press, my eye! I don't believe it for a minute. I can't see you sitting in a hive of undercover information, reading the newspaper."

"Because I'm so curious? Maybe you can indulge that curiosity a bit." McIntire raised his glass to his lips, but placed it back on the table without drinking. "Mia," he said hesitantly, "don't get upset when I ask you this, but could you see Nick when you were on the jump?"

Mia sighed. "I figured you'd get to that sooner or later. I could see him waiting, pacing back and forth. When the train came it blocked my view, and when it pulled away I could see Cindy, but Nick was gone."

"You didn't see him drive away...or hear his car start up?"

"I didn't see his car at all."

Something in the tone of her voice made McIntire look at her curiously. "Did that surprise you?"

"Usually he would just sit in his car at the crossing. But the train was late so I guess he decided to pull off the road and get out. I suppose the car was behind the trees or a stack of pulpwood."

"But you didn't hear him drive away?"

"No, John, I didn't. I told you that, and Nick told you he had to fix a flat. I'm sure by the time he left I had other things on my mind."

A rising note of irritation crept into Mia's voice, and McIntire smiled apologetically. "Did you finish reading Nina's diary?"

She went into the house for a minute and came back with the journal.

"Sorry if I'm sounding cranky. I had a bad shock and I guess I'm still feeling a little spooked."

"I understand that, Mia. It must have been ghastly for you. I don't know how you're holding up so well. I'm having nightmares, and I didn't even see Cindy."

"What? Oh, no. I mean I had a *shock*. I switched on my lathe this morning and was knocked clean across the studio."

"Mia! But you're all right?"

"I'm fine. I called Guibard and he said as long as I feel okay I probably am." She clenched the diary in both her hands. "He also said that if I hadn't been wearing rubber soled shoes, I might have been killed."

"But do you know what caused it? Maybe the wiring in your shop is faulty."

"I opened up the motor. A wire was loose and was contacting the metal housing. My father built that lathe himself. He used the most powerful motor he could get his hands on. He always bragged that it would turn an oak tree.

"It'll be easy enough to fix, and there was no great harm done, but I think it'll be a while before I get up the nerve to go near another power tool." Her grip on the diary tightened, and its binding gave a crack. "It seems like you can't be *sure* of anything anymore. I used that lathe just last week and it was okay then. If a little thing like a slipped wire can kill you when you least expect it…" A smile teased the corners of her mouth. "As opposed to killing you when you do expect it."

She looked at the diary as if she had just remembered that she was holding it and placed it in McIntire's hand. "I read every word. It sure makes you see librarians in a different light."

"How did she manage all this activity without somebody catching on? It's hard to believe that nobody ever saw her and her Nordic god together."

"They made their arrangements at the library. Whispering is par for the course there. They met in Marquette or Escanaba and once even in Chicago, when she was on one of her decorating trips."

"Well, that narrows it down a bit. It has to be someone who frequented the library."

"Are you suggesting we go through the check-out cards and question every adult male who took out a book in the last three years?"

McIntire raised his eyebrows. "My guess is that would not be an insurmountable task," he said. "Especially if we stuck to Nordic gods."

"…who took out books on beekeeping." Mia completed his thought.

"Mia, she didn't say what sort of books he read, did she? Or any reference books he might have used?"

"She didn't say a word that even hints that he might have had any literary interests whatsoever. But as I recall from my Norse mythology, the gods didn't spend too much time engaged in cerebral pursuits." She poured a small amount of wine into Nick's abandoned glass and took a minuscule sip.

"The diaries would give the dates of their assignations," McIntire offered. "It might not be too hard to find out who was out of town on those dates."

"Maybe, but I doubt if that will help much. The trip to Chicago seems to be the only one where they actually spent the night. And that was in late October," she added. "Three-quarters of the men around here might have been away overnight, supposedly trying to put meat on the table."

McIntire brightened up. "Then this should be a piece of cake. There can't be a half-dozen men in the whole county that would schedule a tryst with a mere female during hunting season."

Mia laughed. "That's probably truer than you know." They sat in silence for a time. Mia swirled the wine around the bottom of the glass.

"John," she said at last, "do you think that whoever killed Cindy knew I was there? Saw me, or heard me coming down the jump, I mean. Do you think he could have been hiding somewhere," she asked, "watching me?"

The same thought had occurred to McIntire more than once, and he was as unwilling to face the possibility as she was, though perhaps for different reasons.

"If he had been—or she, we don't know for sure that it was a man—I don't think he would have let you get away. He'd have figured you saw him for sure. You said you heard someone walking away."

"That's what I thought then, but I only heard a few footsteps. He didn't have to go far. Maybe he heard me coming down and was right there watching." Her voice was shaky. McIntire was terrified that she was about to cry.

"Mia, I think if the murderer saw you, you wouldn't be here now talking about it."

Her voice dropped to almost a whisper. "John, this must have been done by a person that we *know*, and I don't know about you, but I can't think of anybody I'm acquainted with who I think could be a murderer. I mean, it's got to be somebody we would never suspect. So what if it was a...a good friend maybe, someone who wouldn't want to hurt me, or someone who hoped I wouldn't say anything? He might have just let me go for the time being, thinking he could deal with me later, and then when 'later' came, found out that I didn't know anything anyway."

Maybe their thoughts weren't so far apart after all, but McIntire still wasn't ready to bring it out into the open.

"I really don't think you were seen," he insisted. "The killer probably panicked and took off and then realized that there might be evidence that he should get rid of—Nina Godwin's diary for instance. But Mia, by now *everybody* knows that you were there. I don't want to frighten you any more, but I do think you should be careful."

"But everybody also knows I didn't see anything."

"They know that you *say* that you didn't see anything. There's always a chance that we're just keeping what you saw under wraps, or that you could remember more later. There's an unbalanced individual out there who knows that you were sitting right on top of him when he broke a child's neck." He gently touched her chin and turned her face toward his. "Please don't take any more solitary walks in the woods until all this is over."

Mia entered the darkened kitchen and softly closed the door behind her. She stood for a moment with her hand on the knob and then pushed the small button that slid the bolt into place. She could not recall that door ever being locked before. Even during the first war, when her mother had so feared for her father's safety and had begged him to bar the doors, Eban Vogel had steadfastly refused to admit to any distrust of his neighbors. Now the latch moved with difficulty. She hoped she would be able to open it again. She hoped she would someday be able to live again without fear clawing at her stomach. She switched out the light and crossed to the living room, moving through the comforting darkness of the familiar home to the stairs where a hulking shape sent her heart rocketing into her throat.

"Mia, are you coming up now?" Nick sat huddled at the bottom of the steps, a blanket thrown around his shoulders.

"Nick, you scared me half to death! What are you doing up?" His eyes were dark caverns in his sallow face, and he was shivering. "Are you sick?"

"What did he say after I came in? Why is he asking all those questions?"

Mia sat down beside him. "Nick, two people have been murdered. Everybody is going to have to answer questions. I've been asked a few myself."

"He doesn't know for sure that Nels was murdered, and for all we know, that girl might not even be dead. Maybe she staged the whole thing. She could be hiding out in some sleazy hotel room in Milwaukee right now. Why is he treating me like Jack the Ripper?"

Mia stood up and pulled him to his feet. "Come on to bed. You're worrying over nothing." She firmly turned him around and led him up the stairs.

The porch light was burning, but the rest of the house was dark when McIntire returned home. He leaned against the warm hood of the car and looked upward.

Since his return to Michigan, he had spent hours gazing up into the night sky, marveling at stars so brilliant and so near that he seemed almost to float among them. Tonight though, the luminous globe of a full moon, hanging just above the barn, created a pattern of silver light and deep shadows on the dew-drenched grass and faded the stars to pinpoints.

He went inside and climbed the stairs in darkness. Leonie was sleeping soundly, the bed covers thrown off despite the coolness, the dim light emphasizing the fairness of her hair and skin. She lay on her side with an arm and a leg thrown over the pillow appropriated from her husband's side of the bed. The book she had been reading was face down on the sheets beside her. McIntire picked it up and placed it on the bedside table. He knew what it would be without looking—Zane Grey. A shaft of moonlight illuminated her face and showed the movements of her eyes under the translucent lids. As McIntire undressed he wondered where she might be in her dreams…riding across the Purple Sage? In a sunny garden with roses climbing stone walls? Sharing a cup of tea with her daughters in a chintz-covered sitting room? Or maybe trying to run, with legs of clay, through a dismal forest of twisted pine, fleeing an unknown monster.

He gently removed the pillow and insinuated himself into its place.

XXVI

Warner Godwin seemed inordinately thrilled with McIntire's offer of his services in translating the Bertelsen business records. He beamed across his desk with an expression of delight which bore all the signs of being hastily assumed to cover his astonishment at learning that a denizen of the backwater of St. Adele could not only converse in a foreign tongue—that wasn't unusual—but was actually literate in several languages. The lawyer was dressed casually, indeed almost ruggedly, his rotund body encased in flannel and denim. This being Saturday there would be no court appearances on his schedule. His entire demeanor was considerably more relaxed than at their first meeting. He even partially dispensed with his conversation-controlling speech tactics.

"You'll see that once Nels himself started handling things, the records are written in English, but that wasn't until nineteen thirty-six. They only run through forty-one. That's when Wylie took over. The first is dated nineteen-six, so that leaves thirty years of Norwegian. If it was just financial entries, I could probably figure it out, but this is like the Great American Novel—or the Great Norse Saga, more like. It's all written in paragraphs with just a number here and there. For all I know it could be weather reports or Ma Bertelsen's recipes for apple pie. I would imagine she had a few. And there are letters, and certificates, and contracts, and God knows what else stuck between the pages, some in English, some not. Don't bother translating all of it—just major transactions— anything you think might have a bearing on the worth of the estate." He paused, and pinched his chubby chin between his thumb and forefinger. "On second thought, just to be on the safe side, translate everything, unless you know for sure it's not relevant. There could be important information hiding in there somewhere...maybe Ole Bertelsen owned an oil well."

As he talked, Godwin stood up, and McIntire watched with downward-spiraling spirits as he pulled a box off the top of a metal file cabinet and dropped it with a huff on the desk. "One for each year for thirty-five years. Like I said, the last five are in English, but I'd like to keep them all together." He plopped the ledgers that were stacked on the desk into the box with the others and shoved the entire collection across to McIntire. "Enjoy."

McIntire made no move to get up, but instead leaned back in his chair and, striving for an air of nonchalance, said, "Speaking of Ma Bertelsen, have you heard how she's doing? Has she been told of her son's death?"

The effect of his words was everything McIntire could have hoped for. Godwin couldn't have appeared more dumb-founded if his new employee had tucked the ledgers under his arm and soared out through the open window. The lawyer's eyes widened and froze. His mouth opened in a perfect O and closed only to open again, but no sound was forthcoming. McIntire was hard pressed to contain his glee. This must be akin to the euphoria Leonie had experienced when she "scooped" the *Monitor*.

When Godwin did manage to speak, he was once again the self-confident lawyer. "I wasn't aware that Mrs. Bertelsen was still living."

"Oh, yes," McIntire told him airily. "She's been incapaci-tated for many years of course, but she's as alive as you or I.

I'd have thought Nels would have mentioned that to you. Frankly, I was quite amazed that, from what you told the sheriff, he doesn't appear to have provided for her in his will." Sure, after letting the state take care of her for thirty-five years.

"Maybe he didn't need to…" Godwin said, more to himself than McIntire.

"What do you mean?"

"John, what exactly is the nature of Mrs. Bertelsen's incapacitation?"

"She was committed to the state mental hospital—or 'insane asylum' then—in nineteen fourteen." The time for being coy was probably over. "Ole Bertelsen had his wife locked up thirty-six years ago. I don't know if he actually said in so many words that she was dead, but he sure didn't set people straight if that's what they chose to believe, and neither did the rest of the family. Now, Mr. Godwin, you know that it looks like Nels Bertelsen's death wasn't any more accidental than Cindy's. We think they might very well be connected. We need to know of anyone who might have benefitted from Nels' death. Just what are the legal ramifications of the fact that Tina Bertelsen is the last surviving member of her family?"

The attorney shifted his weight in the padded leather chair. "There's really no cut and dried answer to that. There are a great many factors involved: the law at the time she was committed, the type of legal actions that her husband took, whether Mrs. Bertelsen owned property in her own right. She could have been deprived of her right to inherit her portion of her husband's estate—her dower rights—on the grounds that she was insane, but if they had joint ownership… and the state or the county could have a claim, too. I'm afraid this is one of those cases that will end up being hashed out in court. Someone will have to be appointed to represent Mrs. Bertelsen's interests. This happened in nineteen fourteen, you say?" The lawyer let out his breath in a heavy sigh. The anticipation of a complicated lawsuit apparently lost some of its shine when he, himself, had a personal stake in its outcome.

He stood up and mounted the short stool that gave him access to the highest shelves of his pine plank bookshelves. Stretching on his tiptoes—resembling a baby elephant performing its balancing-on-a-drum trick—he pulled out a heavy volume and hopped to the floor in a shower of dust.

"When exactly did the elder Mr. Bertelsen pass away?" he asked. "He is actually dead, I take it? Not living the life of Riley in Rio?"

"So far as I know, Ole Bertelsen is well and truly deceased. He's got a stone in the cemetery anyway. He died in thirty-five or six—it would most likely be when Nels started keeping the accounts."

Godwin extracted another book from its spot on a lower shelf and sat down heavily. "I just don't see how something like this could happen. When someone dies people know about it. There's an obituary in the paper and a funeral. They *have* a stone in the cemetery, for God's sake. Didn't people wonder why she wasn't buried at St. Adele?"

"The Bertelsens had only been living in the township for a few years, and they were a clannish bunch. Kept to themselves. They hired some help when they needed it, but usually their workers were transients, lumberjacks in the off season, people who would work for room and board. They didn't mix much with the locals. That's understandable now. They wanted to keep Mrs. Bertelsen's queer behaviors to themselves. And don't forget this was almost forty years ago, and the Bertelsens were dirt poor. Travel and embalming was expensive, and infectious disease was a rampant killer. If people thought that Tina had died from typhoid or flu in a hospital in a distant town they wouldn't have questioned her being quickly buried there.

"And even if they weren't sure, I doubt that anybody would have come right out and asked Ole what happened to his wife. She was sick, she went to a hospital, she didn't come back. She must be dead. If Ole didn't want to talk about it that was his business."

"You don't suppose that the old man actually told Nels that his mother had passed away?"

"Did Nels tell you that Tina was dead?"

The lawyer went back to pinching his chin. "I don't remember if he used those exact words. He sure as hell never mentioned that she was living."

"Maybe these records will shed some light on the question."

Godwin looked for a moment as if he might want to take the ledgers back, file them under "skull and crossbones," and forget he'd ever seen them.

"What was it you said," he asked, "that Cindy's and Nels' death's could be connected? How?"

"It's just more or less of a hunch—happening one right after the other and both in St. Adele." McIntire sidestepped the question. Not that he could have had a good answer for it. They had no real evidence that the murders were connected.

"Has there been any headway made at all? I heard that they finally caught up with her old boyfriend, but they let him go. I called the sheriff's office yesterday and again just before you got here. I haven't been able to get a thing out of any of them, except that they got a specially trained dog in."

He stood up abruptly, leaned with both palms on his desk, and addressed McIntire as he might a recalcitrant witness. "If I had taken her to St. Adele myself that day this wouldn't have happened. I was going out anyway. I could have gone that way and dropped her off, but she insisted that she just loved to ride the train."

"She wouldn't have let you give her a ride," McIntire assured him. "She wasn't really going home, remember. We think that she may have written to someone to arrange a meeting. I noticed that you sent out some campaign literature a few days before Cindy died. Could she have gotten one of your envelopes?"

"Cindy and Annie helped me with the mailing. I addressed some of the envelopes myself, and my secretary did the rest, but the girls stuffed them and sealed them up."

So Cindy could easily have tucked in a message of her own—if she could be sure her note would get into the right hands. "Who were the mailings actually sent to? Were they addressed to specific individuals?"

"To heads of households," Godwin replied. "You can be a little more certain that someone will actually open a letter that has a real name on it."

Well, that would leave out David, even if he had been at home instead of who the hell knew where. "Could Cindy have gotten one of your business envelopes—an unused one?"

"Of course, there are plenty of them in my office at home." David was back in the running—if Cindy knew where to send a letter to him during his defection.

"Then all of the letters mailed out were addressed in either your handwriting or your secretary's?"

"I handwrote the ones I did. Barbara typed the addresses on."

"Did Cindy have access to a typewriter?"

"I have one in my office at home. So you think that Cindy might have used my stationery to arrange a meeting with someone who ended up killing her? If she went through all that subterfuge, it couldn't have been just an ordinary boy-friend. A married man do you think?" He removed his spectacles and rubbed his eyes. "She was so excited that morning, chattering a blue streak. I should have known no aunt could be responsible for that kind of enthusiasm. Pete says that she was all dressed up in my wife's clothes. Can you beat that? To meet some guy in the woods. She must have had such high hopes, and to think of what really happened…" He closed his eyes for a moment.

"The woman who found her was related to my late wife, you know. Although Nina never really knew her. She'd never even met of her until Mrs. Thorsen came into the library and introduced herself. After that she would stop to see Nina at work every now and then and talk a little, just say hello. That's about it. She sent a wedding gift. A jewelry chest that she'd made."

"Was it among the things you gave to Cindy? There was a small chest in her room."

"It's possible. I don't remember seeing it, but it could have been. I didn't look through the stuff to any extent. If it was it might be nice to have the chest back—for Annie, you know. I've heard Mrs. Thorsen's work is quite sought after. I thought that my wife had probably given it away herself."

"That would have been very unselfish of her." Or unfeeling.

"I never saw Nina use it. I figured it made her feel kind of guilty. She hadn't invited her aunt to the wedding."

Nina had, of course, found a use for the gift—to secrete her diaries, and McIntire remembered, the pearls. A gift from the Nordic god?

"I think Mia was actually her *cousin*," he informed the attorney. "But as you said, they hardly knew one another. Mia probably meant the gift as a peace offering. You know, a chance to bring the family together. She doesn't have much family left anymore."

Godwin busied himself straightening some papers on his desk. "Well, there were…other circumstances."

"Oh?"

"Maybe I shouldn't say anything, but my wife is beyond being hurt, and it still galls me when I think of it, and now you're telling me that Cindy was probably involved with some man…" His voice trailed off, and McIntire looked at him expectantly.

"Nina didn't know Mrs. Thorsen, but she was once quite...well acquainted with *Mr.* Thorsen, if you get my drift."

McIntire knew now how the publisher of the *Monitor* felt. He effected his own beached carp imitation.

"I first met my wife when she came to me—her mother brought her—to retain my professional services. She asked for my help in bringing suit against Nick Thorsen. A claim of bastardy. A paternity suit."

"A paternity suit? Your wife bore Nick Thorsen's child? But I never heard...Mia never mentioned..." It was a circumstance that McIntire could hardly grasp.

"Nina didn't come back after that first visit with her mother—didn't pursue the claim. She left town soon after, had the baby, and gave it up for adoption. I imagine she didn't want to face going to court, or maybe Thorsen paid her off. I never asked for the details."

So Nick Thorsen had a child...a child who'd lived while Mia's had died...a child whose mother was Mia's cousin! McIntire tried to focus his attention on the attorney's words.

"I certainly never blamed Nina. She was of legal age at the time, but still only a girl, and I guess we know how impressionable young girls can be." He brought a chubby fist down on the desk. "But, by God, I'd still like to wring that man's neck! Besides being married to her aunt, he must have been twenty years older than her at least. Believe me, I'm not looking forward to Annie's growing up. Do you have daughters?"

McIntire recovered enough to informed him that, happily, his daughters had been bestowed upon him fully grown, complete with husbands to do the worrying.

"But you can understand," Godwin went on, "that my wife didn't feel comfortable about getting on too friendly terms with Mrs. Thorsen."

The phone on the desk gave a short jangle. Godwin answered it with a terse "Yes?" and an, "Okay, put him on." The conversation with his caller was equally abbreviated, consisting of only, "Yes, that will be fine." He replaced the receiver on the hook with a thoughtful look. "That was Pete Koski. He's coming over now. Maybe he'll have some answers."

He stood up, an indication that he had fed his guest enough information, but McIntire had not quite supped his fill. He pushed Nina Godwin and Nick Thorsen to the back corners of his mind. "Miss Delaney seems to be under the impression that Nels intended to embark on some new financial venture," he said. "Would you happen to know anything about that?"

Godwin seemed to be weighing the wisdom of making any further disclosures. Then he replied breezily, "It was nothing definite." He'd had an offer from a firm in Chicago. He was thinking of either selling out or collaborating with them on a resort development.

"Well," he said as he ushered McIntire out the door, "I probably shouldn't have said anything about my late wife and your notorious mailman...but, like I say, it's always stuck in my craw. Anyway, it's all water under the bridge now."

XXVII

McIntire was beginning to doubt that the past ever flowed away under a bridge or any other structure. It just lay like a stagnant pool waiting for the chance to suck the present back into it. Little by little, the past was certainly lapping at the shores of his own complacent present.

Had Mia known about Nick and Nina Godwin? Not Godwin at that time—Everett, wasn't it? Could Mia have joked about Nina's Nordic god, knowing all the while that it could once have been her own husband? McIntire had to admit that she could have; Mia was good at joking, especially to conceal an unpleasant truth. But he found himself deeply saddened by the idea that she would put on such an act for *him*—saddened that she might have chosen to protect her husband of thirty-two years rather than spilling the beans to the jerk who jilted her. Sure. At least she hadn't accidentally thrown the diary into her workshop stove. But she had made that remark about his leaving this investigation to the "professionals." Was she afraid of what he might uncover? Well, Pete Koski could read, too, and would likely be every bit as "curious" about Nina Godwin's paramour as McIntire himself was.

No, the more he thought about it, the more certain he was that she couldn't possibly have known about Nick and Nina. She wouldn't have been chatting up Nina in the library and carving jewelry boxes, risking her nine remaining digits, for a woman who had borne her husband's child. Or would she? Mia was every bit as good at mockery as she was at deception. She might have gone out of her way to be kind to Nina just to grate on her conscience, rub a little salt in the wound. If what Godwin said about the chest making Nina feel guilty was true, it seemed to have worked. And there *had* been a definite note of self satisfaction in her voice when Mia mentioned attending Nina Godwin's funeral.

It struck him for the first time that this information might possibly be considered evidence—Evidence with a capital E, now that he thought of it. Was he going to have to go to the sheriff with this? Thankfully, that might not be necessary. Koski had the diaries—Cecil Newman had come for them on Thursday—and he was on his way to Godwin's office now. The subject was sure to come up. He would have no qualms about asking if Godwin knew of any man that his wife might have gotten involved with, and that would put Nick Thorsen next on the sheriff's list of candidates for "little chats." Sooner or later it was bound to all come out...and when it did Mia would realize that McIntire had known about it all along and had kept it from her.

Should he tell her now? Go to her like a meddling old biddy? No, of course not. Maybe she would never have to know. Maybe Godwin would be able to supply the sheriff with the name of the "Nordic god" himself. Nina's past involvement with Nick might not even be mentioned, it'd be just small potatoes. Godwin hadn't seemed to attach a great deal of importance to it. If he had, he probably would have kept it to himself. Why *had* he mentioned it, anyway? Maybe attorney confidence doesn't extend to dead wives. Well, it was long over and done with. Nina could pose no threat to Mia's marriage now. For Mia to learn about her husband's infidelities—and his child—at this late date would serve no purpose except to hurt her.

On the other hand, Mia had just been an "ear witness" to a vicious murder. She was in a dangerous position. That short in her lathe—Guibard had said she might have been killed. And, as Mia herself admitted, the murderer must be someone close to them all, someone they would never suspect. Could he in good conscience withhold any information from her?

The sound of a Mule Train clippity-clopping through his living room and out the open window told him that, for once, Leonie was spending the afternoon at home. Thank God for Leonie, who said exactly what she meant and let the chips fall where they may. If everybody was as forthright as his wife the world would be a much saner place. McIntire pushed aside the image of an emaciated young soldier cradling his infant sons, Graham and William—a dying man, secure in the belief that he was leaving robust twin sons to carry on his lineage. He stepped over Kelpie, and opened the door.

In addition to Frankie Laine, Leonie was accompanied by several bushels of red, white, and blue crepe paper, which she was fashioning into what looked like miniature patriotic cabbages. Apparently she had been at it for some time; her fingers looked as if she had slammed them in a car door. She was wearing the pensive, preoccupied expression that he had learned to dread. It started before he even had time to sit down. "Do you remember, John," she said, "before I agreed to move here, you made a promise to me?"

He had been expecting it, had even thought he might welcome it, but now that the time had actually come, he took a deep breath and launched into pleading as if for his very life.

"Oh, Leonie, please, you promised, too. You said two years. It's hardly even been one." Was it really possible that all that had transpired since his return had taken place in such a short time? He could hardly credit it. "It'll get better. When this murder stuff is over, we'll take another trip, west this time…to California, Texas. We can go to Washington and drive down the coast, or even go up into Canada if you want."

She looked at him as if she feared for his wits. "John, what the devil are you talking about?"

"Why?" he hedged. "What were you talking about?"

"A horse. You said we could have horses."

He was swamped in a flood of relief.

"I know you don't like horses," she hurried on, "but you wouldn't have to be bothered with them yourself."

McIntire didn't dislike horses. He loathed the evil beasts—loathed them, and they knew it, and returned the feeling in full measure. The proximity of John McIntire seemed to charge even the most docile plug with an irresistible desire to audition for a starring role in Buffalo Bill's Wild West Show. He had gone riding once with Leonie in Hyde Park. He was outfitted with the only horse in the stable tall enough to fit his lanky frame, an equally rangy mare seemingly old enough to have begun her professional career pulling an ice wagon through the streets of London.

The instant he mounted the sluggish creature, it had been transformed into a fire-breathing fiend whose only intent was to leave a healthy portion of its rider's skin on every tree in the park. Even Leonie had not laughed. Her face had remained uncharacteristically grave, and she actually seemed to have tears of sympathy in her eyes. Three days later she had finally broken down and dissolved in a fit of hilarity that was all the more violent for having been so strenuously restrained. He still felt the sting.

But if sharing his home with one of the diabolical brutes would keep Leonie in it, he was ready to make the sacrifice.

"I have nothing against horses, I just don't enjoy riding very much." Now he was doing it, too—lying through his teeth. It must be something in the water. "But you know," he added sympathetically, "it might not be that easy to find the kind of horse that you're used to around here—hunters, or thoroughbreds, or whatever..." *killers, widowmakers..*

"Oh, that's not a problem. Sally Ferguson's got a sister that raises quarterhorses in Wisconsin. She's going to take me to have a look at them. I'll be learning to ride western."

Of course, what else?

Leonie began packing her crepe paper creations into a large cardboard box. "You know, John," she said, "unlike some people, some even in this very room, I have never been under the impression that St. Adele, Michigan is the western hemisphere's answer to Shangri-la. If I should make up my mind not to stay here, it won't be because of the death of some girl I never met. People die in England too, in case you hadn't noticed." After a pause, she smiled. "But that holiday out west sounds like the best idea you've had in a long time."

She appeared to notice his own box and its contents for the first time. "What's all that?"

"Well, Leonie, you'll be happy to know that I've found gainful employment."

"As an accountant? That doesn't look like the usual assignment from your Uncle Sam."

"As a matter of fact, these *are* business records. They're written in Norwegian. I'm translating for Warner Godwin."

She looked at him with a hint of suspicion in her eyes. "And just whose business might they be records of?"

His admission of their source was greeted with a sigh. "Well, I hope you learn something that will help instead of just rattling more skeletons. The more you find out, the more upset you get....Incidentally, I've talked to Mark Guibard about it."

What? Were they planning to have him put away, too?

"About Mrs. Bertelsen, he's going to check up on her. Did he have a hand in getting her committed, do you know? I didn't like to ask, but he was here then, wasn't he?"

"I think he originally came from Duluth, but he's been around for a long time. In Chandler, that is. He didn't move to St. Adele until he retired from his full time practice. There were stories that he ended up here in the middle of nowhere because of some trouble he'd gotten into in Minnesota."

"What sort of trouble?"

"From what I recall, it had something to do with botching up a delivery. A birth, I mean. He'd been at a party and had been drinking, or so the story went. Ma would probably remember more. Maybe it's true. From what I know of it, he's been a strict teetotaler since he's been here. But, I don't know if he was the doctor that declared Tina Bertelsen insane...somebody had to have done it."

McIntire wondered if he should tell Leonie about Nick and his romance with Nina Godwin. Maybe she could advise him on what he should do. Somehow he wasn't quite able to bring himself to mention it. She was right. The more he probed, the more information he uncovered that he really would rather not have known.

But he would let Pete Koski know about Mia's close call with her lathe.

XXVIII

Although it was Sunday afternoon, McIntire left the seductive fly rod in the closet, parked himself at the dining room table with a pot of coffee near his right hand, and prepared to tuck into a large helping of the Bertelsen business accounts.

Instead of accompanying her to church that morning, he had abandoned Leonie to the inevitable onslaught of questions and spent the time driving slowly along the roads, stopping now and then to explore a swaybacked, derelict building or investigate a suspicious area of exposed earth.

After four days spent grilling David Slocum, Warner Godwin, Earl Culver, Lucy Delaney, Mark Guibard, and a few of Cindy Culver's high school friends, the state detectives had left town, taking with them a half-dozen confiscated bottles of Black Leaf 40, and vowing to return after the Fourth of July holiday. Mr. Mowsers had followed suit, voicing his belief that the body had either been taken out of the county or was in the lake, in which case it would probably turn up in the late fall or the next spring, when the change in water temperature would cause the lake to turn over.

McIntire still clung stubbornly to his belief that Cindy's body had not been taken far.

It was obvious that it had also not been left in the open— even if the dogs hadn't found it, a gathering of hungry crows and turkey vultures would have betrayed its presence. That left burial, burning, or simply concealing it somewhere. But where? A forgotten well or unused root cellar? The trunk of an abandoned car? Koski had given him a tepid warning about snooping into private property without a warrant, but the junked cars, half hidden by weeds and brush, that ornamented the majority of homesteads were a tempting target. He would have loved to pop the hubcaps off Nick Thorsen's Dodge to check for evidence of a recent tire change, but neither Nick nor Mia were among those who could be expected to be safely tucked out of the way in church.

The phrase "root cellar" popped into his mind again, and he aimed the Studebaker down the narrow road that led to the old Makinen place. The Makinens had left St. Adele in 1932, part of a large contingent of Socialist Finns from the United States to emigrate to the Soviet province of Karelia. Whether they found the workers' paradise that they expected was unknown. The Makinens, like many of their fellow emigrés, had not been heard from again.

McIntire turned into the end of the driveway, two dim parallel tracks separated by a growth of timothy and foxtails. He stopped the car, took his flashlight from the glove compartment, and stepped out into knee high grass. The house was gone—it now served as the south wing of the Culver home—but overgrown lilacs still showed where its dooryard had been. He walked under a trio of twisted apple trees and across to the barn. The double doors stood slightly open. McIntire widened the gap only enough to allow him to slip inside the single unpartitioned space. For the last few years it had been used by Sulo Touminen to store the hay he cut off the Makinen's abandoned fields. It was empty now, but McIntire methodically crisscrossed its earthen floor, scuffling his feet and raising a cloud of dust as he walked. He found no evidence of digging, and stepped outside regretting that he'd permeated his socks with hayseeds to no good purpose.

At the far end of a weedy clearing—potato patch, probably—the earthen berm that marked the root cellar swelled out of a low hillside.

The thick slab door still hung solid on its hinges. McIntire swung it open to expose the short tunnel leading to the storage space deep inside. McIntire knew what awaited him. A door at the far end of the tunnel, and a third one bisecting it through the middle would divide its length into a pair of two-foot-by-three-foot chambers. The accepted protocol was to close one door before passing through the next, in order to keep warm air from entering the root cellar proper.

Protecting carrots and cabbages was not a priority now, and McIntire had no intention of sealing himself inside the manmade cavern or its iron-maiden antechambers. He kicked a pile of soil against the open door to keep it that way. He switched on his flashlight, ducked inside, and passed through the next two portals, securing their doors in similar fashion, and giving each a hefty thump to warn any possible inhabitants of his approach.

The interior was not only cool, it was cold, and smelled, as was to be expected, of earth. Shelves lined the back wall. A small wooden keg lay on its side near his feet. The beam of his light reflected a silvery coating of frost where the walls met the dirt floor. The shelves sat empty but for a lumpy burlap bag. Livid white tentacles erupted through its rotted fibers, groping and intertwining like a nest of light-deprived vipers. A sack of forgotten potatoes, making one last bid for life. Sulo had apparently also made use of the cellar in the past year or two.

As he bent his head to back out through the narrow passage, the sunlight coming through the open door was suddenly eclipsed. He whirled, losing his grip on the flashlight and striking his head on the low lintel. Sandra Culver stood at the entrance to the tunnel.

"I saw your car," she said. "I thought maybe...you haven't heard something?"

McIntire fumbled for the light and waited for the ringing in his ears to fade before responding. "No, I was just looking around."

In the week since her daughter's disappearance Sandra Culver had grown thin to the point of gauntness. Grim desperation had etched every vestige of grace from her features. The burnished cap of hair was now an oily helmet clinging to her skull. She was soaked to the knees, and her neck and the backs of her hands were raw with insect bites.

"There's nothing here," he added.

She turned her amber eyes to his with a long look that was half searching, half pleading. "I thought I was doing what was best for her, letting her go where she'd have things nicer, where she'd find out that there could be more to life than grubbing in the dirt and having babies."

McIntire put his hand on her shoulder. "You *did* do what was best. Your daughter had a good life, and she was doing a wonderful job of caring for Annie Godwin. You're not responsible for the act of some psychotic maniac any more than you could be blamed if she'd been struck by lightning."

She bit her lower lip and blinked rapidly. Then with a grave "Thank you" she put her hands in the pockets of her too-large barn jacket and stalked off across the fields.

He probably should go after her, try to get her into the car and take her home or to his own house. Leonie would take care of her. She couldn't be doing those seven other kids much good, the shape she was in. He watched until she disappeared into the trees. Better to let her go on with her search. Who was to say that guzzling tea with Leonie would better help to assuage her grief—or her guilt. Maybe tramping around in the woods was all that was holding her together.

McIntire closed up the root cellar and left the Makinen place to its ghosts.

He had stopped at the store, informed Elsie that there was nothing new to report, and received her information that Lucy had come in at least an hour and a half later than usual on the morning of Cindy's death. After purchasing a copy of the *Marquette Miner* and two packs of Walnettos, he drove home.

Immediately after her own return, Leonie had collected shovel and broom, hammer and crowbar, and gone off to render the old barn fit for its prospective tenant. The sound of her enthusiastic singing—wondering why someone "didn't love her like they used to do," and were, in fact, "treating her like a worn out shoe"—waxed and waned as she wheeled load after load of ancient straw and manure out the door and into the barnyard. Leonie might fancy herself the expert on horses, but McIntire could have told her a thing or two about cows. Most particularly that she could get down on her hands and knees with a toothbrush and Lysol, but she was never going to rid that barn of the odor of cow manure, a redolence that would soak into every pore of her being within minutes of entering its vicinity. Well, she'd find out for herself soon enough.

He opened the first of the ledgers. The ruled columns with their red and blue lines had been ignored in favor of scratching down whatever seemed to be uppermost in the writer's mind at the time—the writer most usually being Ole Bertelsen, although an entry in his wife's handwriting appeared now and again.

An hour and a half later McIntire had worked his way through 1909. Warner Godwin had not been far wrong; daily details of weather and not a few recipes did make up the bulk of the entries. Most of the financial recordings pertained to expenses. It would be years before the Bertelsens realized any profit from their enterprise. They received a few dollars each year from the sale of potatoes to a logging company, and Ole had spent the winter of 1908 cutting timber for that same company. For the most part they had lived frugally on Tina's small inheritance.

McIntire carefully recorded what little he felt was of importance: the letters from Norway awarding the estate of Sigrid Guttormsdatter to her only surviving child, Christina Bertelsen, née Bjornsdatter; the price paid for the farmland; the purchase of a team of oxen. On a separate piece of paper he jotted down instructions for a mosquito repellant, an unlikely concoction of vanilla and turpentine.

The occasional protesting screech of a nail being ruthlessly yanked from its longtime bed told him that his wife's efforts had passed the mucking out stage and moved into active remodeling. He carried the coffee pot to the kitchen range and stood staring out the window while he waited for the brew to reheat. Then he poured another cup and returned to wade into 1910.

In September of that year Ole and Christina had acquired another forty acres of land, the property on the lakeshore where the fish house and dock now stood. Late 1912 saw the loss of their only daughter, Julie. The following spring the first of their trees bore fruit.

Inserted between the pages of the subsequent ledger was a certificate, written in more or less plain English, stating that the Honorable Ira Sandhurst, Judge of the Probate Court of the County of Flambeau, in the State of Michigan, after a full investigation of the matter, including filing the certificates of two legally qualified physicians, was granting the petition of Olaf Bertelsen praying that Christina Bertelsen be ordered admitted to the State Asylum for the Insane as a public patient.

The Honorable Ira further ordered that Olaf Bertelsen be appointed to transport said Christina Bertelsen to the above mentioned institution and receive as pay for such services the sum of three dollars per day, together with his necessary expenses—another small amount to enter in the short column representing income not derived from his wife's inheritance, if Ole had kept track of such things.

Leonie had left off her mournful serenade and was talking with someone. McIntire stopped reading and listened. The visitor was female and was speaking in low urgent tones that told him that some crisis had no doubt arisen to throw a monkey wrench into the July Fourth plans. A minute later the kitchen door opened, and Leonie appeared with Mia Thorsen. Mia was in a state of rare animation. Her eyes glittered, and her face was uncharacteristically flushed.

"Mia would like to speak with you, John," Leonie announced. She turned to Mia. "I'm afraid I'm not in any fit state to be serving refreshments, but perhaps John might make you some tea?" Mia shook her head. Leonie, from her position behind their guest, gave a brief lift of her eyebrows and her shoulders and excused herself to return to her box stall.

Mia waved away his gesture toward the coffee pot and gripped the back of a chair. "The state police were out yesterday. They looked around the studio, and they took my fingerprints so they could tell if there were anybody else's on my power tools. Was it you that told them?"

"I told Pete Koski. I was worried about you, Mia. Wires don't just spontaneously pop loose, and anybody could get into your workshop, goose patrol notwithstanding."

He stood up and pulled out a chair. She ignored it.

"The sheriff came. He's taken Nick in."

McIntire had expected that Nick would be questioned again, but was that what Mia was getting at? "What do you mean, taken in?"

"He called this morning and told Nick to get into his office, that he—let's see, how did he put it?— 'needed some information from him.' Nick told him that he drives over five hundred miles a week and he's not about to do it on his day off, so if Koski wanted to talk, he could come to him. Pete sent that scrawny little deputy out, and he took Nick back to the sheriff's office. But first he spent a long time looking over Nick's car."

"Do you mean he's *arrested* Nick?"

"Arrested him? What are you talking about? Of course he hasn't arrested him. Why do you ask that? Arrested him for what?"

"Mia, settle down a minute. What did the sheriff actually say?"

"He said he wanted to ask him some questions, and Nick could come in on his own or he'd have to take him in. He didn't say Nick was under arrest...maybe it amounts to the same thing. What does he want? Has he told you?"

"Pete hasn't said anything to me about it. Nick will probably be back pretty soon. He'll be the one to tell you what it's all about."

"John, Nick won't be able to tell me anything. He can't handle something like this by himself." Her stained fingernails dug into the chair. "If it's something about Nick's *car*...when he's drinking he doesn't always...sometimes he forgets what happens. I have to know what's going on. What does the sheriff think Nick can tell him?"

McIntire opened his mouth to deny any knowledge of what Koski had in mind, but stopped himself. Mia would soon find out he was lying. She was right, she would have to be the one to take charge, and she deserved to have information, no matter how upsetting it might be. Good old Nick, he surely must be enough of a child for any woman. He felt a surge of the most intense dislike for the petty, strutting banty rooster. Afterward he wondered how much that revulsion influenced his decision.

McIntire closed the ledger and patted the chair. "Mia, sit down."

She sat without taking her eyes from his face.

"Mia, I don't know for sure, but I think Pete might have heard something from Warner Godwin. It might be something unimportant, but he's bound to check on every single thing."

"Heard what? What could Warner Godwin say about Nick? As far as I know, they've never met."

"Warner doesn't know Nick, but he says that Nina did."

"I suppose she did. Nina's father owned a garage up on Forty-one where Nick used to take his car. Nina helped out there sometimes." Mia's face turned from rosy to ashen as his meaning became clear to her. "Please don't try to tell me that this Nordic god business…"

"No, not that Nick was the man in Nina's diaries. This was something that happened a long time ago, before Warner met her. She was very young." That wasn't helping. He should never have brought this up, never have said anything. "Warner doesn't claim that they…. He doesn't know how far things went," he lied.

"Nick doesn't do anything halfway, you know that." She looked at him with disbelief. "Warner Godwin *told* you this?"

McIntire nodded.

"That my husband had something going with his wife, my own cousin?"

"That's what Warner *thinks*. Maybe he's wrong." What a tangled web he wove. "She wasn't his wife then, and Nick probably didn't know then that Nina was your cousin. Nina didn't."

She put her forehead in her hands for a long minute. When she raised her head again, her look of bewilderment was replaced by one of anger. "And you're telling me this for my own good no doubt."

"Would you rather have heard it from the sheriff?"

She stood and walked to the doorway, where she turned to face him. Her fury was palpable. "Yes, John, believe it or not, I would rather have heard it from the sheriff. I would rather have read it in the *New York Times*. You are the last person on this earth I would have wanted to hear it from! Didn't you humiliate me enough thirty years ago? You have to find some way to do it again? You left me. You left all of us. What gives you the right to come interfering into our lives now, into *my* life?" Her wrath faded and her mouth was set in a firm line.

"You know Nick is all I have left," she said. "I'm not going to let you take him away from me, too." Her voice had a bitter edge. "Why couldn't you have stayed away? Why didn't you just stay dead?"

XXIX

When McIntire awoke on July Fourth, only the muffled rustling made by Leonie as she dressed told him that it was indeed morning. It was impossible to guess the time. The room was almost as dark as night, due partly to drawn curtains, but mainly because of the heavy blankets that had been draped over their rods, placed there for McIntire's comfort.

He had been typing industriously the previous afternoon, chronicling the day in 1924 that Ole Bertelsen had acquired twenty more acres of land, when the sudden disappearance of his right thumb and the keys f, g, and r had put him in the all too familiar grip of panic at the knowledge that the next thirty-six hours of his life would be lost to him.

He had suffered from occasional migraines since he was a child, and although his brain told him it would pass with no lasting ill effects, the end-of-the-world terror he felt when the malady struck never dimmed. He had crawled to his bed and remained there, leaving it only to relieve himself of his breakfast and lunch, and a good-sized portion of his vital organs, it seemed.

Leonie had returned from her last-minute Independence Day preparations in the late afternoon. After draping the windows and offering him tea, she had sensibly left him alone. Sometime in the waning hours of the evening she had come to him and inquired as to whether she might be of help by getting his blood flowing to some part of his body other than his brain. At his answering groan, she had toddled off to sleep in the guest room, leaving her husband to lie awake through the long night, listening while the cacophony of the frog recital faded away to a dead stillness broken only once by a far off train whistle.

After what seemed like an eon, the raucous voices of crows stirring in the spruce trees outside the window told him that dawn was approaching. A light rain began to fall, its whisper blotted out pain, and at last he had slept.

Leonie finished dressing and, seeing him awake, tiptoed to the bedside. "Are you feeling any better?"

"Not much," was his feeble answer. "What time is it?"

"About ten. I'll be on my way in a bit. It's raining a little. We're going to have to set things up indoors. Can I get you something to eat before I leave?"

McIntire's insides gave a lurch. "I don't think I'm ready to eat quite yet," he said.

"Well, I'll leave you some tea in a thermos. Be sure you drink it *before* you get out of bed."

"Please make it coffee, Leonie. As a matter of fact, maybe I could drink a little right now."

Leonie hustled down the stairs and reappeared shortly carrying a tray laden with a steaming cup, a dented red thermos, and a plate upon which rested two of those carbonized slices that the British call toast, accompanied by a minuscule pat of butter. She placed the tray on the bedside table and smoothed the blanket over his chest. A hat decorated with tiny red, white, and blue ribbons was positioned at a jaunty angle on her yellow curls.

"Jenny Wakefield is picking me up, so the car will be here if you feel well enough to come to town later." She put an arm under his shoulders and eased a pillow under him. "It's going to be awkward, you know, your not being there."

"I know, I'm expected to pin on my badge and make sure the revelries don't get out of hand. If the picnic degenerates into an orgy, call me. I'd arise from the dead to see Inge Lindstrom performing the Dance of the Seven Veils. Anything less and folks will just have to be on the honor system."

"Nobody's going to believe you're really sick. Most likely they'll figure you're taking the opportunity to spade up their turnip patches looking for bodies, while they're all safely out of the way eating ham and baked beans."

The words were hardly out of her mouth when her smile disappeared, and she sat down on the bed with a thump that sent her husband's stomach pitching northward. "Oh dear, there's nothing funny about this. That poor child! And that poor woman, knowing her daughter is lying somewhere out there in the—" her lamentations were interrupted by the sound of a car horn, and a slightly subdued Leonie left the room, closing the door quietly behind her.

McIntire sat back against the pillows and closed his eyes, breathing deeply and letting his body adjust itself to the more upright position. After a minute, he reached for the cup of rapidly cooling coffee. He took a single swallow and set the cup back on the table, slopping a dollop of its contents into the saucer in the process. He felt exhaustion, helplessness, and self-pity. Leonie might have been joking but, as usual, she could have read his mind. With most everybody from miles around in town, he really would have had the freedom to explore the more private areas of the neighborhood…and likely get torn apart by dogs in the process, he admitted.

More importantly, the murderer himself might be planning to use the deserted countryside to his advantage to destroy evidence, maybe better conceal the body, or even move it, if he'd just temporarily hidden it somewhere. Although why any of that should be necessary McIntire couldn't imagine. Cindy Culver had effectively disappeared off the face of the earth. Still, it would be interesting to see which of the township's residents attended the picnic, and for how long.

He might also have been able to watch for unusual behavior. He couldn't imagine that even the most cold-blooded of slayers could conduct himself in a completely normal fashion with his victims' families across the room, or across the table. Koski would be likely to put in an appearance, if only because this was an election year. But he would be making the rounds of the various gatherings in the county; he wouldn't be able to stay long. Well, it couldn't be helped. McIntire could take no action today, at least not for hours. Like Hercule Poirot he would have to resort to the use of his little gray cells. *Zee little gray cells, zay have zee great pain,* McIntire said aloud.

He dozed off again and awoke with no idea of how much time had passed. The coffee in the cup was cold and the room seemed a shade or two brighter. He fumbled to find his glasses. The dark blob on the bedside table was resolved into the familiar alarm clock. Twelve-fifteen. He eyed the browned and curling bread. He wasn't that hungry yet.

After hitching himself up a bit higher on the pillows, he screwed the top off the thermos and took a tentative sip, then, satisfied that the liquid was not hot enough to cause major damage, a larger gulp. Maybe his brain cells could function after all.

It was almost a certainty that the murderer was a member of the immediate community, or possibly of Chandler. It had to be someone who knew Nels well enough to have reason to want him dead, and someone with whom Cindy Culver was adequately acquainted to send her into spasms of ecstasy when he wrote requesting her to meet him—or agreeing to *her* request that they meet.

One question that he hadn't entertained was that of *why* the body had been taken away. Unless the murderer had been aware of Mia's presence, he should have believed that Cindy's disappearance wouldn't even be noticed until that evening when she didn't return to Godwin's. That would give him more than twelve hours to get well away from the scene. He might have hidden the body to try to delay the discovery of the girl's death, thinking that it would appear that she had run away. That wouldn't have bought much extra time. As far as they knew, Cindy hadn't taken anything with her to indicate that she planned to be gone overnight, and she wasn't invisible on that train. Her destination was well known.

After the killing, the murderer either left immediately and then shortly returned for the body and the belongings, or he heard Mia descending the jump and hid until she left. Mia hadn't started down until after she heard someone walking away, but she wouldn't have been able to tell how far that person had gone. If the killer knew that someone—Mia—had already seen the body, he didn't remove it just to conceal the fact that a murder had been committed. But then why? Was there some mark stamped on Cindy's body that would have pointed to her slayer?

McIntire poured more coffee and flipped his pillow over to its cool side. He remained still for a few moments before drinking.

The killer had a vehicle nearby—probably hidden, another point in favor of a local culprit, or at least someone familiar with the back roads of the area. The body had been carried to the vehicle. There were no signs of anything being dragged through the woods. It was a point for the killer being male or an unusually strong woman. Cindy was petite, but even a small body would be difficult to carry, and, if she had been taken out through the gravel pit, the job was accomplished quickly. Guibard parked there shortly after seven o'clock.

The murderer was also someone whose presence on the roads in the early morning hours would not be seen as unusual. McIntire reluctantly came back to Nick. He knew that any suspicions he had about Nick Thorsen were likely to be colored by his personal feelings, although the antipathy he felt for the mailman was balanced by a sincere desire not to give further injury to Mia—regardless of what she might believe.

There was no denying that Nick had the opportunity. He could easily have made a quick loop through the trees, followed Cindy into the woods, and killed her. If he had heard a noise on the jump he would have known immediately that it was Mia on one of her early morning explorations and could have hidden until she left. He was really the only person to fit this possibility, since if the murderer knew Mia was on the jump, he would naturally suppose that she had seen what happened. If it was anyone other than Nick, Mia would have been the next victim. McIntire couldn't believe that Nick would directly harm Mia under any circumstances.

And, try as he might to ignore it, if the blackmail theory was the correct one, Nick Thorsen would fit neatly into that picture, too. But would he commit murder to keep Mia from finding out about a romance that, if rumors were to be believed, was only one of several? Well, an affair was one thing, a child was another—not something Mia would so easily forgive. Did Nick himself even know about the pregnancy? Godwin had said that he might have paid Nina off. If it had been that easy, why not just do the same with Cindy, and take the diary?

Did Nick hate Nels bad enough to kill him? He was out late the night before Nels died, and if he hadn't drunk enough to affect his judgment it would be the first time. The tavern was less than a half-mile from Bertelsen's dock. McIntire could see him planting the bees as a spur of the moment prank. But Nels' death was not the result of a prank. The killer had planned it months in advance and had gotten into his house at least twice: to take one vial of adrenaline and replace its contents with bug killer, and later to switch it with his new one. And getting into Bertelsen's house had been made significantly easier by the demise of the wheel-chasing Truman.

But *was* Cindy blackmailing somebody over the love affair? She had known about the Nordic god for months. It was hearing of the death of Nels Bertelsen that got her onto that train.

So who else was known to be out that morning? Lucy? According to Elsie Karvonen, Lucy had not made her appearance until about nine o'clock. She'd have had plenty of time to throttle Cindy, stuff her body into the trunk of Nels' car, and stroll out onto the road where she was seen by Wylie. But if she'd hidden the car in the gravel pit, she'd gotten it out before the doctor parked there about seven-fifteen, and Wylie said she was back home about that time—on foot.

Lucy's harsh voice could be mistaken for a man's, but Mia said the person she believed to be male had only spoken a few words. That didn't sound like Lucy. And it was hard to picture Cindy going into raptures over a summons from her. Lucy *had* started into town that morning. She was out there when Wylie offered her a ride, which she had refused for the feeblest of reasons.

Lucy could easily have been responsible for *Nels'* death. With Christina Bertelsen still living, she probably wouldn't profit from it, but she might not have known that.

Wylie Petworth, of course, since he generally drove a pickup truck, would have the best means of driving off the maintained roads to conceal his presence. Wylie knew the woods for miles around as well as he knew his own cabbage fields and could have gotten the body out with efficiency. But would he have offered Lucy a ride if he had a body in his truck? And, assuming that Cindy was killed to hush up what she knew about Nels' death, Wylie had no motive that McIntire could see. Nels and Wylie didn't always get along, but two people who are that close seldom do. Of course you never know what might have gone on between them through the years, but Wylie would be the last person to profit from Nels' death, especially since Nels' mother was still alive. By the time everything was laid out on the table and the attorneys had finished picking the bones, Wylie could wave that orchard and its income goodbye.

McIntire would bet that if anybody outside the family knew that the old lady was still alive, Wylie did. He'd had the Bertelsen financial records for years, and you didn't have to be able to read Norwegian to see that they contained no documents relating to the death of one of the farm's owners. Wylie could have had hopes of buying the property after the dust settled, but that would be taking a chance that somebody with deeper pockets and a closer relationship to Warner Godwin or his colleagues didn't come along. Not to mention that some shirt-tail kin could turn up and lay claim to the whole ball of wax.

What about Warner Godwin? He surely wouldn't want his late wife's infidelities to become common knowledge. Although he had chirped right up about her pre-marital shenanigans. Why? To throw suspicion into another quarter? Godwin knew where Cindy was going and when. He could have followed her, killed her, and driven through the hills to Marquette, disposing of the body on the way. The roads through the mountains weren't that good and would have been especially tricky after all the rain the night before, but they were probably passable, and Godwin had that Jeep that Koski envied so much. That route was less distance than the main roads, but it might have taken longer time-wise. Still he could easily have made it. His dentist appointment wasn't until ten-thirty. Cindy might have snooped around and come across some unsavory information concerning her employer and Bertelsen.

Or maybe her death had nothing to do with Nels Bertelsen after all. Maybe she was fleeing Godwin for some reason...all dressed up in his dead wife's clothes, and heading straight for the woods, giggling her head off when she meets him. Hardly likely—even if Godwin could have pulled it off without being spotted or having a coronary trying to move the body.

That left David. McIntire swallowed the last of the coffee and spread one of the pieces of toast with butter. He raised it to his lips, then sighed and returned it to the plate.

Something about David was definitely disturbing, something almost eerie, but oddly familiar. His outward surliness and defiance seemed to have no real target, as if he had already been defeated by life and was just getting in a few last shots at the world in general.

There was no getting around it, the evidence, what there was of it, pointed to David. He had at least as much motive for killing Nels Bertelsen as any of the others, and he had obviously lied about being in touch with Cindy. If her letters were any indication, she'd have gone readily to meet him. He had the best chance of getting her off into the woods and under that ski jump. The idea of an adult male arranging to meet a woman in the bush still didn't sit well, although such an assignation might have seemed irresistibly romantic to a girl like Cindy.

Cindy's appearance would indicate that she was heading off for a lovers' tryst, not a blackmail payoff, although the latter couldn't be ruled out. She might have dressed up and worn the makeup to make herself appear older and more confident, but would she have done that for David's benefit? What's more, if she was only going to meet David for a little roll in the ferns, why would she have brought Nina's diary? To convince him to conspire in the blackmail? But why wouldn't he say so? Why was he not talking, unless to protect himself? Nothing he said could hurt Cindy now.

And where in hell *was* he before he stranded himself at that camp? Where would a seventeen-year-old boy with no money to speak of disappear to without telling a soul? What might have happened to suddenly send him off in a cloud of dust? He disappeared after helping with the funeral preparations. So what could have triggered his leaving? Guilt? Did cleaning up Nels' trash and chauffeuring his old "army buddy" bring home to him the realization that he had committed an abominable crime? Lucy told him that David had spent most of the afternoon mesmerized by Captain Paulson's war stories. Did the tales of Nels' military heroism bring on an attack of remorse…or possibly plant some other notions? McIntire recalled his own hasty departure from St. Adele in the spring of his seventeenth year. If the captain's stories had seduced David into making a similar flight, given him a yen to visit Korea, perhaps, there was only one likely place he would have gone—and a wrong turn on a shortcut home could easily have landed him in that cabin.

McIntire pulled himself all the way up into a sitting position and swung his legs over the side of the bed. It was worth a shot, anyway. In a few agonizing minutes he was in the kitchen, standing weak-kneed by the telephone with a slightly sour-smelling dish towel thrown over his head to shield his eyes from the light. He cranked the phone with as much briskness as he could muster.

"I need to reach the army recruiter in Marquette," he told the operator—Jeannie Goodrow again. "This is something of an emergency. I know it's a holiday, but please see if you can find out who it is and try his home number. If you can't get the officer in charge, I'd appreciate talking to anybody who works in the office. Do the best you can." He hung up, dropped into a chair at the table and, with his head on his folded arms, let himself be submersed in blankness until time again lost its meaning.

The phone jangled and he found himself speaking to Sergeant Sam Kolquist against a background of slamming doors and boisterous children. Roses were in order for Miss Goodrow.

"This is Warrant Officer John McIntire, retired. I'm in law enforcement now, Flambeau County." No need to go into too many details. A township constable might not fit the sergeant's definition of law enforcement. "I'm sorry to bother you on a holiday, but, as you've probably heard, we're investigating a murder here. We're trying to trace the movements of a young man from the area, and we have reason to believe that he may have been in your office sometime around June nineteenth. If he was, I think you'd remember him." McIntire was amazed that his voice could sound so normal, coming, as it was, from a man near death.

Sergeant Kolquist did indeed recognize David from McIntire's description. "I couldn't say exactly what day it was, but yeah, he was in sometime that week. I thought the whole thing seemed kind of funny at the time. So he was running from the law, was he?"

"Not exactly, at least not then." McIntire suddenly thought of something. "David is only seventeen, did he have any kind of consent signed by his mother?"

"No. He was truthful about his age, but he said he'd get a signature after we were done. Of course, there's no question of that now."

McIntire wondered what the recruiter could have heard. "Why do you say that?"

"Well, of course we weren't able to accept him."

McIntire held his breath as a hot knife passed through his left eye. "Not accepted, but he's…are you saying he has some physical problem or some illness?" The poor kid, no wonder he'd been behaving oddly.

"Mr. McIntire," the voice on the line bristled, "you should know we have certain standards. Standards of mental ability. You probably also know that those standards are not particularly high, but I'm afraid they're well out of the reach of your young man."

"You mean he's…"

"To put it gently," Kolquist said, "feeble minded. Not that we got so far as actually testing him. There was no point. He couldn't even begin to understand the enlistment forms let alone fill them out. A real shame. He was in great physical shape too."

"Tell me this," McIntire asked before he hung up, "could he read and write at all?"

"He could sign his name, but not much more."

McIntire replaced the earpiece on its hook and climbed the stairs, gripping the handrail and stepping softly. Only when his head was once again motionless on the pillows did he allow himself to concentrate fully on what he had just heard. So David was telling the truth when he claimed not to have written to Cindy. Whoever she heard from on the Saturday before her death, it wasn't David Slocum, unless he got somebody else to write the letter for him. Cindy wouldn't have known the difference. She obviously wasn't aware of David's illiteracy. Who would David trust enough to ask to write such a letter? Even his own family seemed to have no inkling of his problems. His mother must have believed David could read the letters he was getting from her older son—and the ones she thought were from him. On the other hand, a letter to Cindy only *purporting* to be from David would have served two purposes, to get Cindy back to St. Adele, and to throw suspicion on her boyfriend.

Poor David. It explained so much. Maybe even his irregular working hours. Dorothy had mentioned that he needed her to remind him when he had to be somewhere at a certain time. Maybe the kid couldn't even read a clock. McIntire identified the source of the twinge of familiarity that David had evoked, the vicar's dull-witted son who came to cut the grass and rake up the leaves at the home of Leonie's sister at St. Mary in the Marsh. But Tommy Alworth had found a place in a community of people who understood and accepted him. David Slocum carried his burden alone. Well, David would likely be well advised to borrow a page from the vicar's boy and keep honing his skills with rake and spade.

McIntire groaned aloud as the image of a tree with bulbous roots, dropping into a gaping hole, flashed into his mind. "Oh God. No. It couldn't be. Right in front of us?" He spoke to the darkened room. "Nobody could be *that* stupid…or that imperturbable."

He hoisted himself to his feet once more, and, fighting back waves of nausea, dressed quickly. He picked up both pieces of toast and, putting them together sandwich fashion, took a heroically large bite, chewing as he went down the stairs. It was like swallowing sawdust and brought tears to his eyes. Before going out the door he donned his raincoat— the London-style trench coat that never failed to evoke a few snickers from his neighbors—and pulled his fedora low on his brow. When he caught sight of himself in the mirror by the kitchen door, even he had to smile at the picture he made. All that was needed was a lamp post and a little fog. Kelpie gave two sympathetic thumps with her stub of tail as he went out the door, but did not open her eyes.

XXX

The drive to the orchard was torturous. The growl and vibration of the engine served to screw the vise gripping his temples a notch tighter with each passing mile. Even on this cloud-wrapped day, the light sent his own personal Independence Day fireworks exploding before his eyes, and he pulled the hat even lower until he could see nothing but a few yards of the gravel road beyond the car's hood.

The Bertelsen homestead was deserted and looked more barren than ever in the mizzle. The door to the summer kitchen was now left unlocked and McIntire scanned the assortment of tools at his disposal. He picked up the thin-bladed spade that he had seen David wield with such gusto, then replaced it and chose instead a device intended for the digging of holes in which to set fence posts. Before leaving he noticed a conspicuously empty space on the formerly crowded shelf of handy household poisons.

He shouldered his implement and plodded up the hill, keeping his eyes on his feet except for the occasional quick glance upward to check on his progress.

He studied the two rows of saplings with increasing despondency. There were upwards of twenty newly planted trees with nothing to distinguish one from its sisters. No wilting leaves or greater amount of soil piled around a spindly trunk gave telltale evidence that a particular individual might have an occupant in its basement. He lifted the post-hole digger in both hands and approached the tree that geography told him might be the first to have been planted. Boring straight down on the outside of the burlap-wrapped rootball, he dug until he encountered the firm soil that marked the bottom of the excavation. He examined the mass of roots, probed gently under the burlap. He moved to the next tree and then the next, grasping the digger by its twin handles and slamming its curved blades into the earth, spreading the handles apart and lifting the captured soil to drop it on the grass. Every stab of the implement sent a fireball rocketing between his eyes and out the top of his skull.

He had explored the roots of over half of the young trees and was beginning to feel slightly foolish and decidedly sicker, as well as increasingly apprehensive about this vandalism, when his invasion produced, not the sight of shredded burlap, but one of bare roots snaking through the earth. McIntire placed his palms over the rounded ends of the handles and rested his forehead against his knuckles.

He stood that way for a full minute, then raised his head, wiped the sweat from his eyes with the end of his sleeve, braced his feet, and brought the instrument down a final time. The blades scraped through earth and struck an object from which it elicited a muffled thud that sent a sickening shudder up the handles. McIntire gently lifted out the dirt and added it to the small pile collecting on the grass. Crumbs of soil drifted down into the hole, landing on a tangle of dirty silk and pale, mud-encrusted hair. McIntire turned and, bending double, deposited his coffee and toast alongside the excavated soil.

XXXI

By midafternoon the St. Adele town hall was buzzing with activity. The intermittent rain, which in other years might have kept away all but the truly patriotic and those who would be seeking their vote that fall, had produced no ill effect on the turnout. The community was now drawn together by the common tragedy and a healthy sense of curiosity. The weather had driven most of the festivities indoors, and the hall was filled with the smell of tobacco smoke and baked ham, and the buzz of sundry conversations. Only the older children and adolescents ventured out to play a ragged brand of softball on the waterlogged field or to indulge in the furtive sharing of a handmade cigarette in the lee of the woodshed. In this latter they were not so different from their fathers, who stepped out occasionally into the drizzle for a "breath of air" and a quick nip from a common bottle.

The program had started at one o'clock and played to a packed house. It opened with a shaky-voiced high school student's reading of the Declaration of Independence and wound up with a patriotic medley by St. Adele's own barber-shop quartet. Hard on the heels of the final strains of a rousing rendition of *Yankee Doodle Dandy*, the pot luck dinner had been served, and now the party was in full swing.

Mia Thorsen sat with a group of women enjoying the brief respite that fell between the serving and the cleaning up. She sipped coffee heavily laced with cream and gave half an ear to the conversation around her. With few exceptions, that discussion consisted of one topic only, and the presence of the Culver family necessitated that it be conducted in a muted fashion. A couple of the younger members of the bereaved brood had joined their companions outdoors, but the main part of the clutch sat with their parents and toddler sibling, all of them silently watching the gathering as if momentarily expecting the appearance of a neighbor with a large red "M" stitched to his chest.

Mia, like most of those present, had screwed up her courage and stopped at their table to offer condolences and attempt conversation, but, also like the others, had soon wandered off, leaving the family to keep its vigil alone. Thankfully, neither David Slocum nor any of his relations had put in an appearance.

Pete Koski had also been absent, thus far. This struck Lucy Delaney as a grave dereliction of duty, and for the third time in the past fifteen minutes, she jabbed Mia's arm and demanded testily, "Now why do you suppose that man hasn't shown up? He knows we all want to hear about things."

"That's probably why he's not here," Mia replied. "Anyway, how would it look for the sheriff to be out hobnobbing with us when there's a killer on the loose?" She contemplated the general lack of consideration for Lucy's sensibilities in the discussion of the homicides.

The impending elections had brought one unlikely visitor to the affair. Warner Godwin, with pigtailed daughter in tow, had eaten his dinner with dispatch and was now making the rounds of the tables reminding those who just might be interested that he was a candidate for county attorney. Annie stood at his side, shifting from foot to foot, abstractedly chewing one of her yellow braids. When Godwin spotted Mia, he smiled broadly and spoke into Annie's ear. The child released his hand and walked over to where Mia sat. "How do you do, Auntie Mia?" She spoke her lines firmly and put out a sweaty paw to be shaken.

"Cousin, dear—I'm your cousin." Mia smiled and took the proffered hand, adding to herself, *Not that your father has ever recognized that relationship before. What people won't do for a vote!*

Leonie spoke up beside her. "Why don't you take your niece out for some fresh air, Mia? There are plenty of us to clean up."

Mia nodded gratefully. Leonie herself had spent the major part of the day explaining her husband's absence to skeptical listeners and couldn't be blamed if she had preferred to make her own escape. Mia, however, was beginning to be concerned as to the whereabouts of Nick, whom she hadn't seen since his stint as the barbershop quartet's lead tenor. The entire foursome, which, in addition to Nick, consisted of Wylie Petworth and the Touminen twins, Sulo and Eino, had disappeared—a situation that boded no good.

Annie brightened and danced off to ask her father's permission for the excursion. Mia retrieved her jacket from the row of pegs by the door and left the building with Annie skipping at her side as delighted as any prisoner receiving an unanticipated reprieve. They took the gravel path that ran from the back door of the hall, between the two outhouses, and into the trees.

Mia looked intently into the prancing child's face and was relieved to see the unmistakable stamp of Warner Godwin in her round brown eyes and button nose.

Nick had told her little of what had transpired between him and Pete Koski and he certainly hadn't mentioned any dealings that he might have had with Nina Godwin. When Cecil Newman brought him home late Sunday evening, Nick had gone straight to bed. For the past two days he had continued to wave off her questions about the interview, maintaining that Koski had spent the three hours badgering him about the night before Nels died, an evening of which Nick's recollection was fuzzy, at best. If anything else had been discussed he wasn't saying so, but he clung to her at night like a shipwrecked man to a drifting log.

Finally, in the early hours of that very morning, he had confessed to her that if fingerprints other than her own were found on the lathe, they would probably be his. He had gone into the studio, he told her, looking for wood scraps to burn in the sauna stove and had tripped over the cord to the lathe. He noticed it was pulled out a little from where it entered the motor. He had shoved it back in and forgot about it. It was stupid and thoughtless, he knew, and he was sorry, but if she had told him about the electric shock when it happened, he had emphasized, they would all have been saved a lot of trouble.

After walking a short way, Mia and her charge emerged at the lake. The breeze was barely a breath, and the surface of the water was broken only by softly undulating ripples. Not many yards from shore, water and sky coalesced and were lost in fog.

The beach was made up of fine pale sand, but here and there a small stone would appear, worn smooth and round by the waves, shining with a coat of polish applied by the recent rain. They strolled down the beach, away from the town.

Annie uttered a steady stream of chatter as she traipsed through the sand, stopping every few steps to bend down and retrieve some especially enticing stone. This action was executed while holding two fingers of Mia's right hand in a bulldog-like grip and resulted in a jerk that Mia was sure would eventually wrench her shoulder from its socket. As was the case with her elders, the child's prattle was largely concerned with Cindy, with the added information that she had gone to heaven to be with Mama.

Mia resisted the urge to question Annie about her Mama and sauntered along, listening more to the soft plop of water upon sand than to the little girl's commentary.

When both their pockets were filled with stones they retraced their steps back to the hall.

XXXII

McIntire opened Lucy's unlocked door and began to grope his way through the kitchen toward the living room and the telephone. Even in his state of semi-shock he noticed that the room was in an un-Lucy-like state of disorderliness. Unfortunately, he did *not* notice the open oven door until his shin met it with a crack that brought a yelp of agony and sent him sprawling across the kitchen table. Salt shaker, sugar bowl, and a cardboard shoe box stuffed with papers hurtled to the floor. He sucked in his breath and bent to pick up the larger pieces of broken crockery and the scattered papers, papers which he saw were letters, dozens of them. Some were in envelopes; those that were not were headed *Dear Ma*. Occasional phrases were blacked out, and a few larger portions cut completely away. He'd seen enough of censored mail to recognize it immediately.

He picked up one of the envelopes and examined the postmark. So Lucy had a son in a Missouri state pen. Reason enough to keep her mail from passing through too many hands. Was it also reason enough to make a quick dash back home after absent-mindedly inviting Wylie Petworth into her empty house to help himself to coffee? Did she fear his making this same discovery? McIntire recalled that on his most recent visit to Lucy, she had gone into the house ahead of him and sent him on that water-fetching errand before allowing him to enter.

He stuffed the letters haphazardly into the box and put through his call to the county sheriff's office. Newman was, as usual, holding down the fort. This time McIntire delivered his message with no hedging. He then left the house and crawled into the back seat of his beloved Studebaker, pulling the raincoat over his head and allowing himself to sink into oblivion.

In what seemed like only minutes, he was brought to life by a series of brain-crushing thumps on the car's roof and Pete Koski's thunderous inquiry, "What the hell is going on?"

McIntire got out of the car and pointed him up the hill. The sheriff limped off in his campaign boots with Cecil Newman in his wake. In a few minutes they were both back. "Anybody home here?" Koski asked. McIntire shook his head. "This where you called from?" At McIntire's affirmative nod he headed for the house. The deputy regarded him with a condescending pity. It was clear that his opinion of McIntire's fitness for police work was not altered by the pallid and perspiring countenance the constable presented.

McIntire gripped the top of the open car door with both hands and rested his forehead against them. He made no attempt to explain.

The sheriff emerged, flinching as the tightly sprung screen door slammed behind him with a crack like a rifle shot. "Guibard is on his way, and so is an ambulance. There's no answer at the Culvers'. I'll have to go find them. I suppose they're at that damned picnic. But first we'll take some pictures and get her out of that hole. The state police ain't gonna like it, but there's no way I'll be able to keep Sandra and Earl away for any length of time, and I want that girl out of there and in the mortuary before they show up." He turned to McIntire. "John, try to pull yourself together, for crying out loud. See if you can find some shovels and a couple of blankets—and gloves if possible. She's been in there a long time and we're going to have to be careful if we want to get her out in one piece."

Removing Cindy Culver's body from its place of interment did not take long, but by the time it lay bundled under the trees awaiting the ambulance, McIntire was not the only one of the men to have left his lunch in the grass. Only the doctor, arriving just in time to help in rolling the child onto a blanket and lifting her out of her grave, remained impassive.

The sheriff brushed the soil off his sleeves. "Mark, you'd better come with me. Cecil, wait here for the ambulance and don't let anybody on the place, unless the lady of the house shows up. If she does, make sure she *stays* here. John, why don't you see if you can track down our young Johnny Appleseed. I don't mean arrest him or anything. Just find out if he's at home, and try to make some excuse to keep him there until I can get to him. If he gets wind of this he'll be off again, if he can get his hands on a car."

XXXIII

When Mia returned with her young cousin to the town hall, the crowd inside was as large as ever. Indeed it had grown, since the members of the quartet had reappeared and were now seated at a table with a half dozen other men, casually munching the dregs of the meal. Nick left the group and grasped Mia's free arm. "The sheriff was here," he gleefully reported. "He asked if David Slocum was around, and then he took off. He must have found something."

So Nick's exuberance couldn't only be put down to gin. Mia glared furiously at him and moved away with Annie, leaving him to rejoin his friends. A quick look around the packed room showed that this very group was now being subjected to Warner Godwin's appeal, and Mia threaded her way through the crowd to return Annie to her father. The girl suddenly stopped with another tendon-ripping yank on Mia's arm. "Look!" she said. "It's Mister-ter-teer…" Mia tried to follow the child's line of sight. "Annie, do you know one of those men? Mister who, Honey?"

"No!" Annie's voice bubbled with excitement. "That's what Mama said." Her father waved and started toward them. "But it's a secret," she whispered.

"Annie—" Mia tried again, but Warner was upon them. "Thanks for entertaining my daughter, Mrs. Thorsen. I appreciate it. Annie, tell your Auntie Mia thank you. We have to be going now. Don't forget to vote!"

"Cousin," Mia answered in response to Annie's, "Bye, Auntie Mia," but her eyes were on the circle of variously inebriated men. One of those individuals was familiar to Annie Godwin—and it was "Mama's" secret.

Mia turned away and sought out Leonie to learn what she could about the sheriff's brief appearance. He and the doctor had come in together and had spoken to the Culvers, who had immediately gathered up their progeny and made for the door. The sheriff himself had departed after asking if David Slocum had been there. Doctor Guibard was probably still about somewhere, Leonie said. Maybe he would be able to tell her more.

Mia saw that Guibard was indeed still there, trying valiantly to escape a merciless grilling by Nick and his companions.

Mia wrapped her jacket about her shoulders and slipped out the door. She had had enough and needed to think things through in the open air. She was in no mood to drive home with her drunk and gloating husband who, in any case, did not appear to be in a hurry to leave. As she rounded the corner of the building she heard the door swing open and click shut behind another departing reveler, followed by the sound of rapid footsteps approaching from behind. Nick coming to drag her back? Without looking around, she proceeded briskly down the graveled drive. The sound of steps faded, and she caught a brief glimpse of a hurrying figure before it disappeared between two parked cars. She smiled to herself in relief and at her own absurdity. It was highly unlikely that Nick had even noticed she was gone.

She walked straight across the road and cut between the boarded up hardware store and Karvonen's Grocery to the brushy area behind them. Skirting a collection of junked cars and rusting farm equipment, she continued rapidly along the road that led to the lumber yard and the railroad siding.

Her steps slowed as she left the gravel for the familiar trail through the woods. She removed her jacket, slung it over her shoulder and once again picked up her pace, trying not think about the last time she had traveled this path.

She concentrated instead on the men whom Annie Godwin had seen grouped around her father. Mia wasn't sure she could recall who all of them were. She wasn't even sure that she had recognized everyone, but surely one of them had been Nina's Nordic god. One of them had also been Nick. But if, as it appeared, the sheriff had some new information about Cindy—information that led him to seek David Slocum— maybe the identity of Nina's lover was irrelevant.

Imagine Annie's remembering. She couldn't have been more than three or so. And imagine Nina introducing her three-year-old daughter to her lover and then swearing her to secrecy. No wonder the poor kid stuttered! "Mister-ter-teer, indeed!" she muttered aloud. And it needed to be said aloud. She stood motionless and whispered it again. What were Annie's words?—"That's what Mama said." Could it be that she wasn't talking about a secret friend at all, but rather a secret *name*? The dim spark in Mia's brain glowed and burst into flame. "Oh my God!" she groaned.

XXXIV

McIntire left the orchard with the intention of going straight to the home of Dorothy Slocum and her son. He didn't hurry. If David was at home there was not much chance of his hearing that Cindy's body had been found. Neither the coroner nor the ambulance on its route from Chandler would pass near the Slocum place, and fortunately David and his mother were not members of the telephone party-line loop. The lack of a car would hamper any sudden flight.

McIntire recalled the pickup truck with its load of trees and turned off onto the winding driveway that led to Wylie Petworth's.

Wylie's Buick was absent, but the Ford truck was parked near the garage. A quick dash through the woods would get David here in no time. McIntire parked in the yard and walked up to the pickup. He lifted the hood, grasped a handful of spark plug wires, and gave a quick tug. After closing the hood with as little assault as possible to his throbbing head, he entered the garage. Its interior was swept clean and fastidiously organized, as was everything that fell into Wylie's sphere of responsibility. He placed the wires in an empty cardboard box and stuffed it well out of sight under the uncompromisingly tidy workbench that stood against one wall.

When he left the garage and walked back toward his car, he was struck once more by the sense of contentment and tranquility that prevailed here. Even on this drizzly and somber day—made all the more so by his recent grisly discovery—the old log house showed a warm and inviting aspect. Rainwater glistened on the stone chimneys and on the flagstone walk that passed under the oak trees and meandered between the shrub roses and beds of daylilies to the edge of the yard. There it gave way to the grassy path leading to the pond and the rear boundary of the cemetery where the diabolic Gutter Gulsvagen slumbered. Well, old Gulsvagen could rest easy, his earthly home was being well taken care of.

McIntire walked along the path and through the damp undergrowth to the graveyard. He pushed open the rusty back gate and winced as its hinges gave a protesting screak as if in a desperate attempt to protect the secrets interred there.

A raw wound in the earth was still all that defined the spot where Nels Bertelsen was, once again, buried. A small plaque had been placed in the ground on Ole Bertelsen's grave.

Nearby was a monument about four feet high, a drab white obelisk with no elaborate carving, only Julie Bertelsen's name, the dates of her birth and death, and few lines of verse. McIntire remembered the stir that stone with its accusing verse had caused. "She's slapping God in the face," had been Sophie's contention. *The Rose was Plucked by a Cruel hand, Before it came to Bloom, We are Left Behind to Weep and Wail, to no Avail.* It was a large monument. He had not thought before about what it must have cost Tina Bertelsen financially to publicly defy that Cruel Hand.

He crossed the wet grass to stand before another stone— the one that marked the final resting place of Colin McIntire. He had visited the grave only twice before—once with his mother and again last Memorial Day when Leonie had dragged him here with a bouquet of lilies. He had not yet said a private goodbye to his father, and he wasn't ready to do so today. Not quite ready to sever the ties that bound him so irrevocably to that angry and demanding man. Colin McIntire had never needed to be present in the flesh in order to dominate his son's life.

McIntire had seen his father only once in the past thirty-two years, on this occasion when he had accompanied Colin on a sentimental pilgrimage to his own parents' native Ireland. They had spent a total of six weeks together in three decades—six weeks during which John McIntire had trailed the ebullient stranger in and out of every pub on the Emerald Isle—had listened to him laugh, exchange endless stories with long lost cousins, and sing *The Rising of the Moon* and *O Donnell Aboo*—and had come to know him not at all. Yet the old Colin McIntire, that spirit that perched on his son's shoulder passing judgment on his every action, was with him still. Death hadn't changed that. It would take more than the simple lack of a physical body to separate John McIntire from the man who had given him life and who seemingly felt that the bestowing of that gift gave him the right—no, the obligation—to control every turn that life took. "You might be proud of me today, Pa. I'm about to nab a murderer. Old Gutter always got away, but I think I can nail David Slocum."

An image flitted into McIntire's mind, a memory, for once not one buried beneath the dust of the past, but a recent recollection of a feminine scrawl on a page. He strode back toward the gate through which he had entered. The stone was sheltered by a lilac bush and leaning slightly, pushed off center by the encroaching root of a pine tree. He rubbed the growth of lichen from its face with the heel of his hand, and read the weathered engraving. The name, the place of birth, the dates. It all made sense. As McIntire stood in the fine mist, the full import of his discovery came to him. "Oh, my God!" he said to the ghosts.

XXXV

Mia had no sooner uttered the words that accompanied her own revelation than the Nordic god himself appeared, blocking her path. One look at her face was enough to tell him that she had guessed the truth. "So you've finally figured it out, Mia, and it took Warner Godwin's brat to tell you. And now here you are, strolling along, docile as a lamb to the slaughter." He smiled and shook his head. "There's nothing can compare with the stupidity of a woman!"

Mia made no response except to turn back toward the town. He nimbly stepped around her, again barring her way. "You know I can't let you go. Even you're smart enough to know that."

"And you're smart enough to you know you won't get away with any of this." She took a chance. "They've found Cindy's body."

He didn't bat an eye.

"It doesn't matter by now. They can't prove that I put it there. I didn't like doing that. But maybe you can see why I had to."

Mia looked at the Nordic god and did see…now.

He continued to watch her, malevolently, like a wolf eying the lamb he had alluded to. "It was smart of me to realize that I couldn't let her body be found, don't you think?"

Mia snorted. "How smart can you be if Cindy Culver was on to you?"

An anger that she had never seen before boiled up into his eyes. "That stupid bitch! She was blind as a bat. She had the evidence of murder right in her hand, and all she could see was that I had a little fling with Nina Godwin. That didn't take any brains to figure out. Nina, true to her sex, was dumb enough to write it all down—and the brilliant Miss Culver figured I'd be willing to pay to get the diary. Well, I got the damn diary, all right, and the greedy little sweetheart got her payment!"

Mia lifted her chin and looked him in the eye. "There are four more diaries. Cindy was hoping for installment payments, I guess."

The gloating face registered dismay, and for a brief moment her accoster's confidence wavered. Mia grasped her jacket, with its stone laden pockets, in both hands and swung with all her might. Years of wielding hammer and chisel had given her strength as well as pinpoint accuracy. Her blow caught him on the temple and brought him to his knees. She turned and fled down the path toward home.

McIntire slipped in the back door of the town hall. A large number of people were still in evidence, no doubt hesitant to leave since some news of the murders appeared to be imminent. Two faces, though, were conspicuously absent. He found his wife in the kitchen where she was stacking speckled gray enamel plates in a cupboard. Mia had left alone, and on foot, Leonie said. She couldn't tell him about anybody else.

"Get Koski back," he implored her, as he headed for the door.

He was on his feet and after her in seconds. She knew that he was amazingly quick for one of his age, and she would have no real hope of outdistancing him. She ran blindly, her blood pounding in her ears. The path was smooth, but the grade was steep and her skirt wrapped around her legs, hampering her movements. Still, he stayed always a few paces behind, letting her take him deeper into the woods before he closed in.

Oh, why had she been such an idiot? Why hadn't she taken a chance on getting around him and running back toward town? When she felt that her heart would surely burst with one more step, she reached the point where the ridge leveled off and felt a fresh rush of hope. If only she could reach it. There it loomed ahead—that decrepit, beautiful wooden structure—her long awaited escape.

He was close behind her now, almost touching her. She could hear his breath coming in short gasps. She flung herself onto the jump and began the climb. He cursed as he struggled with mounting the slide, but before she was halfway up, the boards began to creak and sway sickeningly as he followed her. She scrambled upward until she had nearly reached the top. Then she looked up at the tiny platform that was the last stop before nothingness and could go no further. She planted her heels behind the wooden cleat and turned to face him.

He was advancing, slowly now, leaning heavily against the rail, his eyes once more fixed unwaveringly on hers.

"Are you going to do me a favor and finally jump, Mia? Or would you rather I took care of it for you? It doesn't really matter. Once you hit the ground no one's going to be able to tell whether you did it on your own or had help."

He was almost upon her. Her heart seemed to cease in its beat. Tears of terror filled her eyes and blurred his face.

"But thanks for not making me strangle you, too. I'm running out of places to put the bodies."

She heard the scrape of wood against wood as his foot came down on the loose board. His mirthless laugh became a startled grunt. Gripping the rail with both hands and leaning back, gathering every ounce of her strength, Mia drove her foot into his stomach. The stump of his right arm flailed uselessly before he fell backward, crashed through the railing, and disappeared over the edge.

XXXVI

McIntire first noticed the cranelike figure of Mia Thorsen, her knees drawn up under her flowered skirt, perched high above him. Only when he anxiously approached the jump did he stumble upon the twisted body of Wylie Petworth sprawled among the weeds. He passed by with hardly a glance and rapidly mounted the ladder.

Mia's lips were blue in her waxen face, and she shivered violently. He sat down on the boards next to her and wrapped his raincoat around her shoulders, holding her tight to his chest. At length the shaking gave way to a soft sobbing and finally to an occasional sniffle. After a long time, she lifted her head and gulped for air. McIntire produced a handkerchief. She blew her nose robustly and leaned her head back against his chest. "Is he dead?" she asked. Her voice was hoarse and barely louder than a whisper..

"I don't know. He wasn't moving."

She rested against him for a time before speaking again, "John, I still don't get it. I sort of know why he killed Cindy, but why Nels? They were like brothers."

"Not brothers exactly," McIntire informed her. "Cousins. Something like, let's see…half first cousins once removed would be close. Wylie's great-grandfather—you know, our old friend Gutter—was Tina Bertelsen's grandfather."

"Tina?"

"Christina Bertelsen, Nels' mother. She's still alive, Mia, and with Nels dead, Wylie is her next of kin. He could inherit her estate."

"I never heard that they were related."

"I suppose they didn't realize that they were. Wylie must have figured it out when he got the old records from the apple business. Nels' grandmother, Tina's mother, was called Sigrid Guttormsdatter, or Guttorm's daughter. Her father left Norway for good before Tina was born. Wylie's grandfather came from Norway about that same time and his first name was Guttorm."

"That doesn't prove a thing. The Norwegians only have about twenty names that they divvy up amongst themselves. They just juggle the order."

"Which is why they needed to choose a family surname when they came to this country. Like a lot of people, Guttorm adopted the name of his home village, Gulsvagen. An extremely small village, I might add. The letters in the Bertelsen records show that Christina also came from Gulsvagen. Wylie just put two and two together—maybe with some help from Nina at the library."

"You mean Christina Bertelsen lived practically next door to her cousins and never knew it? That's pretty hard to swallow."

"According to Laurie Post, Guttorm's first wife—Sigrid's mother—died. He remarried—to Wylie's great-grandmother that would be—and emigrated to the United States after Sigrid was already grown up and married. Tina thought that people from her village had settled somewhere in this area. That's why she came here. She probably didn't know that her own grandfather ended up in this part of the world, but it's not such a coincidence that he did. Many people who lived together in communities in Europe stayed near one another when they came to America, and it wasn't hard to lose track of family in those days. Maybe it still isn't." He smiled. "Do you think Nina Godwin's descendants will recognize you if you meet them on the street?"

"Depends on who's running for office," Mia observed. In response to McIntire's questioning look she only went on, "I still can't believe Wylie would have murdered his best friend for a few acres of sand and rock." She shivered again, and he wrapped the coat more tightly around her. "Is it true, has Cindy's body been found?"

McIntire told her about the burial under the apple tree. "She was so small that he was able to bundle her up with the roots and put her right in the truck with the other trees. I suppose he had left the burlap hidden back in the woods when he met her. When he left the scene of the murder, he was leaving to fetch it. He just tied her up with all her belongings—except her coat, it was too bulky—and carried her out. I still can't understand why he felt he had to dispose of the body in such a hideous way. He wasn't going to be able to keep her death a secret for long. He could at least have allowed her family to bury her."

"The magnanimous murderer? He had strangled her, John. He knew an autopsy might show that it was done with only one hand."

Mia let her head fall back upon his shoulder. McIntire's hand went up to smooth back the strands of hair tear-glued to the side of her face but was arrested by her words. "John, we can't just let him lie there. He might still be alive. At least," she added, "I don't hear the approach of the Valkyrie."

"Valkyrie? So Wylie's our Nordic god, too?"

"Tyr, Norse god of war—how fitting. He had his arm chewed off by a wolf or something. Annie called him Mr. Tyr. I thought she was stuttering."

"Good grief. Nina Godwin was quite the romantic soul after all, wasn't she?"

They gingerly descended to solid ground and turned to the place where Wylie Petworth lay. His position hadn't changed, but his eyes glittered in his ashen face.

"Well, if it isn't Tweedledum and Tweedledee. God, you two still look like a pair of scarecrows." He attempted to raise himself, but fell back, his face contorted with pain. When he spoke again it was through clenched jaws. "Lend a hand, will you?"

"I don't think you should move." McIntire bent over him. Wylie lay on his back in the wet grass. His right shoulder was twisted up and caught on the rotting trunk of a fallen tree, leaving his unsupported head hanging to the side. A deep purple bruise blossomed from his left temple. The arm that had until recently been undamaged dangled uselessly, and his left leg below the knee was bent at a revolting angle.

"You think it matters now? Just get something under my head."

Together McIntire and Mia lifted, turning him until his head and shoulders were supported on the log in a half-sitting position. McIntire removed his hat and rolled it into a fat sausage which he slid under the injured man's neck. Lastly, he took off the raincoat and tucked it around the inert body.

"Thanks, Mac, you're a real prince. I don't remember you being so generous with the covers when we all shared a bed. Those were the good old days, eh?" His words burst forth in short explosions, like a water tap with air in the pipes. "But that's a tradition the two of you carried on, isn't it? From the cozy pair you make, I imagine you've picked up where you left off. What would the proper English lady say if she knew you'd been screwing each other since you were fourteen?" His laughter sounded hollow and ended in a choking cough. "You never dreamed I knew, did you? You thought you were being so cagey when you'd get rid of me and sneak off together. There are plenty of people that would be surprised at what I know...and the secrets I've kept."

"Like the fact that you and Nels were related?" Mia ventured.

Wylie's eyes widened. "Well, aren't we clever? God, I would have loved wringing your scrawny neck, Mia." He sucked in his breath, and spoke through his teeth. "The whole world would have found out about the Bertelsen clan being my dear cousins before long. I made sure of that when I brought those records to Warner Godwin."

"But how could you have done such a thing, to Nels Bertelsen, of all people?" Mia persisted. "You were such close friends. After all he—"

"Saved my life. Jeez, if I had a nickel for every time I've had to hear that! Nels, the great hero. Rescues bumbling Wylie from death by fire, and then goes off to save the world from Kaiser Wilhelm, leaving the poor crippled kid home to watch the sheep and play Prince Charming to a bunch of giggling females!"

Mia gaped at him, uncomprehending. "But if it wasn't for Nels you'd be—"

"He'd be whole, Mia." McIntire recalled Laurie Post's puzzling statements about a young boy's short memory or forgiving nature. It looked like Wylie had neither forgotten nor forgiven. "Nels Bertelsen started that fire. Is that what happened, Wylie?"

"Ah, the great detective strikes again." He suddenly gasped, then held his breath for a time before he went on. "We'd been fishing through the ice, and we were in the shack. I mentioned to Nels that the nurse that was looking after his mother seemed to be taking pretty good care of his father, too. He came at me like a wild man, slammed me into the kerosene stove. It went up like a torch. He held me down until the oil soaked my coat and was burning right through to my skin, and he still wouldn't let me up. When the hut caught fire, I guess he came to his senses and got us both out. I'd passed out by that time. When I came to, I was in the snow and he was there with that whore. They threw me into the sled and hauled me into town."

"But why didn't you say anything? Why let him get away with it?"

"You think he got away with it? If I had told what really happened he *would* have gotten away scot free. Boys will be boys, you know. They're expected to get into a tussle now and again. Damned if I'd let that happen! When they told me they were going to cut off my arm, I decided I would wait as long as it took, but I'd get my revenge." Wylie began a convulsive shivering. Mia pulled the coat up around his neck.

"When he hit that nest of hornets and ended up in the hospital, I was scared he'd die and cheat me out of it. Turned out to be my lucky day. I unselfishly consented to take over the orchards. I got those old records and figured out that Nels' mother was my cousin, and she didn't appear to be dead at all. Everything was falling into place. I could get even and get back the land that should have been mine if my mother hadn't..." His cough sent a spasm through his body.

"Also very fitting." Mia spoke under her breath, and McIntire turned to her. "Tyr was god of war *and* of justice," she explained.

Wylie ignored, or didn't hear, the exchange. When he continued his voice was softer, but steady.

"Anyway, I fed Nina a cock and bull story about how I wanted to 'do something' for the old friend who had saved my life, and would she please suspend her high morals long enough to slip me a look into her husband's files, so I could see what sort of financial shape he was in. I found out he and Godwin were cooking up a scheme to go into cahoots with some company in Chicago to turn the place into a resort. I had to do something before they ended up selling out, or the old lady kicked off...or, God forbid, that woman should talk Nels into marrying her.

"When he actually died, it was almost a letdown. I spent my life getting to know that stubborn Norwegian as well as I know myself, planning for that day, working for it, and then—bang!—it was all over. I accomplished what I set out to do. I got rid of my worst enemy...and to do it I had to lose my best friend. Nels was gone, and the challenge was gone…kind of took the spark out of life…until I opened Godwin's campaign pitch and found that note from the High School Extortion Queen.

"Everything would have gone smooth as silk if that idiot Nina Godwin hadn't written it all down. Behind every unsuccessful man there's an asinine woman!"

"But," McIntire said, "there couldn't have been anything in Nina's diary to prove that you killed Nels. She didn't know what you were up to. Cindy must have learned from the diary that Nina was having an affair with someone who wanted to repay his best friend for saving his life when they were boys…and from what I told her she figured out that it was you. But there was still no *evidence* that you murdered Nels, nothing that was worth killing that little girl over."

"There didn't need to be. Once that little girl opened her big mouth, it would have all gone haywire. I had the ledgers. I had snooped into Nels' lawyer's files. I called the nut house to find out if his mother was still living. Ole's old whore knew that Nels started that fire." He turned watery eyes on Mia. "And your dashing husband might even have come out of his alcoholic stupor long enough to remember the little fender bender we had that night when we were both headed home, even though I had left the Waterfront considerably earlier."

He seemed to sink back into himself, and his voice could barely be heard. "No, Cindy had to be shut up." He looked again at Mia. "And so did anybody else who guessed the truth. Don't you see? I owed that much to Nels.

"But I've failed, and Nels died for nothing, all because of those two imbeciles, Cindy Culver and Nina Godwin."

"Nina," McIntire said, "you didn't…"

"No, Nina was enough of a moron to drive off a cliff with no help from me." Another coughing spell racked Wylie's body and left him lying spent and gasping against the log. "I would never take a mother away from her child."

The distant sound of slamming car doors and male voices heralded the imminent arrival, not of the Valkyrie, but of Pete Koski and his men.

The three waited in silence as the sun slipped below the cover of clouds and cast their shadows across the grass to merge with the darkness of woods beyond.

To receive a free catalog of other Poisoned Pen Press titles,
please contact us in one of the following ways:

Phone: 1-800-421-3976
Facsimile: 1-480-949-1707
Email: info@poisonedpenpress.com
Website: www.poisonedpenpress.com

Poisoned Pen Press
6962 E. First Ave. Ste 103
Scottsdale, AZ 85251